I0613558

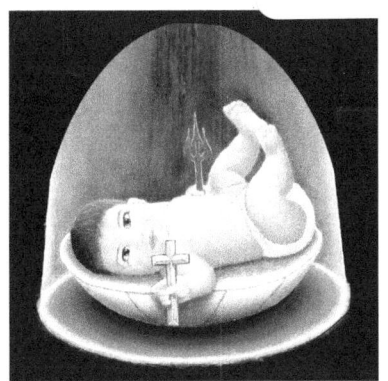

The **Pregnant Pope**

Satan never sleeps. If he did, we would all be in heaven.

by Mit Sandru

Chivileri Publishing

Copyright © 2014 by Dumitru Sandru

This is a fictional story. All names, persons, organizations, businesses, occurrences, and some places are fictitious and spring from the imagination of the author. Any resemblances to actual people or events are completely coincidental.

Acknowledgements

Many thanks to my family

Table of Contents

Chapter 1. The Pope Is Pregnant

"The Pope is pregnant," Claire told Travis as he entered the plush conference room.

"Not again," Travis lamented, and sat in the high-back chair around the oval walnut conference table. He figured it was a kinky joke before the start of a serious meeting in, of all places, the offices of the Archdiocese of Los Angeles.

Claire was capable of inappropriate jokes, but this time her big brown eyes showed no such intention. "This is more serious than the Pope Joan incident of one thousand years ago." Claire's words carried a mysteriously grave undertone.

"Indeed it is. You are not referring to Pope Julius Urban Pius, are you?" He pointed to the holographic portrait of the current pope at the head of the conference room.

Claire nodded, pursing her lips.

"How could a 92-year-old man be pregnant?" Travis swiveled in his chair and stared at the Pope's portrait. He narrowed his eyes, thinking that this information was even stranger than the evening news. "No wonder we were asked to meet here, under the cathedral."

"We'll find out more details as soon as Maximus initiates the holopresence," said Claire, interlacing her fingers and resting her arms on the polished table.

Travis frowned and turned back to face her. "Where's Prescott?"

"He's on his way." Claire shifted her glance sideways as she listened to her aural earpiece. "He's getting out of the elevator."

Travis glanced around at the conference room. The walnut wood-paneled walls were adorned with religious artifacts, paintings of saints, and portraits of past archbishops of the Archdiocese of Los Angeles. The hologram portraits of the Pope and of Cardinal Molino, the leader of the archdiocese, hung in a preeminent place at the head of the conference room, flanked by three flags: the golden yellow and white flag bearing the crossed keys of Saint Peter and the Papal Tiara of Vatican City, California's state flag and its grizzly bear, and the USA's Stars and Stripes.

The Italian marble floor was covered with a thick maroon carpet. Candleholders as tall as a man were unlit. Tall red velvet chairs surrounded the conference table, indicating a place where the Catholic Church makes powerful and secret decisions deep underground, below the Cathedral of Our Lady of the Angels. This room belonged in centuries past, not in Anno Domini 2066.

"What's going on?" Prescott asked as he entered the conference room.

"You'd better sit down. The Pope is pregnant," smirked Travis, curious to see Prescott's reaction.

"On the *sede stercoraria*?" asked Prescott, referring to the medieval papal seat with a hole in it on which a newly elected pope would sit. The cardinals could verify his "male jewels" and thus his eligibility to be sworn in.

Travis chuckled. Prescott lowered himself slowly into a chair, his expression a mixture of concern and surprise.

"This must be a guy thing, and I don't find it amusing," said Claire. "Maximus will join us shortly."

"Did the Pope—"

"No 'coming out of the closet' jokes," Claire cut Prescott off.

"I was about to ask if the Pope has had transgender surgery," said Prescott flatly.

"We'll find out soon," replied Claire, maintaining a businesslike tone.

Claire German, Travis St. John, and Prescott Alighieri were the three members of the Capuchin Trinity Team—the CTT—an investigating unit that belonged to the Trinity Investigation Organization, or TIO. Although *tio* meant uncle in Spanish, it was a good acronym to use, because it never raised suspicions whenever someone mentioned it. Officially, it was a little-known entity that specialized in paranormal and supernatural crimes that science and law enforcement could not resolve. In other words, weird stuff, as in, "the Pope is pregnant."

"I think Maximus wants to start," said Claire.

"Why were we asked to meet here, under the cathedral?" Prescott asked.

"I'm sure Maximus will tell us," replied Claire.

Each CTT member would view the meeting on his or her personal audio-visual-hologram-visor, or PAV. Commercial PAVs used for communication, entertainment, study, work, and any other personal holographic displays resembled an ordinary pair of glasses. When in use, they would shade the eyes of the user to indicate the "on" status. The CTT's PAVs did not shade their eyes, although their PAVs could act as shades, if needed. The CTT's PAVs were much smaller, made of two units, with earpieces worn behind the ears. A small knob extending forward from each unit provided the visual hologram in front of their eyes. Along with many other capabilities, like the holographic display, their PAVs could silence the sound of their voices by issuing countering audio waves, or going "silent." If someone were to observe Claire, Travis, and Prescott talking, he would have seen three individuals staring into the distance while, occasionally, their lips moved without emitting a sound. What Claire, Travis, and Prescott saw and heard in their PAVs was an audio-holographic presentation, while their surroundings were semitransparent. During a meeting, their three PAVs created a simulated joint session.

The bust hologram of a businessman wearing dark glasses appeared in front of their eyes. Maximus was a computer-generated human with artificial intelligence who existed only as a hologram. "We were asked to meet here, in this conference room of the Cathedral of Our Lady of the Angels, because this matter involves the Roman Catholic Church and the Holy See," said Maximus. "This is a very delicate and extremely confidential matter. Not even Cardinal Molino was invited to this meeting, and I'm not sure if he's aware of this subject. In any case, the topic of this meeting is that Pope Julius Urban Pius is pregnant." Maximus paused for effect. "This happening could have civilization-shattering implications."

"Just to make sure—are we talking about the 92-year-old male pope in the Vatican?" Prescott asked, rubbing the bridge of his nose.

"The one and only."

Claire, Travis, and Prescott shifted apprehensively in their chairs. Hearing the news from Maximus made the information even graver.

"Why are we being called to investigate this? Why isn't the Vatican taking care of it?" Travis asked.

"The Vatican asked explicitly for the Capuchin Trinity Team. You." Maximus pointed at them.

"Why?"

"Your reputation in how you handled the case about the Second Coming of Jesus a few years ago," answered Maximus.

Travis laced his fingers behind his head and made a face, as if to say, *It's about time we're recognized for our superb accomplishments.* Prescott and Claire permitted themselves small, appreciative smiles.

"And because you're not Catholics," continued Maximus.

The three exchanged puzzled looks. A Catholic matter involving non-Catholics?

"Yes, I know," said Maximus, as understandingly as his artificial intelligence would allow. "Something like this should be kept in utmost secrecy within Vatican walls. Well, it seems the Holy See wants an unbiased investigation."

Claire, Travis, and Prescott leaned forward, inviting clarification, as if Maximus were a real person in front of them instead of a hologram in their PAVs.

"The Holy Father did not undergo any sex change," continued Maximus. "A week ago, when His Holiness did not feel well, his staff thought he might have a tumor. Afterward, more detailed scans revealed that he had a fetus growing in his lower abdomen."

"A mutation? A parasite?" Claire asked.

"No. A real human fetus. Male, to be precise."

"Why are we to be involved?" Prescott asked. "This is a medical issue."

"Yes, it could be a medical issue," said Maximus. "Although it has never happened before, the self-cloning of a fetus in a mature human body is hypothesized as possible but extremely unlikely."

"That should be the only believable explanation, shouldn't it?" wondered Prescott.

"The Holy See does not believe it is so," said Maximus.

"Do you mean someone abducted him, performed surgery, and implanted the embryo in him?" Prescott asked.

"Along with the entire female reproductive system?" added Claire.

"There is no evidence of any misdoing," said Maximus. "And no other female organs were found, other than the ones necessary to ensure the well-being of the fetus."

"He could have ingested a robo-bug," speculated Prescott. "Or perhaps he inhaled nano-robots."

"They searched for a week and traced everything under the sun, but they found no proof of foul play," said Maximus. "They need an independent assessment, and that would be a job for you, CTT." Maximus motioned toward them.

Claire, Travis, and Prescott glanced at each other questioningly. They were seasoned investigators, and, by now, nothing could shock them, but they were intrigued about this.

"Before we dive deeper into this, I want to know if you'll take the assignment," said Maximus.

The three members of the Capuchin Trinity Team, the CTT, were not part of any government, corporation, law enforcement, or religious establishment, but a private non-profit organization. They were paid for their services—and paid very well—but their moral and ethical values prevented them from aiding any person, entity, or establishment for the employer's own self-advancement or selfish motives. There was no need to reiterate that what was being said in this conference room was highly confidential; however, they were not obligated to take any assignment that they felt was inappropriate or that might force them to turn on their employers. That situation had happened in the past, to the regret of their employer, and, in one case, with fatal consequences to one particular individual.

"Is the Vatican open to all outcomes?" Travis asked.

"Affirmative," Maximus answered. "The Holy Father personally asked for this investigation and for the CTT to conduct it."

"Do you mean to say that the Holy Father has suspicions about what may be at play here, including supernatural forces?" Claire asked.

"Supernatural. Paranormal. Metaphysical. And any other possibilities. That is my understanding."

The Capuchin Trinity Team exchanged discreet, knowing glances.

"We'll take the assignment," said Prescott.

"Excellent," said Maximus. He looked at them anew. "And I see you are dressed for action."

Dressed for action signified a special dress code that Trinity members wore on assignment: dark-gray silk suits, buttoned up to the neck but allowing four centimeters of Roman collar to show. It was not the white Roman collar worn by priests, but it designated the Trinity's Roman Catholic origins. Nor were they priests, but the collar—with its inverted triangular TIO insignia—kept the people around them somehow respectful during their investigations or when they mixed with civilians. The white collar and the insignia contained monitoring sensors. The information gathered was channeled to their PAVs. The suits were bulletproof and capable of changing into different colors, even camouflage, if needed. More important than the protection from physical injuries that the suits provided them was the insulation from any paranormal energy fields during their investigations.

"Since this is rather urgent, I've reserved three seats on a commercial suborbital jump from LAX to Leonardo da Vinci in Rome," said Maximus. "It departs in two hours."

The CTT acknowledged with brief nods of their heads.

In recent decades, and especially in this year of 2066—the year of Satan, as many called it—there seemed to be an increase in paranormal cases. Maybe because law enforcement investigators were more open to such events, or perhaps because the supernatural occurrences were indeed greater, especially since the near end-of-the-world that humanity had experienced in the 2020s. Back then, the economic, financial, and government establishments around the globe had collapsed. The whole world had been gripped by massive famines and energy shortages caused by the unwinding of the financial pyramid schemes that governments and financial institutions alike had perpetrated. The bill came due, and there was no "real" money to pay it.

The world had recovered, but the new normal hadn't been the same since. The supernatural and paranormal effects on some people's lives increased. Nothing like ghosts or poltergeists, but real, unexplained phenomena that science could not figure out. Was this the result of an increased global population of 20 billion, or of extraterrestrials, or of divine—or not-so-divine—intervention? Speculation abounded, but no conclusive answers were ever found. It seemed as if the fabric of reality were tearing.

The Trinity Investigation Organization was able to help. It was an old organization, originally established by the Roman Catholic Church hundreds of years in the past. The men and women who formed Trinity Teams had an unusual ability to detect paranormal and supernatural occurrences. Their talent had nothing to do with being Catholic or even being religious. It was strictly a natural ability among a few individuals who worked at their best when they worked as a Trinity Team.

Mit Sandru

Chapter 2. The Fetus

"Before you depart for Rome, Dr. Stark will present to you the available medical information." Maximus's holopresence retreated into the background.

In his place, the hologram of Dr. Stark popped to life. Dr. Stark was not exactly an example of vitality. With his bald head and wrinkled, liver-spotted skin like that of an Egyptian mummy, he seemed to be an apparition from the crypt. He wore a white lab coat with lots of blinking contrivances on his sleeves, upgrading his status from a corpse to a modern mortician.

"Good afternoon, or is it morning where you are?"

"Good afternoon, Doctor," said Claire for her team. "It is shortly after the noon hour here in California."

"Well, boys and girl, we're starting a new investigation," he said with a poker face.

Claire raised an eyebrow, displeased by the "girl" reference. But then—she told herself—he seemed to be ancient, and, compared to him, she was a girl.

"Dr. Stark, what a pleasure!" Travis exclaimed. "You look great. Have you had some work done?"

Dr. Stark closed his eyes. He was not amused; he was never amused about anything. "Shall we start?" He deployed a hologram of the Pope's body, some parts pixelated to protect the Pope's privacy. His lower abdomen bulged.

"The Pope is a heavyset man, and the growing fetus went undetected until he complained of not feeling well a week ago. That was when the fetus was discovered."

"Morning—" Travis started to ask.

"Not exactly morning sickness," interrupted Dr. Stark, anticipating his question. "High blood pressure is what caused his discomfort." The hologram began to zoom in on the Pope's belly. "The fetus is carried in the lower abdomen's cavity, as you see here." In the hologram, the outer layers of the Pope's body dissipated. The amniotic sac appeared, containing the fetus and the umbilical cord connected to the placenta.

"Is the fetus normal? Healthy?" Claire asked, fascinated by what she was seeing.

"A perfectly healthy, six-month-old fetus. Male," said Dr. Stark.

"OK, Doctor, give us the scoop," said Travis. "How could this happen?"

"It starts with the sperm and the ovum, the female egg, that is fertilized," Dr. Stark intoned. "Therefore, after fertilization we get a zygote, which evolves into an embryo and later on into a fetus, which is what we have now."

"I understand that," said Travis. "But in which of these stages—the zygote, the embryo, or the fetus—was it implanted in the Pope's body?"

"At none of these stages was it implanted in the Pope's body," replied Dr. Stark.

"I know others have asked this question before, but are you sure?" Prescott asked.

"Absolutely positive," replied the doctor. "The Pope's body was scanned in detail at the micron level, and no external intervention was discovered."

"A genetic alteration of any kind?" Prescott did not give up. "Modulated radiation exposure that mutated his genes?"

"The Pope's genetic schema has not changed, other than with the normal effects of aging. His genes don't account for his situation, nor is there detected a change toward a female condition."

"Is this mutation self-cloning?" Claire asked in disbelief.

"No self-cloning either," replied the doctor. "The fetus has DNA from the Pope and from a woman. In other words, it was conceived just like any other fetus."

"Has the woman been identified?" asked Claire.

"The genetic code is not registered," said the doctor. "She is unknown."

The "civilized world" identified its citizens from birth by each individual's genetic code, referred to as GeneID. However, less than half the global population was registered, either by refusing such personal intrusion on the grounds of religion or civil liberties, or by not being part of established socio-economic populations. These men and women were absent from the GeneID data banks.

"I see." Claire was pensive. "But then, aside from the fact that the fetus was procreated, what caused the Pope's male body to develop female organs that support and nurture the fetus?"

"Not all the female organs. The Pope does not have a uterus, ovaries, lumen, or vagina. In other words, the fetus has no exit, no way of being born, other than through surgery."

"Then, what's going on?" asked Claire.

"We have no idea." Dr. Stark threw his hands up in the air.

"Wait a moment," said Travis. "Let's get back to the procreation. How did the female egg get into the Pope's body to be fertilized by his sperm?"

Maximus's holopresence increased. "The Holy Father has not produced any sperm in a long time. In a very unscientific way, it's a miracle. That's why we need you to be involved. Science cannot answer these questions. This could be a paradox or a metaphysical incident."

Dr. Stark scoffed. "Why don't you include divine, or not-so-divine, intervention while you're at it?"

"The Trinity Teams, including this Capuchin Trinity Team, have resolved many cases that were not solvable through science," Maximus retorted.

"Hocus-pocus," said Dr. Stark. "None of their evidence would stand in a court of law. No one else seems to see, hear, or feel the proof for the conclusions the Trinity Teams arrive at."

"And yet, they've solved impossible cases," replied Maximus. "So far, they've always found the cause or the villain, and justice has been served, even if some cases have never ended up in a court of law. The end result is what counts. Isn't it?"

"Well, I'm a man of science. If it cannot be verified experimentally, it is voodoo. So I'm skeptical. However, I'll be open-minded. How would you, CTT, explain what happened to the Pope? Science does not have an answer. Yet."

"Well, we believe that every living entity is a trinity composed of the body, the mind, and the spirit," said Travis. "The body exists in the Physical Realm, or, as some people refer to it, the real world. The Mind Realm is where the memory resides, and the soul is in the Spiritual Realm. We also exist in the White Energy Universe. What happened to the Pope is in the real world, where science reigns. But the transformation may not have happened in the Physical Realm."

"Then where? Behind some curtain, or veil, as the psychics call it?" Dr. Stark, his hands on his hips, could not hide his derision.

"Yes, physical existence is a manifestation of a metaphysical state," replied an unperturbed Travis. "The Pope's body of today may not be the same as before the fetus appeared."

"You mean someone switched the Pope's body with a clone?"

"Or altered it in the metaphysical world."

"So what you're saying is that we are virtual realities in the physical world. Altering the body in the metaphysical world is like changing a software program, and, voilà, just like that, a different body appears in the physical world." Dr. Stark folded his arms, frowning.

"That is as good an explanation as any," said Claire.

"So, you three will go behind the 'veil'"—Dr. Stark used air quotes—"and find out what happened or who the wrongdoer is?"

"No living soul can do that," said Prescott.

"Well, that's a pity," ridiculed the doctor.

"No, it's for safety." Claire was serious. "If we had the ability to alter the Physical Realm, we would be gods. People with such a capability could change whatever they didn't like in this world and replace it with their own design."

Dr. Stark shuddered. "You don't have to spook me with that make-believe nonsense."

"That's why we're still here," said Claire. "Our physical reality continues because no mortal can alter the metaphysical."

"But you said someone did. Who?"

"It is one explanation out of many possibilities," said Claire. "As far as who? God and Satan are two who come to mind."

"Then how are you going to find out the truth?" asked Dr. Stark.

"We have ways of finding out what happened," said Travis.

"I'm listening," said the doctor.

"We will perform a TAP," said Travis.

"A tap?" The doctor narrowed his eyes. "A spinal fluid tap?"

"A trans-axiom-paranormal analysis on the fetus's mind," clarified Travis.

"Ah, that TAP," said the doctor. "But why?"

"Every living thing, from inception until death, connects through a link from his or her mind to the Mind Realm," explained Travis.

"Oh, yes. The 'big library' in the sky," quipped Dr. Stark. "I guess the brain has no function in this matter?"

"The brain is part of the body. It is a processor, a transmitter, and a receptor." Travis didn't react to the doctor's amused expression. "The database is in the Mind Realm. Anyway, before a baby is born, his mind-link is coiled alongside his mother's link to that realm. Since the fetus is not in the body of his mother, we may find some clues of what, or how, it happened."

"What if it coils along the father's, the Pope's, link?" wondered Dr. Stark.

"If that's what we find, it will be something new and very revealing. Perhaps the link may lead us to the mother," Travis said.

"Do you think you could find the mother, then?" The doctor perked up.

"It's a possibility." Claire smiled to see the doctor finally getting it.

"I understand." Dr. Stark returned to his usual composed self. "And what if you find something different, like its own independent link?"

"It happened with Adam and Eve," said Travis.

Dr. Stark stared at him for a few seconds. "Whatever," he said dismissively. "Well, my job is done here. Call if you need me." His hologram disappeared.

"You'd better get going," said Maximus. "You've got a little bit over an hour to departure."

"In that case, we're ready," said Prescott. He, Claire, and Travis activated the dark shades on their PAVs to signal the beginning of their investigation and to maintain anonymity from that point on as needed. Maximus's hologram extinguished, and they were left alone in the conference room.

"Therefore," Travis said after a moment of contemplation, "a 92-year-old male is pregnant with a fetus that was conceived with his DNA and the DNA of an unknown woman. There's no evidence that the man has had any gender reassignment surgery, and the science says that the embryo was not implanted in the man's body through exterior means."

"And the man is the Roman Catholic Pope," added Claire.

"Who could have done it?" Prescott crossed his arms.

"And why?" Travis wondered.

Chapter 3. The Vatican

The conference door opened. Cardinal Molino, dressed in a black clerical suit with a Roman collar and accompanied by a young assistant priest, entered. "Good afternoon." The portly cardinal smiled pleasantly. "I hope you concluded the meeting on a positive note."

Claire, Prescott, and Travis nodded and smiled politely back at the cardinal, although only their mouths were visible. The cardinal's assistant stood respectfully by the door.

"A fair start, so far, Your Eminence," said Prescott. "We were surprised you were absent from this meeting."

"Oh, this meeting was not for me to attend," said Cardinal Molino, interlacing his fingers on top of his plump belly. "The Holy See asked us to facilitate the meeting. If we are needed to provide further assistance, we will be informed."

The conference room's intercom announced, "A shuttle to the airport is here for Ms. German, Mr. St. John, and Mr. Alighieri."

"I believe this is the call for your mission," said the cardinal pleasantly. "Have a safe trip." He blessed them with three fingers.

"Thank you, Your Eminence," replied Claire.

They exited the conference room and took the elevator up to the shuttle parking lot. The unmanned, four-seater robo-shuttle waited with its doors open. Once they were aboard, the doors slid shut, sealing them hermetically inside. The shuttle took off smoothly on its gravimag track, and, in seconds, it exited the underground parking lot. The shuttle skirted Los Angeles's downtown skyscrapers and joined the gravimag freeway that ran at an altitude of 1,000 meters above the old Interstate Freeways 110 and 105 to the airport. Like four giant Eiffel Towers, the airport's four skeletal suborbital launch towers dominated the skyline in the distance.

Surprisingly, the traffic was heavy at this midday hour, and the gravimag paths expanded to almost fifty lanes, channeling vehicles at different intervals, speeds, and altitudes south toward the airport and Orange County. From the ground, it seemed as if the vehicles were flying, but they were actually gliding over gravitational-magneto paths high above the old freeway infrastructures. Their shuttle's speed peaked at 500 km/h, and it arrived at the suborbital flight gates in six minutes.

The CTT departed from LAX at 2:03 pm and arrived near midnight in Rome. A forty-five-minute flight across nine time zones turned day into night. Claire, Travis, and Prescott, along with a few others, walked toward the VIP exit, leaving behind the crowd on their flight. Instantly identified by their GeneIDs, they moved quickly through customs, and, not having any luggage, they proceeded to the private shuttle transportation exit.

"Who do we meet here?" Travis asked.

"They've identified us." Claire read the information inside her PAV. "It's that fellow over there." She nodded her head toward a tall, dark, mustachioed man leaning on the side of a black private limo.

They set their aural PAVs for an instant translator from English to Italian and Italian to English.

"*Buona sera.* Good evening," said the man, standing up straight. "I'm here to escort you to Vatican City." He offered no name. The doors of the limo slid open at his voice command. "Please enter." He was probably an agent of the Vatican's security detail, assigned on a need-to-know basis. The limo whisked them quickly over the Autostrada Fiumicino-Roma's gravimag. Their escort sat silently in the driver's seat, letting the limo's robo-chauffeur do the driving. From time to time, when a car filled with women passed, he turned his head to look at them, just as all pure-blooded Italian males who appreciated the finer things in life would, even in the dim light of night.

Ten minutes later, they arrived at the Vatican through the back gates reserved for deliveries. The limo descended to an underground parking garage. A small, open vehicle arrived near the limo.

"It will take you to your destination, *signori*," said the mustachioed man, indicating the shuttle with his open hand.

Claire, Prescott, and Travis took their seats in the shuttle and departed for the ground level of the Vatican. They arrived inside a small cobblestoned courtyard surrounded by Renaissance architecture and well-manicured bushes lit by green spotlights. Here, time stood still in the 16th-century, and it seemed to replace the 21st-century modern world.

A priest, dressed in a cassock with a red silk sash around his waist and a red zucchetto on his head, approached with a smile. "*Buona sera*, and welcome to the Vatican. My name is Monsignore Giuseppe. I am the Holy Father's personal secretary. I trust your flight was pleasant." He offered his hand.

Claire, Prescott, and Travis each shook his hand while introducing themselves and turning off their shades.

"May I introduce to you Oberst Albert Glauser, head of security?" The Monsignore indicated a man dressed in civilian clothes who stood behind them. He was in his forties, tall and blond, with steely eyes. "Oberst, these are Clair, Travis, and Prescott with the CTT from the TIO."

Claire, Travis, and Prescott turned and nodded. Glauser nodded curtly back, assessing the strangers dressed in dark gray suits. All three had brown eyes. The taller man, Travis, had black hair and the other, Prescott, light brown hair. There were no handshakes. As usual, law enforcement people, including the Swiss Guard, were weary of paranormal investigators like the CTT.

Albert Glauser, a colonel in the Swiss Guard, watched them coolly. He then said, "If you don't mind, lady and gentlemen, please step on our scanner." He indicated the round scanner pad on the pavement.

"No need, Oberst Glauser," said Monsignore Giuseppe, raising his palm. "They are cleared by the Holy Father."

Oberst Glauser touched the comm-device behind his left ear to confirm the clearance from his own sources. He nodded and stepped aside. "Do you need me to come along, Monsignore?"

"*Grazie*, no need. I'll take them to the Holy Father's quarters myself." Monsignore Giuseppe smiled at his guests. "May I offer you refreshments? Perhaps you'd like to use the bathrooms?"

"We are fine, Monsignore. The sooner we see His Holiness, the better," said Prescott.

Mit Sandru

Chapter 4. The Pope

"This way. The Holy Father is waiting for you. Their Eminences, a small group of cardinals, will be present as well." Monsignore Giuseppe invited them to follow him. They walked on marble floors covered by red, velvety carpets through sumptuously decorated corridors. Crucifixes and miniature statues of the Madonna and Jesus, lit by discrete wall lamps, and many religious oil paintings, banners, and tapestries hung on the walls. It smelled of incense and wax, which was not surprising, considering the number of chapels connecting to the corridor. The Apostolic Palace was a large compound, requiring them to traverse the Cortile di Sisto V to enter the Papal Apartments.

"The Holy Father is waiting for us in his living room," said Monsignore Giuseppe as they entered the vestibule. An usher opened the doors to the living room and let them in. Several nightstand lamps and a few candles softly lit the room. The melting candle wax gave a silky feel to the ornately appointed quarters.

The Pope sat on a white armchair trimmed in gold, holding a rosary in his hands. He was dressed in simple white papal robes with a white zucchetto on his head. His red shoes protruded from underneath his robes. The Pope was a heavy man with slumping shoulders and a kind, serene face. He looked at the Capuchin Trinity Team almost as if he were relieved to have them in his presence.

On a side sofa at the Pope's right sat three cardinals. They were dressed in black cassocks with scarlet piping and buttons. Around their waists they wore scarlet watered-silk sashes, and each one wore a scarlet zucchetto.

At the Pope's left stood a civilian of about fifty years of age. His dark, wavy hair was shiny from the oil he must have used on it. His brown eyes, with a glint of skepticism, fixed on them.

Monsignore Giuseppe genuflected in front of the Pope and then stood to address him. "Your Holiness, allow me to introduce the Capuchin Trinity Team from America. Claire German, Travis St. John, and Prescott Alighieri."

Each of them bowed slightly as they were introduced.

The Pope extended his hand, and, since none of them were Catholic, they shook his hand— except for Claire, who, after shaking his hand, bowed and lowered her forehead to his ring. The Pope raised his eyebrows in surprise but then regained his passive expression.

"Your Eminences," said Monsignore Giuseppe, addressing the cardinals, "allow me to introduce the Capuchin Trinity Team from America." The three cardinals nodded toward them.

Monsignore Giuseppe continued the introductions starting with the farthest cardinal to their left. "Cardinal Bertrand, the Camerlengo." Cardinal Bertrand was a stout, black-haired man with a Mediterranean complexion. As the Camerlengo, he was responsible for the Pope's secular affairs, and, in case of the Pope's death, he would act as the Vatican's head of state.

"Cardinal Navarro, the President of the Pontifical Commission for the Vatican City State," said the Monsignore, extending his arm to the cardinal seating in the middle. Cardinal Navarro was a plump, round-faced man with white hair.

"Cardinal Cellini, the Secretary of State." Monsignore Giuseppe indicated the slim, seemingly tall cardinal who sat closest to the Pope, at his right hand. He had dark, penetrating eyes.

"And, of course, Dottore Pietro, the Holy Father's personal physician," concluded the Monsignore.

"Hello," Dr. Pietro said.

Claire made a mental note about the people at this meeting. These were the most powerful men in the Vatican. If something were to happen to the Pope, the cardinals would be instrumental in electing the new pope. They all had a stake in the condition of the Pope's health, for, perhaps, better or worse.

Monsignore Giuseppe pulled out three armchairs, and the Pope invited them to sit down.

"It is a pleasure to meet you, Claire, Travis, and Prescott," said the Pope.

"And so it is ours, Your Holiness," said Claire for the Capuchin Trinity Team.

"Dottore Pietro, my personal physician, will provide you with any scientific and medical assistance that you may need." The Pope indicated the doctor.

The doctor bowed his head slightly and said, "I am glad that you are here. Considering the delicacy of this matter, your confidentiality is most essential."

"We consider this matter highly confidential," said Prescott.

"That is understood," said the Pope. "Tell me something about yourselves." He glanced from one to the other.

"My name is Claire German," began Claire. "I'm educated as a medical doctor, but I joined the FBI instead of pursuing a medical career. Five years ago, we formed our Trinity Team after Maximus discovered us. And I've been a member of the Capuchin Trinity Team since."

"Hmm, a doctor and a law enforcement professional," said the Pope. "How about you?" He looked at Prescott.

"I'm Prescott Alighieri. I graduated as an electronics and security engineer, but, shortly after starting my engineering career, I joined the US National Security Agency, the NSA, as a countersurveillance specialist. Maximus was instrumental in forming our Trinity Team."

The Pope smiled and then turned to Travis.

"I am Travis St. John, and I studied history, but, instead of teaching, I aspired to become a spy. The CIA agreed and hired me as a field operative. Maximus saw my potential and raw talent, and invited the three of us to meet in person to discuss a fascinating career opportunity. And so we became the Capuchin Trinity Team."

"Interesting," remarked the Pope. "All of you are professionals and former law enforcement or intelligence agents."

"Is that unusual, Your Holiness?" Dr. Pietro asked.

"They are the only Trinity Team with such backgrounds," said the Pope, gesturing toward them. "The Chinese tried to organize a similar Trinity and failed. Maybe God was watching."

The doctor did not seem to understand the Pope's remark.

"Not because they were Chinese, but because they were trying to assemble a Trinity Team made of secret police agents to serve the motives of their state apparatus. God works in mysterious ways."

"Forgive my ignorance, Your Holiness, but isn't the Capuchin Trinity a United States government organization?" the doctor asked.

The Pope's smile invited the Capuchin Trinity Team to respond.

"We are part of the Trinity Investigation Organization, also known as TIO," said Prescott. "Our team, just like all the Trinity Teams in the world, is independent of any government, political, or religious organization."

"Which perhaps invites the question: Why is the Vatican Trinity Team not involved?" Travis asked.

The doctor made a face, as if he were surprised to learn that the Vatican had a Trinity Team. It seemed that he did not know everything there was to know about the Vatican's institutions.

"Well, the Vatican Trinity Team answers to the Holy See," said the Pope. "And their aptitude is more spiritual. I think your team is very well-suited for this case."

"Your Holiness, I'm curious. Why did you specifically request our team?" Claire asked.

The Pope smiled. "Whatever happened to me could be divine intervention, and I pray it is. I and the Holy See are prepared to accept this fact." He glanced at the cardinals, who bowed their heads. "However, what if this is not divine intervention and it is perpetrated by evil? An act like this could destroy our faith in God, or our faith in the Holy Church, or our faith in humanity. Perhaps, this could be the beginning of Armageddon." The Pope and the cardinals made the sign of the cross. "In any case, your reputation as incorruptible impressed me."

"Your Holiness, you mentioned evil," said Claire. "What kind of evil?"

"Of the unholy kind. That's why I asked for your team to investigate. We must be absolutely sure about what we have here. If it is a malignancy, a living malignancy induced by the unholy one, I have no problem removing it from my body. However, if it is the work of God, we must be prepared and make arrangements for a new era." The Pope raised three fingers in the sign of the Holy Trinity.

"Your Holiness, what do you exactly want us to do?" Prescott asked.

"I ask you to determine what has happened to me and what is the cause. Then and only then can I and the Pontifical Council determine what action to take."

"Your Holiness, we will try our best to resolve this mystery," said Claire. "Who else knows about your condition?"

"Just those of us in this room," said the Pope. "And, of course, your organization."

Claire had a feeling that the Pope was not divulging the whole truth. There was someone else aware of his situation, but she let it rest for now. "Your Holiness, could you tell us what happened?"

"Certainly. A week ago, I started feeling unwell." The Pope looked at the Monsignore for agreement; he gave a short bow. "The Dottore was not available, so, instead, Monsignore Giuseppe had the robot at the papal clinic diagnose me. It was unclear what the problem was, but it seemed that I carried something in my belly. The Dottore returned immediately from his trip and gave me a more thorough analysis, and he almost fainted. I'd better let him tell you the rest."

Dr. Pietro cleared his throat. "As His Holiness said, after I returned I gave him another examination and, to my surprise, when I checked his abdomen, I heard a heartbeat. I thought I was imagining things, so I took him immediately to his private medical clinic. Luckily, just last year we received a state-of-the-art scanner. The hologram transmitted by the scanner made me lightheaded." The doctor paused. "At first I thought it was a malignancy, but soon I realized it was a fetus. I scanned again and did a complete genetic analysis, but the results confirmed it as a male fetus. The good news is, it is not a cancerous malignancy. The not-so-good news is, it is a fetus, and I have no idea how it happened."

"Any signs of exterior intervention?" Travis asked.

"None," said the doctor. "I performed epidermal and muscle tissues scans, and there is no external intrusion anywhere on the body. It is as if the fetus just grew inside His Holiness, all by itself."

"In your professional opinion, is this possible?" Prescott asked.

"A healthy fetus is unheard of," said the doctor. "I searched for any similar cases, but I found none. I thought it was a genetic mutation and the Holy Father's body was recreating his own clone, but the genetic code indicated that this fetus is not a clone. This fetus is no different from any other fetus conceived between a man and a woman. Forgive me, Your Holiness."

"Not to worry," said the Pope. "I did not violate my celibacy vows. I am a man, and, in this unusual circumstance, I'm carrying a baby just as if I were a female. Is that correct, Dottore?"

"That is correct, Your Holiness," confirmed the doctor.

"But how could this be?" wondered Claire. "You must have scanned the Holy Father in the past. Did you detect any anomalies before?"

"Nothing at all," said the doctor. "I performed a complete scan six months ago. His Holiness was as normal as any man of his age."

"Therefore, whatever happened, it occurred within the last six months," said Claire.

"Possibly," agreed the doctor. "When exactly it happened is a subject of debate."

"Do you have any explanation as to how a male body could transform itself to sustain a fetus?" Travis asked.

"His Holiness's body did not transform itself into a female body," said the doctor. "But it developed the fetal sac to nourish and grow the baby. The hormone levels have changed, taking on very much the characteristics of a pregnant woman."

There was a long pause. It was unprecedented and impossible. However, there he was: a pregnant old man. Monsignore

Giuseppe bowed his head and started praying silently.

"I pray it is divine intervention," concluded the Pope. "God will help us as much as we will help ourselves. And that's why you are here."

"We will do our best to be of assistance, Your Holiness," said Claire.

"I'm sure you will, I'm sure you will," the Pope said with a trace of tiredness in his voice.

"Forgive me, Your Holiness," said the doctor. "But I'm not sure what more the Capuchin Trinity Team could do for you, besides what science can and will do."

"Find the truth." The Pope steepled his fingers as if in prayer.

"How, Your Holiness?"

"Dottore, I'll have to explain. The Church created the first Trinities many centuries ago. We realized that certain people had abilities to see and sense the supernatural. They were not possessed by the unholy—they were God's children with special abilities. What's even more astonishing is that, when three of these special people were teamed up, their abilities expanded beyond our mortal comprehension. That's how the Trinities were started."

The doctor nodded, but seemed intrigued.

"There are certain things that religion and science cannot explain," continued the Pope. "A Trinity Team can. That's why we formed these groups—to help mankind live and prosper under God and not be vanquished by the unholy one."

"I never knew of their existence," said the doctor.

"Few people do," said the Pope. "Trinities are rare. They are called upon to investigate when men can do no more."

"Are you Catholics?" the doctor asked the CTT.

"We believe in God, but we are not of the Catholic religion," said Prescott.

"Then how…"

"The Roman Catholic Church could not keep this all for itself," said the Pope. "Their rare talent is present throughout the world's population. The Capuchin Trinity Team happens to be American."

"One more thing, Your Holiness, if you permit me," said the doctor. "Why do they take the name of a monastic religious order? They are not monks."

"The original Trinity members, long ago, used to be monks. And they named their teams after their religious orders," answered the Pope. "The new Trinity Teams kept the naming tradition."

"Thank you, Your Holiness," said the doctor. "Although, as a scientist, I'm skeptical of their abilities."

"And you should be, Dottore," said the Pope. "However, in this circumstance, please work with them."

The doctor bowed in agreement.

"Well, Claire, Prescott, and Travis, what do you suggest we do?" the Pope asked.

"We would like to do a trans-axiom-paranormal assessment, or TAP," said Prescott.

"What would that be?" Monsignore Giuseppe appeared apprehensive.

"Yes, what would that be?" asked Cardinal Cellini.

"A trans-axiom-paranormal assessment is a non-intrusive observation of the mind's link from the brain to the Mind Realm," said Prescott.

"Are you saying that you will be invading His Holiness's mind?" Cardinal Cellini and the other two cardinals looked concerned.

"Nothing like that, Your Eminence," responded Prescott. "Let me explain it in more detail. What we do in TAP is to examine the link of the fetus's brain to the Mind Realm."

That explanation seemed to be news to the cardinals; their eyes widened, but, in Cellini's case, they narrowed.

"The widely held belief is that our brains are our minds," said Claire. She caught the doctor frowning in disagreement. She smiled and continued, "That is not so. Our minds continue to exist even after we die and our brains become dust. The brain is an organ, just like the heart. The heart is not responsible for our feelings, so is the brain not responsible for our minds."

"Then what are our minds?" asked the doctor with a slight smirk.

"Our minds are our recorded experiences," said Claire. "The brain is the processor, but our experiences, our memories, are stored in the Mind Realm, which is located in the White Energy Universe. Every living creature's brain has a link to this realm. That link is what we will examine."

"But what would that tell you?" asked the doctor.

"The mind link of a normal fetus, in a woman's body, coils around the mother's link, guided to the right destination. It stays that way until the child is born, after which it separates from the mother's link and becomes independent."

"And this fetus's link would be coiled around its mother's link, too?" the doctor asked.

"That's what we hope to observe, since there is not a proper mother involved here," said Claire. "When the fetus is not procreated from normal intercourse between a man and a woman, such as in test tube babies, the fetus's mind link is different."

"How different?" the doctor asked with slight trepidation in his voice.

"If the woman is artificially inseminated, the fetus's link follows the mother's link, but it does not coil around it. If the woman carries a test tube fetus, its mind's link is completely independent of the mother."

"I would say this is fascinating but not scientifically proven," said the doctor.

"Correct, only a Trinity Team would be able to observe this phenomenon," said Claire.

"Then you would be able to deduce how the fetus came into existence?" Cardinal Bertrand asked.

"That's what we hope to find out," confirmed Claire.

"Any ill effects on His Holiness's being?" Cardinal Navarro asked.

"It will have no effect on Your Holiness," said Travis, addressing the Pope. "We will not physically touch you or mentally disturb you. With your permission, Your Holiness, we would like to perform this assessment when you're ready."

The Pope exchanged quick glances with the cardinals, and then he nodded at the CTT. "I'm ready right now."

"Your Holiness, please stay seated where you are. If you don't mind, Monsignore and Dottore, we need you to stand away from the Holy Father so that you will not interfere with our observation." Prescott and Travis walked slightly behind and to the side of the Pope. Claire stood in front of him.

The Monsignore and the Dottore did as they were asked and retreated near the sofa, where the cardinals sat quietly. The Monsignore looked uneasy. The doctor looked doubtful. Cardinal Cellini placed a finger on his lower lip, staring at them from under his thin eyebrows. Cardinals Navarro and Bertrand seemed to be praying.

After taking their positions, Claire, Travis, and Prescott stood with their feet apart, their hands folded on their chests, and their heads lowered. They began.

Mit Sandru

Chapter 5. The Trans-Axiom-Paranormal Assessment

The minds of Claire, Travis, and Prescott amalgamated into one. From that point on, they were not three individual minds, but one. They no longer considered each self as "I," but addressed one common thought as "we."

We are one. We observe everything through our human senses, although we know that our senses are limited. The realm we enter is the realm of mental ether that scientific instruments cannot detect. This is a realm where time flows into the future and the past, and where it could even stop. This is a realm of unknown spatial dimensions, changing from one, two, three, four, or more dimensions continuously. It is a strange realm, and hallucination would only begin to explain what we see, feel, hear, taste, and touch. Although we have no corporal body, our sensory perceptions are as sharp as ever. We see now what ordinary people do not see until after they die.

There is a random pinging noise coming from an undetermined direction. We are orbiting two nebulae of mental energy. The small one is the fetus and the other one, much bigger, is the Pope. We see the mental energy flashing within and around the surfaces of the nebulae like storms of colorful light. Some of these storms pulsate or change colors. From time to time, tiny lightning flashes randomly discharge. We observe the thoughts in action. We are here to observe the fetus's connection from the mind's nebula to the Mind Realm.

The Pope's mind nebula is brighter, and it floods its surroundings with diffuse light. Calm and tranquility emanate from it, accompanied by the sweet smell of jasmine flowers. Filaments of slow light in rainbow colors uncoil from the Pope's mind like tendrils of smoke dissipating in the ether. Other filaments resemble solar flares, expanding and then collapsing back toward the sphere. The Pope's mind is relaxed, judging from the slow activity of mind energy discharging within and along the mind link. The Pope's mind link exits its nebula, coiling halfway around the orb cloud before it vanishes into the infinity toward the Mind Realm in the White Energy Universe. The link resembles a bundle of colorful, fuzzy conduits, pulsating away from or toward the Mind Realm. Some of the pulses of the mind's energy are instant. Others travel slowly, like colorful liquids flowing in transparent tubes. Some pulsate at different frequencies, with or without changing colors.

We approach and see the fetus's mind nebula. It is smaller than the Pope's, and it is under development. The link is our interest. A small raceway of light threads exits the nebula and curls halfway around it, just as we observed with the Pope's link. The link departs toward the Mind Realm in the White Energy Universe. But this link does not coil around the Pope's link, as it would around the mother's link. It flails around it, sometimes halfway coiling, sometimes following a parallel path into the infinity toward the Mind Realm.

We move closer to observe the fetus's nebula and its link. As we go toward it in a semi-elliptical path, a strange phenomenon happens. We enter a dimensionally undetermined universe. The nebula is no longer a fuzzy sphere but an incomprehensible shape that seems to evolve and collapse on itself all at once. From one of the poles of the indescribable shape a white light link unfurls, which changes shape at random, from a line to a tape to a tube to an indeterminate and strange link heading toward the Mind Realm. From the antipode of the fetus's mind, we see another link. It is a link of Dark Light. This is unusual, as most humans' Mind Realm connects to the White Energy Universe. This connection shoots straight like an arrow into the void toward to the Dark Energy Universe.

We get closer to the dark energy link, which manifests itself in a four-dimensional universe. We are confused by a world that we cannot comprehend, and we make an effort to convert some of its dimensions into three dimensions. We struggle to maintain a steady picture. We cannot. It shifts too radically for us to make sense of what we see. We must take another approach. We must split into our three individual minds while staying connected to each other. Each one of us will observe one of the three-dimensional universes that make up the multidimensional universe. We, individually, must penetrate the dark energy link.

I, Prescott, am first to break loose. I feel Claire and Travis nearby in the other three-dimensional universes. I am inside a link of dark rainbow colors. This is definitely dark energy. It is as if I am in the middle of a bundle of dark color flows of indefinable surface textures. The flows are opaque, and I can't see what is roving through them. But wait: As I get closer I enter its channel, and the flow of dark energy resemble snakes, black snakes with shimmering scales, coiling and interlacing as if in a braid. A putrid smell like rotten meat emanates from them. I need more information. Where is the fetus's mind? Behind me or ahead of me? It is above me. I move outside through the twisting bundle of snakes and observe that this link has transformed into a helix now, coiling itself around another dark-blue link. There are two paths: one straight, the other circled by the helix link. I look toward the hazy light of the nebula. The link exits out of the nebula like a flower stem coming out of a smoky surface. At the opposite direction it disappears into a dark hole. I'm tempted to follow it, but I feel something deadly awaits . . .

I, Claire, sense Prescott and Travis in two of the other universes. I am in the middle of a gray shaft. Bolts of dark light travel at low speeds to and from the mind, the dimly lit mind nebula I see in the distance. At the other end, the bolts of dark light dissipate into black tendrils. Or perhaps they are not tendrils, but black lightning. I must be careful about those bolts of black lightning. If I am hit, it will take me to a dark hole, and I have a feeling that I will not ever return from it. I sense a very unpleasant taste, as if I've put my tongue on the terminals of a battery. It tingles sourly . . .

I, Travis, exist in a globular universe. I sense Claire and Prescott, but Claire is concerned about her safety. I feel as if I've emerged in a dark-yellow fog, like a toxic sulfuric cloud. The transparent, gaseous globules move in haphazard directions. I see no perimeter on this universe. In all directions, it expands forever. It is perhaps infinite. Nearby, two globules collide. A blue flash, like an electrical discharge, sparks between them, after which they unite into a larger globule. I sense the reverberation of the collision as if two bells were clanged together. The reverberation diminishes and returns as an echo of hot energy . . .

I, Prescott, observe the coil of snakes changing in color from black to velvety violet.

Sprouting from the mind's nebula like veins, a pulse of glowing red-purple radiance travels along the snakes, and it disappears in the far distance as a red flash of light. Another radiance follows the one I just observed, and it explodes in another red flash, but much closer. What is going on?

I, Claire, determine that the bolts of dark light are increasing in speed. If they continue to increase at this rate, I may be hit by one of them soon. It's getting perilous here, as if I were standing among a fusillade of dark lasers. It is getting cold . . .

I, Travis, see an increase in the collision and aggregation of the gaseous globes. They grow in size. I wonder how big they will become. Will this entire universe become a giant globe? Suddenly, one explodes into small molecular silver bullets. Some of these pierce through the other globes, and they explode in turn, releasing more of the silvery bullets. It resembles a nuclear chain reaction. I feel the pressure from the explosions. This doesn't look good . . .

I, Prescott, perceive the red flashes as explosions that are arriving nearer and nearer my ethereal location. The flashes are burning my senses, and they thunder all around me . . .

Danger! Danger! Danger!

Claire, Travis, and Prescott regroup.

We are one. We must leave. We exit from the link back to our three-dimensional universe. The fetus's mind orb is sparkling with dark energy, a storm is raging inside, and the link is glowing with dark light. Even the white-light link is pulsating with information of different frequencies. The fetus's mind is trying to understand our intrusion into the dark energy link. It has become hostile.

We must return.

Prescott, Claire, and Travis raised their heads. They were back in the present time. This was the first time they had witnessed such an event. Instead of finding an answer, they discovered a deepening mystery.

"Thank you, Your Holiness," said Claire, and she sat down.

Travis and Prescott returned to their seats.

"Did you change your minds?" The doctor exchanged dumbfounded looks with the Monsignore. "You are not going to perform your, your TAP?"

"We did. That's all it takes," said Claire.

"I don't understand. Aren't séances longer than this?" asked the doctor.

"Let me explain, Dottore," said Prescott. "We did not conduct a séance. Séances are for speaking with the spirits of the deceased. They are marginally successful even for experienced mediums. We are not mediums."

"Then what are you?"

"We are a Trinity," said Prescott. "Our three minds amalgamate as one, and we are able to explore other realms. In this case, we explored around the new fetus's mind and his link to the Mind Realm. To you, it seemed that we took only a second. In reality, our minds spent considerable time performing the Trans-Axiom-Paranormal assessment while amalgamated. We were in a different time frame."

The doctor widened his eyes in disbelief. "And what did you find out?"

"You see, every unborn life has unique link characteristics, but they are predictable to a certain extent," said Prescott. "What we experienced with the link of this fetus is unusual."

Everyone except the Pope leaned forward. The cardinals sat on the edge of their sofa.

"How unusual, CTT?" Cardinal Cellini asked, his eyes wide.

Claire took a deep breath before giving them the news. "To begin with, the fetus has a link to the Mind Realm in the White Energy Universe. This link shows characteristics of both normal procreation and artificial insemination."

"What does that mean?" Cardinal Bertrand asked.

"It could mean that there was a dual conception," answered Claire.

"Dual, like in twins?" The doctor was pacing behind the Pope's chair, disturbing the flames of some of the nearby candles.

"No. As you found, there is only one fetus."

"Then what? Dual brains, dual minds?" The doctor looked shocked.

"Neither," said Travis. "The fetus has only one brain and one mind. However, how it was procreated is the mystery, as if it were both naturally and artificially created."

There was silence; the group was afraid even to breathe.

"But that's not all," said Travis. "The fetus has another mind link. A link to the Dark Energy Universe."

Explosive gasps erupted from the cardinals and the Monsignore.

"Would you explain?" asked Cardinal Cellini, troubled by what he heard.

"Well, we've never experienced a dual link phenomenon, but from our predecessors we have learned that a fetus with a dark energy link is rare. Some may say it is an anomaly," Travis said.

"What kind of an anomaly—good or bad?" Cardinal Navarro asked.

Travis understood what the cardinal was alluding to. "Dark energy could be interpreted to be the realm of the devil, and—"

"*Dio mio!*" exclaimed the Monsignore.

"However, that hasn't been proven," said Travis. "Evil people have mind links to the White Energy Universe, while perfectly good people could have links to the Dark Energy. A few of them were believed to have been geniuses."

"His mind is exposed to two different realms?" the Pope asked, and he looked at his belly.

Travis nodded. The Pope and the Monsignore made the sign of the cross. The cardinals sat stiffly as if they were unsure of what to say or do.

Travis cleared his throat. "But we've just begun. With Your Holiness's permission, we've finished our assessment and would like to review the genetic results that our good Dottore collected." Travis took notice of the time. "However, it is late, and we will do that in the morning."

"Certainly. Dottore Pietro will offer his full support." The Pope glanced at the doctor, who smiled and bowed slightly.

"May I ask if that is all you can tell us?" wondered Dr. Pietro. "I feel that we're not any further along in uncovering this mystery."

"Have a little bit of faith, Dottore," said the Pope. "In due time, we will get a complete explanation from the Capuchin Trinity Team." The doctor bowed his head. "Please see that they obtain what they need." The Pope blessed the Trinity Team, and they were dismissed.

The Monsignore invited the CTT to follow him. Dottore Pietro, eager to ask more questions, excused himself and followed them outside the papal quarters.

"If you don't mind me asking you," said the doctor, catching up with them. "How many realms are you able to see?"

"We don't see them—we sense them," said Claire as she followed her teammates and the Monsignore to their sleeping quarters. "To explain what we sense, we have to convert the information into our five senses: sight, hearing, taste, smell, and touch. For example, the sense of sight while we are in a particular realm is omni-directional. We sense-see at once in every direction, unless something blocks our view. It is very difficult to describe what we see because it happens all at once."

The doctor nodded, his mouth slightly agape.

"And as far as how many realms we can sense," continued Claire, "we always see new ones, and it is difficult to categorize them as they change and interconnect and convolute in infinite ways."

"But isn't heaven made of seven circles?" the doctor asked.

Travis chuckled. "Dottore, humans are limited in imagining how all God's realms are assembled. God has no limit, and his realms are infinite."

"Including . . . " the doctor hesitated, "Satan's realm?"

"Including Satan's," said Travis.

The doctor froze in place, his eyes wide in disbelief and fear.

Mit Sandru

Chapter 6. May God or Man Help Us

After the door closed, the cardinals stood up and went to the three chairs in front of the Pope. They sat in silence, thinking about and analyzing the information the CTT had divulged to them. When God and the Roman Catholic Church are one and the same, the decisions that need to be taken have to be thought out most carefully.

"God works in mysterious ways," said the Pope thoughtfully.

The cardinals nodded in understanding.

"The information imparted by the Capuchin Trinity Team is disconcerting," continued the Pope. "The living thing inside me may be human or may not. If it is human and it is an act of our Heavenly Father, we will commit an unforgiveable sin to remove and kill him. He could be the new Messiah." The Pope raised his eyes to the heavens. "Of course, if this is the doing of the unholy one, I may be carrying the Antichrist. We cannot be nurturing the destroyer of our God's kingdom." The Pope sat quietly with his palms together as if in supplication. "Please, Heavenly Father, guide us! We must be certain of who exactly is inside me."

The cardinals nodded in concordance.

"Therefore, whatever the outcome will be, we need to prepare our Holy Church for the aftermath. I know that this situation was kept in the utmost secrecy. Nevertheless, from now on, we must prepare our most devout cardinals for the potential of a most happy outcome or a most tragic one.

"I am an old man. Someone will need to take my place and lead the Church into the 22nd century. Either through my dying from this," the Pope waved his hand over his belly, "or my resigning before our conclusion on the fate of the fetus." The Pope sighed.

Cardinal Cellini spoke up. "Your Holiness, permit me to say that we will support you in whatever decision needs to be made." The other two cardinals murmured words of agreement.

"May God bless you and guide your path into the future." The Pope blessed them, and the cardinals, one by one, kissed his ring.

Cardinal Bertrand entered his chambers. In his chapel, he kneeled in front of the crucifix and the Madonna. After a quick prayer, he went to his desk and initiated a holopresence with an elderly cardinal.

"You seem very distraught, brother Bertrand," said the older cardinal.

"Cardinal Le Pere, thank you for staying up late to have this conversation with me," said Cardinal Bertrand.

"For my disciple, any time." Cardinal Le Pere smiled.

"There is graver news about our Holy Father's health. You are my mentor, and I need to confer with you regarding a most delicate situation in case our Holy Father is unable to carry out his duties."

"Is it that serious?" Cardinal Le Pere raised his eyebrows. "I am sure that you, as the Camerlengo, will be able to conduct the business of papal affairs most diligently."

"Yes, I am. I've prepared for this mission under your guiding hand all my life." Cardinal Bertrand made the sign of the cross. "I would also like to offer my candidacy as the next pope, should such a need descend upon us. I realize that this is not proper for me to ask, however, you are my mentor, and a capable hand will be needed at the helm of the Church in the trying times ahead of us."

"I see," said Cardinal Le Pere. "What makes you think that?"

"The passing of our Holy Father into heaven in the very near future is an almost certainty."

"*Mon Dieu!*" exclaimed Cardinal Le Pere.

Cardinal Cellini did not waste a moment after he left the Pope's quarters. He spoke into his secure comm-device, "Emergency meeting in five minutes."

The cardinal entered his quarters, positioned a PAV on his nose, and initiated the holopresence. "Are we all here?" he asked in Latin.

"All but one," answered one of the cardinals.

Cardinal Cellini collapsed into his sumptuous chair in front of his desk. Cardinal Le Pere was absent. "Let's begin." He looked at the circle of eleven holograms of the present cardinals in his PAV. "I, Cardinal Cellini, the Secretary of State of the Vatican, proceed with this emergency meeting regarding the affairs of the Holy See and the health of our Holy Father. I've selected the twelve of you from the Curia to be members and overseers of the Secret Holy See Emergency Council. We have an emergency on our hands. A grave emergency."

The Secret Holy See Emergency Council members did not move or say a word but waited to hear the news.

"Our Holy Father is gravely ill. The outcome of his illness may affect the Holy See in such a fundamental way that it may cease to exist." That information drew gasps from most of the council members. "In short, our Holy Father has a growth in his belly that resembles a male fetus."

Exclamations invoking God, the Madonna, and all the saints erupted from the group. Some were waving their hands, and others made the sign of the cross several times, while two of them started an argument.

Cardinal Cellini raised his hand, demanding silence. "May I remind you that this council is the most powerful body in the Curia and is righteously responsible to save our Holy Church." Nods and reassurances followed. "The reason that this affair is so monumental is because our Holy Father has not performed any medical procedure to avail himself of a son."

"Then how is it possible?" demanded Cardinal Molino of Los Angeles. "It cannot be an immaculate conception. He is a man!"

Cardinal Cellini leaned forward. "It is not an immaculate conception. It is an unholy conception."

The Secret Holy See Emergency Council members were so shocked that they did not utter a word.

Finally, Cardinal Tobutu Goba of Mozambique asked timidly, "Do we have proof of this transgression?"

"*Certo*! A Trinity Team, the Capuchin Trinity Team, was summoned to assess the Holy Father's condition. They found," Cardinal Cellini raised a finger, "they found the fetus's mind connected to the Dark Energy Universe."

"*Dio*, no!" some cardinals shouted.

"I, myself, sensed a dark, cloaking shadow around the Holy Father," said Cellini. "I believe that our Holy Father is a victim here. How and why it happened is unknown. Nevertheless, we need to take steps to preserve the Holy See and our Holy Church."

Cardinal Navarro walked slowly along an out-of-the-way path to the Sistine Chapel. He needed time to think, and he needed to pray, to pray hard, for an answer out of this dilemma. The Roman Catholic Church had never been faced with such a predicament. Was this the arrival of Armageddon? Or was this a test for the faithful?

He kneeled in front of the altar in the Sistine Chapel and looked up at the fresco of Jesus suffering on the cross. Will he be able to save us from all the devastation and the perils humanity is suffering today? Will he be able to resolve the enigma surrounding the Holy Father? Will he be able to save the unborn child that is contained not in a woman's womb but in a man's belly?

Will Jesus Christ, the Son of God, save us from the evil that may have a hand in this challenge? Or is it all-divine and immaculate, commensurate with the trying times we are facing? God, give us guidance to take the right path and help our Holy Father. Is the unborn one flesh from the flesh of the Lord? Is the unborn one the new Messiah? Will he be able to deliver us from evil?

Two other cardinals approached Cardinal Navarro, and they kneeled on each side of him. One of them was Cardinal Le Pere. They began praying as if of the same mind, hoping for deliverance and divine intervention.

Chapter 7. Genetic Paleontology

The next morning a bell, sounding somewhere in the courtyard, woke Claire, Prescott, and Travis. The ultrasonic sleep inducers they always carried with them had done their job, and they had slept well and peacefully. Their biological clocks were on Italian time now. Written notes—paper was still in use at the Vatican—were slipped under their doors telling them where their suitcases were and that breakfast was available in the mess hall. Their suitcases contained their usual travel wares, including special weapons, compliments of Maximus and TIO. After a quick vibratory shower, they dressed in their suits and met outside their chambers. Exchanging short "'Mornings," they followed the directions to the mess hall.

And it was a mess hall of the monastic type, with long wooden tables and benches. A variety of breakfast foods were available on a large table adorned with crucifixes. They must have been late for breakfast, because the room was almost deserted, except for a couple of priests in a far corner who ate quietly.

Claire took her time to assess the breakfast table. It had many baskets with breads and buns, platters with fresh-cut fruits, cheeses, and cold cuts, three types of freshly squeezed juices, boiled eggs, and an assortment of pastries. Several brands of cereals and carafes of milk completed the assortment. An incredibly elaborate brass espresso machine was placed in the middle of the table, flanked by lit candles—Italians took their coffee seriously. After careful inspection, Claire filled her plate with fruit and picked a roll. Travis and Prescott were already sitting at the table. Travis was sipping from his double cappuccino, while Prescott was chipping methodically at his soft-boiled egg, as if he were creating a work of art.

"Boy, they know how to make a good cappuccino here," said Travis with a satisfied smile.

"They probably have Capuchin monks on duty just to make cappuccinos," commented Prescott, spooning into his perfectly unshelled boiled egg. He took a bite and let the egg swirl in his mouth. He sighed with content. "Where do they get these eggs from? They taste devilishly good." He covered his mouth with his napkin. "Oops! I meant heavenly."

"Oops is right. Saying such a word in the Vatican," admonished Claire, as she bit into a plump grape. "It is the blessing that makes the food taste better."

"Indeed," Travis said. He looked over the rim of his cup, inspecting the empty hall.

Claire observed a robo-bee cleaning the melted wax on an extinguished candle, after which it reignited the candle. "It's all clear. No listening bugs," she said to Prescott and Travis.

"Let's go to cloak anyway," said Travis. They turned on the audio silencing. "Interesting mind link on that fetus, don't you think?"

"Yes, probably it freaked them out when we told them about the dark link," said Prescott. "Frankly, I'm sort of freaked out myself. Two links, one to the white energy and the other to the dark energy." After a moment he added, "Like Jesus."

Clair and Travis were thinking of what they had discovered.

"You saw the helix of snakes," said Travis to Prescott after a while. Prescott nodded. "Anything to do with the DNA helix?" Travis asked Claire.

Claire thought for a moment. "It could be. This could be a hint about where to look next."

"You think that Satan made a mistake by leaving that information in the link?" wondered Prescott.

"Satan or whomever else," said Claire, tapping her chin with the handle of her fork. "It definitely transferred information to the Dark Energy Realm when we disturbed it."

"Let's not jump to premature conclusions about Satan," said Travis. "He is not the king of the Dark Energy Universe. He may be just an opportunist, arriving after the damage was done to the Pope and to torment humanity as a bonus."

"Then it is human misdoing," said Claire.

"We need more information," said Travis.

"We definitely need to follow the genetic trail," concluded Claire. She dabbed her mouth with her napkin while watching the robo-bee extinguish the candles. Breakfast was now over.

Prescott initiated audio contact with Dr. Pietro. "*Buongiorno*, Dottore. How are you today?"

"*Buongiorno*! *Molto bene*, very well, Prescott," said the doctor jovially. "Any more information about our very strange case?"

"Actually, we would like to obtain some information from you, if you don't mind," said Prescott.

"But of course. What can I do for you?" he asked.

"We would like to see the fetus's genetic scans," said Prescott.

"*Certamente*, sure," said the doctor. "But why, may I ask?"

"Well, we cannot leave any stone unturned. Procedure, you know," said Prescott.

"I understand. I'll set a tracer for you to follow to the medical quarters, where I shall meet you shortly."

"*Grazie*." Prescott concluded the communication.

They followed the tracer in their PAVs to the papal medical quarters. The doctor met them in front of the door. "Welcome." He smiled broadly. The papal clinic was as well-equipped as any emergency medical and dentistry unit would be. "I am surprised that you wish to see the scientific facts. I thought you were more into, you know, the world beyond."

"We are all over—jacks of all trades," said Travis. "And Claire is a medical doctor."

"By education, not practice," added Claire.

"Oh, you could have made such a good doctor," Dr. Pietro flattered her.

"She faints at the sight of her own blood," said Travis.

"*É vero*? Is it true?" asked the doctor in disbelief.

"Not if she draws blood from someone else," Prescott pitched in.

"They're kidding, Dottore," said Claire, shaking her head at the other two.

"A joke, of course." The doctor laughed.

They entered the laboratory, which was adjacent to the operating room. By voice command the doctor turned on the holopresenter unit. The holographic form of the fetus, its placenta, and its umbilical cord, all enclosed in the transparent fetal sac, hung in the air at eye level. The fetus's pink form was curled up, head down, seemingly asleep. Claire, Prescott, and Travis walked slowly around it, examining it intently.

"How long ago did you take this scan?" asked Claire.

"Six days ago," said the doctor.

"How old do you think the fetus is?" asked Claire.

"Six months, judging by its maturity."

"And the last scan you took before this was six months ago?" asked Travis.

"Yes."

"So the start of the abnormality happened shortly after that scan?" asked Travis.

"I presume so," acknowledged the doctor. "But it is not an abnormality—it is a fetus."

"Of course. Did anything unusual happen after the last exam six months ago?" Travis continued his questioning.

"No. As a matter of fact, the Holy Father took a month's sabbatical for prayer and meditation after the last scan," said the doctor.

"Hmm," said Travis, thinking.

"Examining this hologram, I see there is no way of giving birth to this boy," said Prescott.

"No, not at all. It will have to be removed surgically."

"When are you planning to do that, Dottore?" Prescott asked.

"Whenever the Holy Father, or the baby, decides it's time." The doctor seemed as if he hadn't considered this until now. He glanced at a corner of the room, and they followed his glance. A preemie incubator stood by, ready for use; it was a strange object in the Vatican, where babies were not supposed to be born. "We're ready for all eventualities," said the doctor, catching their glimpses.

"A living human inside the belly of a man," said Prescott, more to himself than anyone else.

"Could we see the genetic report, Dottore?" asked Claire. She was curious to see what clues they may find in it.

"Of course." With another voice command, the doctor displayed the genetic diagram on the wall screen. Color bars of different lengths appeared on the screen.

"So these are the male genes." Claire pointed to a group of bars.

"Yes, and the other sixty percent belong to the female."

"The female's genes look kind of unusual, don't you think?" proposed Claire.

"Perhaps," said the doctor, squinting at the bars.

"Can you project the DNA ribbon, Dottore?" Travis asked.

"Certainly." The doctor activated a hologram, and the DNA ribbon unfolded before their eyes. "The computer would have picked up any anomalies and mutations, but there are none."

"Were you able to identify the mother by her genes?" asked Travis.

"They're not registered in any data banks," said the doctor.

"It couldn't be that easy to just find Mary and her genes down the street," quipped Travis. He noticed the unappreciative looks of the other three. "Well, aside from my poor choice in names, if the female genes had been registered and we could know who she is, we would pay her a visit, and this wouldn't be a mystery any longer."

The doctor lamented, "Of course that would have been so much easier."

"Are you equipped to perform regressive analysis on the female's genes?" Claire asked.

"We have full capabilities, but I don't see what that will tell us." The doctor was mystified.

"You'd be surprised," said Prescott.

Claire and Travis nodded in concurrence.

"Have you named your computer, Dottore?" Claire asked.

"*Sì*. I named her Magdalena," answered the doctor.

Travis and Prescott exchanged quick glances in their PAVs.

"Please give me access to Magdalena, Dottore," said Claire.

"*Certamente*. Magdalena, please allow Claire full access to your databanks."

"Acknowledged," responded Magdalena. "Hello, Claire! How may I help you?"

"Hello, Magdalena!" Claire did not have to start with a hello, but computers seemed to respond to requests better if you treated them courteously, just like any other human being. "Please display the female genes of the fetus in alphanumeric and chromatic table format."

Claire pulled up a chair next to the flat holographic display and sat down. The table displayed alphanumeric figures in different colors.

"Please indicate the closest association with a registered female gene bank."

Magdalena boldfaced the genetic figures that were similar to existing registered genes. "60.7 percent match," informed Magdalena.

Claire looked at Prescott and Travis in puzzlement.

"I wonder what are the lowest percentage similarities found between registered and unregistered gene banks," said Prescott.

"Magdalena, please research," asked Claire. "As far as I know, the lowest percentage match found between registered and unregistered people is eighty percent. Let's see what Magdalena will tell us."

"The lowest match found between registered and unregistered females is 79.3 percent," came the answer from Magdalena.

The doctor's eyes widened in surprise. "What does this mean? Why would the fetus's female genes have a lower percentage match with other registered female genes?"

"The woman does not exist," said Travis. "It's possible that the genes were artificially fabricated."

"Or the woman existed once upon a time," added Prescott.

Claire understood immediately what Prescott said. "Magdalena, please run a paleontological analysis against the closest registered female-gene group."

"Closest registered female-gene match is in the Germanic gene pool," replied Magdalena. The genetic table converted into a three-dimensional chart, with the current matching codes remaining in the foreground while the other gene codes receded toward the back. Between the receding codes and the foreground codes calculations were made and the regressed gene codes appeared in gray. It took two seconds for the paleontological regression calculations to be completed. "The female genes of the fetus are one thousand years old," declared Magdalena.

Dead silence descended in the room. They exchanged confused looks.

"Incredible!" The doctor threw up his hands in surprise. "Do the genes belong to a thousand-year-old woman? How could this be?"

"Or the genes belong to a woman who lived one thousand years ago," said Claire. "That's why her genes look unusual."

"The plot thickens," said Travis. "Question is, why old genes, when modern ones are plentifully available?"

"And why from a thousand years ago?" wondered Prescott as well.

"Pope Joan?" Travis raised his eyebrows, looking at them conspiratorially.

"Impossible!" The doctor chuckled. "Pope Joan did not exist. It's only a legend." He shook his head in disbelief.

"Maybe," said Travis. "However, we might be able to verify that."

"How?" the doctor asked sharply.

"By locating her long decayed body."

"And how are you going to find her?" The doctor was no longer amused. Now he was curious.

"You see, we have sixty percent of the mystery woman's GeneID," said Travis. "We also know where Pope Joan's supposed demise happened. If we locate the essence of her genes at that location, we could speculate that Pope Joan had lived once."

"You mean you will walk down the old Via Sacra, now known as the Shunned Street, and perform your TAP?" the doctor asked incredulously.

"Yes and no. We will not perform any TAP," said Prescott. "We have other means of detecting her essence, if she frequented that part of Rome."

The door opened, and Monsignore Giuseppe came in. "*Buongiorno*! Well, I heard you were here and decided to see if you have fresh news. Any progress, may I ask?"

"*Sì*. The female genes belong to Pope Joan!" The amazed doctor gesticulated with both hands.

"*Madonna!*" The Monsignore froze in surprise.

"It could be Pope Joan," said Travis, trying to tone down his conclusion.

"What if you don't find the woman's genes anywhere in Rome?" the doctor asked.

"Then our supposition is false, and Pope Joan may or may not have existed after all," said Travis.

"You see, we're not after discovering Pope Joan," said Claire. "We have sixty percent of the woman's genes, and we know approximately how old they are, but, without a grave site, we won't be able to identify her."

"Therefore, let's chance it and explore the possibility at the location where Pope Joan might had traveled," added Prescott. "With the information we have, we may have a chance—otherwise, we would be looking for a needle in a haystack."

"It could be a long shot, but, if we walk down the Shunned Street, we may be able to detect her presence," said Travis. "And if the legend is true, her remains might be nearby, which we can also trace."

"Can you do that?" The Monsignore appeared dismayed.

"If all these elements are there, yes," said Travis.

"Even if it happened a thousand years ago?" the doctor asked.

Travis and Prescott nodded.

"Unbelievable!" The doctor lifted his hands as if giving praise. "Monsignore, wasn't the Basilica di San Clemente your former parish?"

"Yes, it was," said the Monsignore. "But what does that have to do with the Shunned Street and Papessa Giovanna?"

"The basilica is just around the corner from where it happened." The doctor gave him a knowing look.

"Yes, it is very near," replied the Monsignore in a flat voice.

"Why don't you be so kind and escort them over there?" said the doctor, with a wicked glint in his eyes.

"Me?" The question startled the Monsignore. "Yes, I suppose I could."

"*Grazie*! That would be great, Monsignore," said Prescott. "Shall we make it for 1 pm, after lunch?"

"That will be good," said the Monsignore. "But no, I have a conflict. Let's make it at 4 pm." He bowed slightly and departed.

"Did you record the gene schema?" Prescott asked, and Claire nodded.

"It is uploaded. I can see it," said Travis, viewing the schema in his PAV.

"Well, that's it. Have a nice day, Dottore Pietro," said Claire. She headed for the door, followed by Travis and Prescott.

The doctor was staring at the gene chart with his hands behind his back. He turned around absentmindedly and said, "Have a good day!"

After they were outside, Prescott said, "It still doesn't make sense. Why use old DNA to create an embryo, and for what purpose?"

"Would God need thousand-year-old DNA?" Travis wondered.

"Man would," said Claire.

"Or the devil," commented Prescott.

"What if the DNA is from the real Pope Joan?" speculated Travis.

"If she were real, it must signify something," said Prescott. "But what? Why her DNA?"

"This was definitely by the hand of man," said Claire.

"One way or another, we'll find out the answer to both questions." said Prescott, and then he added, "I hope."

"How should we approach our investigation on the Shunned Street?" Claire asked Prescott and Travis.

"Since we have her DNA, we could use her DNA-essence ghostly resonance," said Travis.

"We also know the approximate temporal marker." Prescott was the expert in temporal perception. "I would say a thousand years, plus or minus twenty-five years."

"That will be a good start," said Claire. She stopped and concentrated on a thought. The other two waited patiently. "Also, if this is Pope Joan, she had a traumatic experience shortly before her death."

"Are you suggesting the Black Fog of Fear?" asked Travis, furrowing his eyebrows.

"Yes, exactly," said Claire.

"It makes sense," said Prescott. "Her DNA-essence ghostly resonance would cease in the temporal travel in the Black Fog of Fear. That makes three markers by which we can track her remains."

"We have to be careful." Travis was concerned. "The Black Fog of Fear has a great appetite for souls, and it could swallow us, too."

Mit Sandru

Chapter 8. Via Sacra

"There you are," said Monsignore Giuseppe when he saw the Capuchin Trinity Team. "I'm at your disposal. This way, please." He extended a hand with a barely visible clear-film bandage on it, showing them the way. They followed the Monsignore to the same inside courtyard where they had arrived the night before. A small FIAT automobile waited for them.

Travis was incredulous. "Is this a gasoline-engine car?"

"Yes, it is. It's a vintage FIAT 500."

"Why don't you get a hydro-engine vehicle? This must cost you a fortune," said Travis.

"It was my father's," said the Monsignore proudly. "I know. It is an antique—built in 2012. But I enjoy this old car, and it has a manual transmission. Finding gasoline is becoming a problem, though. Just a minor inconvenience, and I don't drive it that much."

They all squeezed inside the small car. Claire sat in the front passenger seat, while Prescott and Travis sat in the back. Travis had to sit sideways, almost with his chin between his knees. The Monsignore started the engine—which took some time until it lumbered to life—shifted the gears, and drove to the gates. As they exited through the south gate of the Vatican and turned onto Via della Stazione Vaticana, protestors holding holographic placards demonstrated against the right to life.

Some called for the separation of church and state, as if it hadn't happened for centuries now. One protester held up a large sign with the numbers 666. A larger group held a red banner with white letters proclaiming, "God is Fraud."

Some protestors took pictures of their car. It must have aroused their conspiratorial suspicions to see an old FIAT driven by a priest in a large-brimmed black hat and carrying three passengers wearing dark shades. Some top-secret inquisition squad, perhaps?

"Are they here often?" asked Claire.

"All the time in the past decade." The Monsignore sighed. "They are holding the Catholic Church responsible for world overpopulation, poverty, greed, the environment, and many other unholy reasons."

"Is it any one particular group demonstrating?" asked Travis from the back seat, lowering his head to check out the crowd left behind.

"It seems to be a coalition of many different groups, even Catholics who want to rescue the planet," said the Monsignore. "It's like someone is organizing a continuous protest."

"Any violence?" asked Claire.

"Thank God, no," said the Monsignore. "Just demonstrations. Although one time, the fascists got into a brawl with the communists." He turned onto Via di Porta Cavalleggeri, heading toward the bridge across the Tiber River. "Where would you like to start?"

"Do you know the approximate spot where the legend says the incident happened?" asked Prescott.

"It is said that it happened around the intersection of Via Dei Querceti and Via Dei Santissimi Quattro, but nobody knows for sure."

"Please take us to just before that location," said Prescott. "We would like to retrace that route. On foot."

"*Bene.* What exactly are you going to do?"

"We will attempt to detect the woman's DNA-essence ghostly resonance," said Travis.

"What would that be?" asked the Monsignore while they were crossing the Tiber.

"As it happens, every person's DNA imprint remains behind after he or she dies," clarified Travis.

"Like a ghost?" The Monsignore looked back at Travis, astounded at what he was hearing.

"No, not a ghost, although we call it a ghostly resonance. You see, the DNA is the code that is responsible for every person's corporal body. After one dies, that code remains in the metaphysical realm. We can detect its existence in a space-time location by its ghostly resonance."

"Provided that we know the DNA code," added Claire.

"*Madonna*! You can see all that? But what and where is the space-time location you mentioned?"

"You are driving us to the location where it could have happened," said Prescott. "That's the space. Then we will regress in time to that specific period and at the space where this woman might have walked by. And, if this woman suffered great turmoil before she died, we will feel her anxiety, pain, and fear, even if it happened one thousand years in the past."

The Monsignore shook his head in acknowledgement and disbelief. "It sounds to me like you're looking for a needle in a haystack." He shifted the gears on his car.

"It could be, but we have a small haystack," said Prescott. "First, we're looking for the DNA-essence ghostly resonance in an approximate location and specific time frame. Great suffering is bonus information in identifying this woman."

"Unbelievable." The Monsignore was still dismayed. "However, even over a short period of time, there are bound to be many suffering souls at that spot."

"It is not an exact science," said Travis.

"Not even a science, Monsignore," added Claire with a mysterious smile.

"It seems to me that you can solve any mystery in the world." The Monsignore honked his horn at someone who had cut him off, who most likely was another human driver, not a robo-car.

"It is not that easy. We need preliminary information and a strong reason to pursue this investigative method," said Prescott. "It can be dangerous."

"I don't understand, but I'm sure you know what you're doing," concluded the Monsignore as he drove on. He took them expertly to the Coliseum and around it to where the defamed street began.

"I think this is a good spot in which to begin your investigation." The Monsignore stopped the car on the one-way street on Via dei Querceti near Via Marco Aurelio. Claire, Travis, and Prescott exited the car. The Monsignore rolled down his window. "I will park my car over there"—he pointed up the street to a church—"at the Basilica di San Clemente, and I will join you shortly at the corner of this street, Via dei Querceti, and Via dei Santi Quattro. From here to the corner over there, at Via dei Santi Quattro, is the likely spot it may have happened." The Monsignore drove on and made a left turn onto Via Marco Aurelio.

Claire, Travis, and Prescott looked around. A few people were going about their business on this quiet dead-end street. They walked in the direction the Monsignore had indicated and stopped at the descending stairs in front of the round brick tower of the Cardinal Palace of the church of Ss. Quattro Coronati. On their left was Via Capo d'Africa; ahead was Via dei Santi Quattro. This was supposedly the "hot zone" where the big event had happened, but it possibly had been erased from history. Or maybe it was a legend, after all.

"What do you think?" wondered Claire.

"Not much of a street," commented Prescott.

"It wasn't this way back in the eleventh century." Travis pointed to the round brick tower on their right. "This place, a thousand years ago, was in ruins. The three- and four-story buildings around us did not exist in their present shape, although some of their foundations were supporting smaller buildings. And these streets were located at a lower level."

"Lower than where the stairs end." Prescott looked downward. Travis nodded.

"So what's the plan?" said Claire.

"Supposedly, the event occurred one thousand years ago, in 1066. I think we should regress back to 1100 and descend back in time from there while we probe the DNA-essence ghostly resonance," said Travis.

"There is one problem with that," said Prescott. "If we encounter first the Black Fog of Fear, we may fall into it."

"Then let's regress back to 1000 and ascend in time while we probe the DNA-essence ghostly resonance," said Claire.

"It's a plan," concluded Travis. "According to legends, she was pope for only two years. It will happen very quickly, and it should end up in the Black Fog of Fear."

"You know, why do we think that the woman was Pope Joan?" Claire wondered. "It could have been anyone else."

"A thousand years old and German. Elementary—it's Pope Joan," said Travis.

Claire smirked at him.

"OK, that's the only clue we have," said Travis.

"We're not after Pope Joan," reiterated Prescott. "We're after the psychic fingerprints of who did this and why he used this old DNA."

"He?" wondered Claire. "It could be she or it."

"Or they," said Travis.

Claire, Travis, and Prescott walked slowly toward the infamous location while inspecting their surroundings. It was an ordinary location in the old section of Rome. There were multi-level yellow and sienna-colored apartment buildings built, and rebuilt, over foundations that went back to the Roman Empire. The street layouts could have been very similar to what the ancient Romans may have walked on to go about their daily lives or even to go to the Coliseum to see gladiator fights.

"How do we keep track of the temporal flow?" Travis asked.

"I'll issue one ping per month," said Prescott. "I think we'll detect the resonance as we pass the place and time when she was here."

"That would take a long time," said Claire. "How about if we go back to 1061 and cover a shorter span? If we don't find anything, we can go back another five years."

"I like that better," agreed Travis. "We will be exposed to the street traffic for less time that way. According to the legend, this was a procession, so it will pass by on this street. We know for sure that the procession came along Via Dei Santissimi Quattro and turned left on Via Dei Querceti, or the other way around. I suggest we take positions at that intersection."

They walked to the intersection. Travis glanced up Via Dei Santissimi Quattro. "Claire, why don't you take the northeast corner? Prescott, you take the southeast corner, and I will walk across to the southwest corner. In this way, we're flanking the procession."

"Once in position, take my lead and let our minds regress in time," said Prescott.

They took their positions and set their PAVs to video overlay. People passing by would think that they were watching the news on their PAVs. The actual streets around them became a semitransparent background. Unlike when they performed the TAP, their minds did not join together. They were three individuals able to communicate with each other, while their minds regressed back in time.

"Get ready to unbalance the temporal flow in our minds," said Prescott. It started with a dizzying jolt. The panes of time swirled around them, as if they were entering a spiraling descent. "We are halfway there," announced Prescott. "We are three-quarters of the way there. We are ninety percent there. We are ninety-five percent there. We are in the year 1061."

Their minds sensed a large space void, with the semitransparent modern Roman streets as the background.

"Commence the DNA-essence ghostly resonance," announced Prescott.

Four columns of pale multicolored light formed, representing DNA's guanine, adenine, thymine, and cytosine, also known as G, A, T, and C. These are the information pillars of life. The team's PAVs were able to emit this information in a temporal realm. At rhythmic intervals, pulses of brighter light traveled up the genetic columns. At predetermined location on the columns, a circular disturbance would occur, just like waves on water after a rock is thrown in. The hazy rings propagated from around the four columns and then dissipated into nothingness. A harmonic note would sound simultaneously with each disturbance. Each column emitted a different tone. The four notes were C, E, G, and B.

Shortly after this harmony would occur, a dissonant sound would echo back. This indicated no match. Only when a pitch-perfect echo resulted from the emitted harmony from the columns would they know they had found their mark. Prescott started the ascending beat count. Every ping was a month.

After a while Prescott announced, "Year 1063." The pings continued, followed by the harmonic sound of the disturbances and the response of the dissonant echoes. "Entering the year 1064." The harmonic resonances were followed by less dissonant echoes. They were getting closer to a target, a DNA essence that was close but not exactly the same as their emitted DNA signal. It faded. The pings continued as they ascended in time. "1065."

A perfectly resonant echo match could be heard coming from Via Dei Querceti. It moved around the corner onto Via Dei Santissimi Quattro.

"Oh my God, a perfect match!" Claire gasped.

"Let it go," said Travis. "This must be from earlier processions going to the Basilica di San Giovanni in Laterano. But it's her."

A ping later, the echo match announced the return of the procession. "Keep an eye on this one, although it is only 1065," said Travis. The echo diminished in time down Via Dei Querceti.

Several pings later and after some more perfect resonances, Prescott announced, "Year 1066."

They listened as the pings—the months—passed, until they heard the perfectly resonant echo approaching them again. It was coming up Via Dei Querceti. Prescott slowed down the time flow. They waited, holding their breaths in anticipation of what would happen next. The echo resonances were in harmony.

And then the resonance stopped. It was eerily quiet; only the harmonious vibration and the resonant echo pulsating in time could be heard. Around them they felt vortexes of gray smoke flowing toward the spot where the procession stopped. The vortexes became darker and more violent. It felt as if a hurricane were forming right before their eyes.

"Don't move!" shouted Travis. "Stay perfectly still!"

A black vortex of dense and putrid smoke began spinning on Via Dei Querceti. The DNA harmonic sound pulsed rhythmically, and the resonant echo emanated from the black vortex. Shouts and cries of despair and fear came from many invisible mouths. Thunder and lightning flashes discharged inside the vortex. Suddenly, the resonant echo stopped. A life, the life of the woman—perhaps Pope Joan's life—had ended.

The black vortex collapsed. It became a black fog with its tendrils spreading as if searching for other lives to take. Travis and Prescott were the first ones to feel the deadly dread of the fog. They, intruding into this realm, were in danger. Pain, fear, hopelessness, and agony swirled around them. Panic, hatred, and loathing radiated from the center. The hatred and fear amplified until it became a small tornado. And suddenly it died down. It was replaced by horror, convulsing terror, and much anxiety. And then a peaceful feeling flew away from the dark fog.

Claire noticed the tendrils floating and curling around like octopus tentacles, sniffing for life. It passed between Travis and Prescott. One tendril coiled around Prescott's legs, but it moved on. She just could imagine the fear that must have passed through Prescott's mind. The Black Fog of Fear was approaching her.

Travis observed as the fog passed between Prescott and him. He cringed, seeing the tendril coiling around Prescott. A feeling of desperation and coldness engulfed him in dark agony and pain. The Black Fog moved on and now was advancing toward Claire. Travis noticed that he and Prescott made a gate through which the fog passed. If the fog turned right on Via Dei Santissimi Quattro, it would pass through the gate made by Claire and Prescott. Would that be a factor that would diminish the behavior of the fog toward Claire and Prescott?

The Black Fog of Fear moved slowly down Via Dei Querceti and did not turn right on Via Dei Santissimi Quattro, but continued straight ahead. Claire had no counterpart at the northeast corner from the west side of the street, and the fog sensed her standing alone. It moved nearer and engulfed her. Travis knew that the fog had to be distracted immediately away from Claire. Based on the semitransparent images of their location, he crossed Via Dei Santissimi Quattro like a blind man to the northwest corner. In the far distance, he heard the long honk of a car. He must have crossed the street in front of a car that he couldn't see.

The fog stopped engulfing Claire. As if sensing a new life, it sent whiffs of black smoke vines toward Travis. He steadied himself, bracing for death's visit. Fortunately, the procession carrying the murdered woman—because the crowd did murder her—moved on, and the fog lost contact with them, retreating hurriedly. The Black Fog continued moving north on Via Dei Querceti, not letting go of its dead victim.

On Via di San Giovanni in Laterano, it made a left turn. Travis realized that there was a good chance of it going to the Basilica di San Clemente. "We need to follow it," he told Claire and Prescott. The three of them walked blindly after the Black Fog of Fear. They bumped into poles, walls, people, and hoped that no car would run them over. All three came to a sudden stop against a wall. They could see the fog dissipating, but they remained with a feeling of sadness, pity, and emptiness.

"We jump to now," said Prescott. The same spiraling process repeated, but this time upward, and they arrived back into the present time.

Prescott, Claire, and Travis came out of their trances. They stood in front of a pale green wall with their noses against the cool stucco. A few passers-by wondered what these three people were doing—praying to the wall? The three looked around and found they were in the front of the Basilica di San Clemente, facing the wall on Via di San Giovanni in Laterano. They turned, leaned their backs against the wall, and inhaled deeply to recover from the shock of what they had just experienced.

"I think they took her into the crypts under the church," said Travis.

"We need to find the Monsignore to get in," said Claire.

Just as she said that they heard him asking, "Are you well?" He stood a few steps away with a concerned stare. "I saw you coming toward me, and, how shall I say, I had a feeling of watching the walking dead."

"We're better now, Monsignore," said Claire, wiping her brow. "It was awful."

"*Madonna.*" The Monsignore made the sign of the cross. "All three of you are shaking. Shall we find a place to sit down and perhaps have a drink of water?"

"A stiff drink would be better," said Travis. "But we don't have time for that. We captured a certain feeling that we don't want to lose, and we must find its resting place."

"Resting place?" the Monsignore asked. "Like a tomb?"

"I don't know what, but it sank in there, behind it." Prescott pointed to the wall.

"There are crypts in there," said the Monsignore. "Last April, I buried a good friend of mine there, Brother Luca. May his soul rest in peace." He made the sign of the cross.

"Sorry to hear that, Monsignore," said Claire. "Can you take us in?"

"Certainly. Follow me." Monsignore led them down the steps to the basilica's entrance on Via Dei Querceti. "What exactly did you do, while you were doing whatever it was you were doing?"

"We traveled back in time to the approximate year of the DNA, and we found the ghostly resonance of the DNA essence," explained Claire.

"Wait, you traveled back in time and saw what happened back then?" asked the Monsignore with great interest.

"Not exactly, Monsignore," said Claire. "We did not see anything like that, neither humans nor old Rome, only echo remains of the woman whose DNA walked on that street at that time. And then we saw the Black Fog of Fear, which almost got me if it hadn't been for Travis." Claire smiled at Travis, who saluted with two fingers to his brow.

"*Madonna*! You were in mortal danger?" asked the Monsignore.

"We had a close call. Part of our job description," said Claire, as if she were describing office work.

As they were crossing the interior courtyard, a workman called out to the Monsignore, "*Le erano utili, gli strumenti idraulici?*"

"*Grazie! Molto utili*," replied the Monsignore brusquely, and he entered the basilica followed by Claire, Travis, and Prescott.

The Basilica di San Clemente was a splendid medieval church, built on old Roman foundations. The ornately designed ceiling was gilded in gold, and it took their breath away. The wall behind the altar glowed from the red color of the fresco of the twelve apostles' robes. The Monsignore took them expertly down the stairs to the crypts.

It was nearly dark in there, with sparse illumination from a few lights. The crypt was a long chamber with a flattened, barrel-shaped brick ceiling. The brick walls had niches filled with stone coffins. Many more marble funerary boxes, some resembling sarcophagi, perhaps dating back to the Roman Empire, lined the walls. Marble statues, not necessarily religious icons, adorned niches in the walls.

The Monsignore paid his respects to his old friend, Brother Luca, by lighting a small candle, placing it on a candleholder on the side of the vault, and saying a quick prayer. Claire stood at his side, observing the wall full of crucifixes adorning the vault covers.

Prescott and Travis wandered in the crypt, as if they were two hounds on a trail. They returned shortly.

"Is there more than this?" Travis asked.

"Yes. Although that entrance has been barred for a long time." Travis and Prescott invited him to show them. The Monsignore took them behind Brother Luca's vault wall. In a well-hidden niche, they found a rusty wrought-iron gate. "It is pinned shut," said the Monsignore.

"Let me take a look," said Travis. As he expected, the gate was rusted through, and it came off its hinges. He pulled it out and leaned it against the wall.

"We'll have to replace this," murmured the Monsignore.

The entrance, large enough for only one person at a time, led down into a narrow spiral staircase made of stone. They descended into a damp, moldy-smelling passage that led into the catacombs. Claire, Travis, and Prescott had no problem seeing in the dark with their PAVs, which were equipped with microwave radar that converted the signals into digital images of their surroundings. Their PAVs needed no light. At the bottom of the stairs, the Monsignore flicked his lighter and found an old torch, which he lit. The deeper they advanced, the older the crypts were. Some were just ossuaries filled with human skulls and bones piled in niches and corners, or in lidless stone containers.

Travis, who was leading the party, halted suddenly. "It's back there."

Mit Sandru

Chapter 9. Pope Joan?

They retraced their steps and took a side corridor that was lower than the others. This corridor did not go far before it dead-ended. A round stone gate, resembling a fat cookie, blocked the narrow corridor. Travis removed the blocking rock on the lower-left side and, without much effort, rolled the round stone away from the entrance it was obstructing.

"I never knew this was here," said the Monsignore.

"It was not meant to be easily discovered. On either side of the round stone, there are these two columns, which also hold it in place," explained Travis. "The columns mask the stone gate."

Prescott was first to enter. "It looks like this entrance has been sealed for hundreds of years." Prescott pushed aside a gauzy sheet of medieval cobwebs. "We're so far down below ground that there are no more tree roots reaching down here."

They descended into another catacomb, even more dank and humid than the ones before. Over hundreds of years, this one had been filled to capacity with more stone and marble tombs. Some had their lids pushed over, and the remains lay broken on the ground; some had their lids partly opened, just enough for grave robbers to access the contents inside. Many more were intact however, but these had crosses engraved on the lids. These were

Christian burials, and, later on, the church prevented entrance to these catacombs.

"Do you feel it?" Claire asked, referring to the dark impression they had discovered earlier.

"Yes, it is this way," said Travis as they advanced deeper into the underground labyrinth.

"What do you sense, Travis?" the Monsignore asked.

"The ending of a dark impression," said Travis. "The tragedy we sensed above ground ended down here, somewhere here." He continued advancing.

After a short while, they came across footprints left in the moist soil.

"Perhaps we've been walking in circles," said Travis.

"It must be behind this wall," said Prescott. He walked between two sarcophagi and touched the wall, as if feeling something emanating from behind it.

"I think there is another chamber here, behind this wall," said Claire.

"It's right here, behind this statue," said Prescott as he squeezed in.

They followed him inside a circular chamber that contained a few unadorned stone burial sites. Prescott, Claire, and Travis went directly to a specific stone box and placed their hands on the lid.

"It ended here," said Prescott. He exchanged glances in his PAV with his teammates. "Let's remove the lid."

"Is that wise?" questioned the Monsignore, slightly nervous at the prospect of opening the box. "Disturbing the peace of the dead?"

"Judging by the shoe prints around the box, someone has already disturbed the dead," said Claire, pointing to the ground.

Travis investigated the footprints. "Recent, but not that recent." He thought he noticed two indentations of knees, as if someone had prayed by the burial box. "Let's see what's inside. On the count of three: one, two, three." They rotated the lid, exposing half the interior of the box.

The four of them bent down and looked inside. The Monsignore raised his torch high above them to shed more light on the interior of the vault. The bottom was covered with dusty stones.

"What is the meaning of this?" the Monsignore asked.

"It's in there," said Prescott, and he climbed inside the box.

Claire and Travis pushed the lid to enlarge the access to the box. Travis joined Prescott inside and together they began removing rocks, dropping them outside over the edge. It did not take long until they saw the first femur, the long bone of a human leg.

"*Dio mio*," whispered the Monsignore, as he made the sign of the cross. He planted the torch in a crack on the wall to illuminate the site.

"Stand back," said Prescott. "We need to remove the remaining stones."

"Hold it," said Travis. "Let's see where the bottom is before we become human excavators."

"OK. How about this corner here?" Prescott replied.

They removed rocks from that corner exposing more bones, and soon they reached the stone floor. Satisfied that there weren't that many more rocks in the box and under Claire's supervision, Prescott and Travis methodically removed, over a half-hour, as many rocks as possible to uncover the skeleton without disturbing the bones inside. In spite of the catacomb's moist environment, their removing and dropping the rocks outside the box gave rise to a cloud of dust that engulfed the crypt, dimming their ability to see through their PAVs.

Travis and Prescott climbed out, stepping on the rocks that abutted the outside of the box's wall. They walked a few steps away, coughing and waving their arms to clear the air. When the air finally cleared, all three climbed inside. The dim light from the torch revealed the broken skeleton of an adult, lying on its side, and on top of its rib cage laid the skeleton of a small baby. An infant.

"*Madonna*," said the Monsignore, who had been quiet during the removal of rocks. He peered over the edge and quickly started praying.

"Judging by the pelvic bones, the adult is a woman," said Claire. "And the infant is definitely a newborn. The cranium, although collapsed, is unformed at the top."

"This is where the tragedy finally ended," said Prescott, and he produced a small plastic bag. "We should take a small bone from each skeleton for DNA analysis." He took a finger bone from each skeleton, placed them in the plastic bag, and dropped it in his breast pocket.

"What a mess," said Travis, looking outside at the pile of rocks. "We can add to our résumés the title of grave robbers."

"Who are they?" the Monsignore asked, showing his dread at what the answer might be.

"A great mayhem and melee happened in the streets above a thousand years ago," said Prescott. "These two were the victims. After they were killed, their murderers dragged them in here, dropped them in this stone vault, and covered them with rocks. After which they closed the lid to make sure the bodies would never be discovered."

"*Madonna*! Who were they really?" insisted the Monsignore.

"If you're wondering if they were Pope Joan and her baby, that we'll never know," said Claire. "Just because we found two skeletons matching the legend may be just a coincidence.

There were no GeneIDs one thousand years ago."

"Heck, there were no GeneIDs fifty years ago," commented Travis.

"There are no inscriptions of any kind on the lid," said Prescott. "And no significant remains of any clothes. Probably they stripped the woman of her clothes, especially if they were expensive. This was intended to be an anonymous burial."

"Shall we place the lid back?" wondered Travis.

"By all means," said Claire. "We found what we wanted."

Travis and Prescott raised the lid and placed it back on.

The Monsignore looked amazed at the strength of those two and asked, "How are you able to move that lid as if it were made of foam?"

"Mind over matter, Monsignore," said Prescott.

They squeezed out into the main corridor of the catacombs. Travis took the lead, retracing their steps toward the exit. When they arrived at the round stone gate, it was closed.

"What the hell?" Travis pushed against the stone. "Someone rolled the stone back over the entrance and locked it." He pushed again, but without any success. "We're trapped. It cannot be moved. The blocking stone is on the other side."

Chapter 10. Entombed

"Who could have done this?" wondered the Monsignore, turning around as if looking for a culprit.

"That's a good question," said Claire. "It seems someone took an interest in what we were doing here." Travis and Prescott acknowledged that with a short nod.

"Why can't you move this stone? You were able to move the lid back there," said the Monsignore.

"This stone is obstructed. We cannot move it," said Prescott.

"We need to find another way out," said Travis. "Maybe there is another exit at the other end."

"Good idea," said Prescott.

They turned back into the catacombs, retracing their steps.

"I hope there is another exit," said the Monsignore, holding his torch high, which occasionally burned the hanging cobwebs.

"It smells like gas," said Prescott.

"I don't smell anything," said the Monsignore.

"Don't you sense that distinctive odor of gas?" Travis asked.

The Monsignore sniffed the air.

"Who is using natural gas nowadays?" wondered Claire.

"A lot of people in Roma," said Monsignore.

"It doesn't matter if it is natural or otherwise—put the torch out, Monsignore," said Travis.

"How am I going to see?" he asked.

Travis snatched the torch, threw it on the ground, and stomped on it.

"I can't see!" cried the Monsignore.

"Don't worry, Monsignore, we can," said Claire. "Just stand still until we figure this out."

"We cannot run out of here," said Prescott. "We need to flame it."

"Flame it? What's that?" asked the Monsignore nervously.

"We've got to stop the gas inflow," said Prescott.

"*Bene*, good," said the Monsignore. "But how?"

"That box looks big enough," said Claire, pointing to a large and sturdy sarcophagus ahead of them, which only the CTT team could see through their PAVs.

"Let's go," said Prescott, heading for the sarcophagus.

Travis grabbed the Monsignore by the wrist and led him along in the dark.

"*Dove* . . . where are we going?" asked the Monsignore.

"To safety," replied Travis. "Here, Monsignore, hold onto these while we open up this box." Travis took the Monsignore's hands and placed them on the breasts of a female stone statue nearby. The Monsignore couldn't see what he was cupping in his hands and didn't complain.

The Capuchin Trinity Team positioned themselves around the one-ton stone lid and shifted it partially aside.

"Not too bad," said Travis, peering inside. It was a large stone burial container containing only one skeleton of some very important person, judging by the richly embroidered, decayed garments. Luckily, it was dry and smelled only of dead dust.

"Don't worry about a thing, Monsignore," said Travis, acting as his guide. "I'll lift you and place you in the vault for protection, and we'll join you as well."

"Let's hurry—the gas smell, it's getting stronger," warned Prescott.

Claire was inside when Travis dropped the Monsignore in like a sack of potatoes. The bones at the bottom crunched like crackers. Prescott and Travis climbed in quickly.

"Monsignore, you don't mind if we use your sash to flame out the gas?" asked Prescott politely, while tugging at it.

"Of course not," said the Monsignore, pulling off his sash, which Prescott grabbed unceremoniously. "But what do you mean by 'flame out'?"

"Can we have your lighter, please?" asked Claire, and, without waiting for his approval, she snatched it out of his pocket faster than a pickpocket.

"What is this crunching below my feet?" asked the Monsignore. "Don't tell me we're in a tomb." His voice was anguished. "This could be the earthly remains of a saint."

"If we don't hurry, the four of us will be saints," said Travis.

Claire struck the lighter and ignited the sash. Prescott held it outside and made sure it was on fire before throwing it on the ground.

"Ready," said Travis. They lifted the lid and placed it back on the box, enclosing themselves inside the vault.

"What's happening?" The Monsignore was frightened.

They were crammed inside, but safe. The Monsignore kneeled and bent down, with his head below Claire's crotch. Travis smirked, which Claire noticed, but she did not admonish him.

"No need to be alarmed, Monsignore," said Claire. "Please pray for all of us."

The Monsignore prayed like he'd never prayed before. Travis was biting his knuckles to keep from exploding with laughter, seeing Claire holding the Monsignore's head down between her legs, while the man was doing his best job to appeal to God and all the saints.

Claire pointed a finger at Travis and said, "Shu–"

A big boom thundered outside. Streams of air, dust, and smoke jutted through the cracks between the lid and the box. It was not built the way they used to build them during

Egyptian times—water- and explosion-proof, that is—but it held. Nevertheless, despite the ringing in their ears, they had survived.

"*Dio mio*, what was that?" asked a shaking Monsignore.

"Hopefully we're safe after this bang," said Prescott.

"Give it time to vent," said Claire, alluding to the gases outside.

After some time, they cracked the lid open. The air was breathable, although smoky and dusty. They slid the lid some more to allow their exit, and after they helped the Monsignore climb out, they respectfully put the lid back on.

Prescott discovered a small padlock brass key on the stony floor and picked it up. Travis placed a finger on his lips and patted his pocket. Prescott placed the key in the same pocket with the bones, without uttering a word.

The gas leak was burning someplace down the catacombs, and that provided some dim illumination. The Monsignore looked around, dazed, as if trying to comprehend the aftermath of the explosion. Stoically, he accepted the situation and followed that up with a quick prayer. He blessed the Capuchin Trinity Team for good measure.

"I hope we burned the whiskers of whoever did this," said Travis. "Let's go toward the flames."

They arrived at the spot where the gas had leaked out. It was a blowtorch gushing out of a pipe up high, close to the blown-out ceiling. Daylight was showing through the cracks where the flames were escaping up aboveground.

Farther away, stone steps led to what seemed to be a door. They climbed up and found a heavy wooden door still standing, held up by a chain and padlock, but ripped off its hinges by the explosion. They pushed it aside and walked out into another passage. Prescott lagged behind but quickly caught up with them. After a few turns, their tunnel ended in the underground storm drain. From above police sirens were wailing, approaching the site of the explosion.

"We need to find a manhole," said Travis, checking the ceiling of the tunnel. "There." He pointed to the iron rungs leading to the round cover of a manhole. He climbed up and pushed the cover open. A shaft of light descended upon them, followed by fresh air and street noises. They got out and about quickly.

"Where are we, Monsignore?" Prescott asked.

"We're on Via Labicana," he said. "East of the church. We traveled far in the catacombs."

"Yes, and we found what we were looking for," said Prescott, patting his breast pocket.

"And then some," said Travis, smirking. "The hand of man is in this."

The Monsignore flinched at what Travis said.

"Monsignore, we need to ask you not to divulge to anyone that we were trapped inside when the gas explosion happened," said Prescott.

"But why?" he asked, startled.

"This is an ongoing paranormal investigation, and, from what we just experienced, it is a criminal one as well now. The less information we give out, the better we will be, and the worse off the perpetrators will be, kept in the dark about what we did to foil their assassination attempt."

"I see. But I cannot lie to the Holy Father if he asks me, and he will."

"Can you commit this sin now and ask for forgiveness later?" Prescott asked.

"Please," added Claire.

"Besides," said Travis, "this could have been an accident. The stone could have rolled back and locked itself in position. We didn't see what was holding it locked on the other side of the wall. And rusty pipes may have caused the gas leak. We don't know, but right now it is best to keep this as an accident."

"*Va bene.* Certainly. Let's go. My car is parked on the opposite side at the Basilica di San Clemente, on Via dei Normanni," said the Monsignore.

They walked back on Via Labicana, passing the crack in the street east of Via Dei Querceti, from where smoke was coming up from the burning gas below. Fire trucks, paramedics, and *carabinieri* stormed around the location of the explosion. Yellow police tape commanding "Do Not Pass" delimited the crime scene. No one seemed to be hurt, although many windows were broken in buildings that surrounded the hole created by the explosion. Luckily, the explosion had been contained mostly underground.

Travis spoke into his PAV: "Claire, Prescott, we need to arm ourselves when we get back. This investigation is getting hot."

Chapter 11. Old DNA

The following morning at 8 am, Prescott, Travis, and Claire entered the papal medical quarters where they found Dottore Pietro analyzing new data from the fetus. "Good morning! There was an explosion yesterday, I heard, near the Basilica di San Clemente, where you were. Terrorists are suspected of setting it up."

"That's what the media says?" Claire asked. "Did they find the bomb?"

"They didn't say," said the doctor.

"It was a gas explosion, actually," said Claire. "I wonder why they didn't say that."

"Probably the mayor is covering it up. A bomb is a bomb. Blame the police. But rusted infrastructure is politically troublesome," said the doctor. "The Monsignore told me that you were able to travel back in time. You could solve all history's mysteries." The doctor was looking excitedly at them.

"I wish that were possible," said Travis with a wistful smile. "We go back in time, but we are unable to see the past, like you would see a movie. Just traces of very specific information that we were seeking."

"Oh." The doctor was disappointed.

"But we were lucky and we found what we were looking for," said Travis.

"Which brings us to the reason we came here," said Prescott. "Dottore, we would like to genetically analyze these bones we found."

The doctor looked a bit confused at first, then curious. "Bones? Where did you find them?"

"We have two bone samples we found in an underground tomb," said Prescott. "Can Magdalena identify the genetic make-up?"

"Certainly," the doctor said, studying the bones in the plastic bag that Prescott handed him. The doctor placed each bone in an analyzer tube and gave verbal orders to Magdalena to sterilize and commence the genetic analysis. "It will take about an hour."

"Excellent. That will give us time to have breakfast," said Prescott.

An hour later, they returned to the medical quarters.

"Ah, there you are," said the doctor. "They corrected the news and admitted that it was a gas explosion from a ruptured pipe after all."

"Not a terrorist bombing?" said Claire.

"No," said the doctor. "The analysis of the bones was just completed, and you'll be surprised at the results."

"Please show us," said Clair.

The doctor smiled broadly. "The smaller of the bones belongs to an infant, and it is related to the sample of the bigger bone. The bigger bone's genetic signature is the same as the female's genes from the fetus the Holy Father is carrying."

"Well, well, well," said Travis. "Considering that the bones were not disturbed for centuries, how did the woman's genes become part of the fetus's DNA?"

Mit Sandru

Chapter 12. Genetic Regressive Reconstruction

"We need to perform a genetic regressive reconstruction of the fetus's DNA," said Claire.

"But, but why?" the doctor asked, wrinkling his eyebrows.

As he asked that, Cardinal Cellini entered the room. He nodded to the others, acknowledging their presence. "The Monsignore told us about the bones you brought back from the skeletons you found buried under stones. I'm curious about this latest development."

"The female genes match," said the doctor.

Cardinal Cellini couldn't hide his surprise, but he said nothing. He exchanged glances with Claire as if inviting her to expand on the news.

"We were about to perform a genetic regressive reconstruction," she said. "We could find out when the woman's genes became part of the fetus's DNA."

"At conception, of course," said the doctor confidently.

"What if there was no conception?" Claire proposed.

"Now that would be a miracle, wouldn't it?" Cardinal Cellini placed his palms together.

"But the fetus . . ." The doctor became agitated. "The fetus contains genes from that woman, and she's been dead for centuries. And, according to the CTT, her tomb was not disturbed."

"Intriguing," said the cardinal. He placed his hands behind his back.

"What if these genes belong to Pope Joan?" asked the doctor.

"Pope Joan did not exist," said the cardinal in a stern voice. "Besides, the identity of the long-ago dead woman is irrelevant. Please do what Claire requested, Dottore."

"Certainly," the doctor acknowledged as the cardinal exited. The doctor stared at Claire with a perplexed look on his face.

After an uneasy pause, Claire said, "We'll have to make use of Magdalena." The doctor invited her with his hand to go ahead. "Magdalena," called Claire.

"Hello, Claire! How may I help you?"

"I need you to do a genetic regressive reconstruction of the fetus's DNA. Specifically, analyze the female genes and determine when they were introduced into the fetus's DNA make-up."

"Certainly, Claire," said the computer.

"I don't know what that is going to accomplish." The doctor had his doubts.

"I don't know, either," said Claire. "That's why I want to see the devolution of the fetus's DNA. It may shed some new light on this matter."

"Can you project the analysis in regression?" asked Prescott.

"Magdalena, please display the retro-analysis," asked Claire.

A flat hologram appeared on the wall displaying alphanumeric codes as they were regressed one day at a time. Not much changed as day-by-day regression occurred until the date of April 11, 2066.

"Regression stop," said Magdalena. "The female's genes have disappeared."

"How come?" Travis wondered as he approached the flat display hologram.

"That's not possible," said the doctor, turning pale.

"Magdalena, go back a week, and then reverse to when the genes appear," asked Claire.

The computer did as commanded.

"The analysis must be erroneous," said the doctor. "Magdalena, perform self-diagnosis of your analysis."

A second later, the computer replied, "Self-analysis completed. No malfunctions were detected."

"What's going on?" the doctor wondered dumbly, his hands shaking slightly.

"It seems that the female genes were spliced into the fetus's DNA about two months ago," said Prescott.

"Any news?" Cardinal Cellini asked as he re-entered the lab. Cardinal Bertrand accompanied him, a look of concern on his face.

"Yes, the mystery deepens," said Claire. "The female genes were introduced into the fetus's genes after the fetus was conceived, which is hard to do."

Cardinal Bertrand asked, "How sure are you of this?"

"As sure as Magdalena is," replied Claire.

"Let's presume that is so," said Cardinal Cellini. "Are you suggesting that the Holy Father immaculately conceived a human embryo six months ago? Possibly via self-cloning? Then, about two months ago, a new set of female genes was introduced that mutated the fetus? And the genes belong to a woman who lived a thousand years ago and whose bones have not been disturbed until now?"

"That would be our conclusion. So far," said Claire.

"Is this a miracle or a curse?" wondered Cardinal Bertrand, looking at Cellini.

"Why don't we have Magdalena perform a fetus regressive reconstruction?" said Travis.

All eyes turned to stare at him.

"Let us see how the fetus itself appears in time. It may answer our question," clarified Travis.

The doctor shook his head vigorously. "It will tell us nothing."

"I think it will tell us a lot," said Cardinal Cellini. "Please proceed."

"Magdalena," Claire asked. "Please perform a fetus regressive reconstruction, one day per second, starting from today's date."

"Right away, Claire," said the computer.

A hologram appeared, displaying the fetus as it was currently. Every second, the fetus was reconstructed, but a day younger. It shrunk in size, and the definition of its details, such as its fingers, toes, mouth, ears, eyes, even its eyelashes, regressed. It looked like a normal fetus until April 11, when the female genes first were introduced.

And then, in a split second, the fetus transformed.

"*Dio*!" screamed the cardinals in unison.

Mit Sandru

Chapter 13. The Abomination

The fetus had morphed into a hideous creature. It had a spiny back, horns on its head, claws on its fingers and small bat-like wings. A long tail curled around its legs. Even the shape of its face elongated into a lizard-like appearance.

"What is that?" Prescott asked.

"The devil," said Travis, nonplussed.

The fetus continued regressing back in its devilish form to an embryo and then to nothing. The witnesses stood still, stunned by what they had seen. Incredible as it seemed, the fetus before the introduction of the female genes resembled the devil. A pale pink devil.

"Oh, my God!" whispered Cardinal Bertrand, and he made the sign of the cross.

"Did you notice the date?" asked Claire, pointing to the countdown of time. "March 6, 2066. That's when the embryo was created."

"The new analysis of the fetus indicates that he is more than seven months old, not six, as we had thought. But he was conceived only three months ago—" The doctor stopped speaking abruptly. His face darkened, and he looked as if he were about to be ill. "*Cardinali*, we must remove this abomination from the Holy Father. It's aging faster than we thought. Today is the first of June—at this rate, it will come to full development and be ready to be delivered by June six . . . " The doctor's voice trailed off.

"June six, sixty-six," said Cardinal Cellini. "The year and date of the devil."

"Not a good sign," agreed Cardinal Bertrand.

"*Cardinali*, please, I beg of you, ask the Holy Father to consider the surgical removal of that thing." The doctor clasped his hands together, as if begging them.

"That would be an abortion. Unacceptable," concluded Cardinal Bertrand.

"But that thing is an abomination! Created from the genes of Pope Joan!" argued the doctor.

"It is a mystery, Dottore," said Cardinal Bertrand. "We don't know if the fetus is an abomination. That's why we have the Capuchin Trinity Team here. And Pope Joan did not exist."

The doctor's shoulders slumped.

"We need to consult with the Holy Father," said Cardinal Cellini. The two cardinals left immediately, without another word.

There was a moment of silence after the cardinals left. The doctor was fidgeting, nervous and tense. Drops of sweat formed on his brow.

"Let's see the evolution from the beginning," said Travis.

Magdalena started the simulation from March 6. This time it was magnified, showing how the cells multiplied until the embryo was formed. At first, the fetus looked like a tiny snake. And then it evolved into a lizard. The front arms developed first, followed by the hind legs. The head sprouted tiny horns. Even fangs could be seen in the elongated, dinosaur-like jaws. The nails—or perhaps claws—appeared, and the tail stretched longer. The body was covered in pink scales. From its shoulder blades two appendages grew that, at first, resembled fins. Then, delicate bones with thin, blood-loaded vessels grew into two bat-like wings. The devil fetus grew healthily and then suddenly transformed into a human fetus.

"Magdalena, stop the evolution," said Claire. "Reverse to 00:00 April 11 and restart the evolution in hourly increments."

The computer displayed the devil fetus again. It did not evolve as rapidly since the evolution time slowed down. At 10 o'clock on April 11, the devil fetus went through spasms, and suddenly it begun to re-evolve. The horns retracted into the skull, the face shortened. The wings shriveled and disappeared. The tail shrank back into the body. Pink, smooth skin replaced the scales. In a mere six hours, the human fetus had replaced the devil fetus. By the end of April 11, there was no trace of what once was.

"It seems that the female genes corrected the mutation," said Claire.

"What makes you think it was a mutation?" Prescott asked.

"You believe that was the devil?" said Claire.

"Then what was that?" Prescott asked.

"It was the devil, not self-cloning," interjected Travis.

"What do you mean to say?" the doctor asked.

"That thing was induced to procreate in the Pope's body," said Travis.

"But there was no external intervention," argued the doctor.

"Just like there was no intervention when the female genes appeared," said Travis. "But there was a culprit, or culprits, at work here."

"Culprits?" wondered the doctor in a shaky voice. "You mean to say that the devil didn't do that?"

"Oh, that was the devil," said Prescott. "But flesh-and-blood humans helped him out."

"Who could have done that?" Dottore Pietro stopped and listened to his earpiece. "*Scusate.* The Holy Father would like to see the evolution of the fetus." He gave several commands to Magdalena and exited the room.

"Paranormally capable culprits," Claire said, raising an eyebrow and nodding her head slowly.

"That's our specialty," said Prescott.

"Indeed," agreed Travis. "It seems that someone wanted to compromise the Pope. Then, a month later, the damage is reversed. Same perpetrator, or a different one?"

"Or the devil and the angels," said Claire. "This is going to be tragically interesting."

Chapter 14. The Timeline

"We know the time the angel intervened—10 am on April 11—but when did the devil do his dirty work?" wondered Travis.

"Let's find out," said Claire. "Magdalena, please give me the date and time the zygote began meiosis."

"March 6, 2066, at 14:00," Magdalena answered.

"Therefore, it seems that the essence of Satan contaminates the Pope's body on March 6 at 2 pm," said Prescott. "That essence causes the Pope's body to create a new life form in the devil's image. On April 11 at 10 am, the essence of God, represented by the woman's genes, is introduced into the Pope's body, and Satan's creation is defeated."

"And the fetus is growing at an alarming rate, as if ready to surprise us with its appearance in this world," commented Claire.

"And to be born on June 6, '66, the devil's date," said Travis.

"There are many omens about such an occurrence," said Prescott.

"Lots of them, including doomsday and Armageddon," said Claire. "Although we supposedly already had an Armageddon."

"No, that was the end of the world," joked Travis.

"You know, I'm still curious," said Prescott. "If the woman's genes corrected Satan's fetus into a human fetus, what caused the zygote to take hold in the first place? I mean, what brought the devil's genes inside the Pope?"

"Let's see what story the genes may tell us," said Claire. "Magdalena, please compare the genetic code of the fetus before April 10 with the genetic code of the Pope."

"The genetic codes are identical to a 99.9999% accuracy," replied the computer.

"That's impossible," said Prescott, now agitated. "Unless..."

"Unless the Pope cloned himself?" Travis speculated.

"Or the Pope was induced to clone himself within his own body," said Claire.

"Any dormant genes?" Prescott asked.

"Two dormant genes." Claire read the display. "Those must be responsible for the devil fetus."

"Yes, but we're looking at this from the wrong direction," said Prescott. "We need to do the analysis from the conception, forward."

"I see what you mean," said Claire. "Magdalena, please analyze the genetic code of the fetus from the creation point, increase the resolution to one second, and report the first anomaly when it disappears."

Magdalena took two seconds to respond: "From the creation, there were two genes that do not belong to the human genome. The genes went dormant after eleven minutes and six seconds."

"Eleven minutes and six seconds—666 seconds? Is this a joke?" wondered Travis.

"Or a coincidence," said Prescott.

"It is the real thing," said Claire. "The number of the beast."

"I wonder if the dormant genes are present in the fetus now," said Claire, getting back on track. "Magdalena, verify the presence or disappearance of the two pairs of dormant genes in the fetus from April 10 to now."

"The dormant genes disappeared at 10:00 on April 11."

"Magdalena, please display the fetus's evolution and the gene analysis side by side, in seconds, from 9:59:30 to 10:00:30, on April 11," asked Claire.

The computer displayed the hologram of the fetus's evolution, and it showed the genetic codes on a holographic panel, with the two dormant genes highlighted. Everything seemed normal until 10:00:05, when the fetus started to spasm. The dormant genes disappeared, and the rest of the genetic makeup started rearranging itself.

"Did you see that?" Claire asked excitedly.

"Yeah," said Travis. "The first thing the woman's genes did was to kill the two foreign, although dormant, genes that were responsible for the devil fetus."

"Good girl!" said Claire. "A woman's genes saved the day."

Mit Sandru

Chapter 15. The Possible Suspects

"Let's have lunch and talk about this," said Prescott, stretching.

"Indeed, I've missed my cappuccino," said Travis.

They arrived at the mess hall, half-full now, and managed to have a quiet lunch, each thinking about and analyzing the situation at hand. Travis had his double cappuccino to complete a satisfying meal.

"Why don't we take a stroll through the Vatican gardens and draw a list of possible suspects?" said Prescott. "We'll silence our voices." Their PAVs went to audio cloak mode.

It was a beautiful day, and the Vatican gardens were delightful—green, well-manicured, flowering, and smelling like fresh-cut grass. Birds frolicked around the trees and bushes. It was paradise, or the way paradise should look and feel, according to many paintings in the Vatican museum. The sounds and smells were an added bonus.

Travis was the first to break their silence. "Who did it and why? What is the motive?" He was walking with his hands behind his back. "Is there one entity, or are there two?"

"It's obvious there two entities," said Claire. "One wanted to destroy the Pope and the Church, and the other prevented it."

"Or he changed his mind and corrected the misdoing," speculated Travis. Then he changed his mind: "No, not likely."

"The assassination attempt on us in the catacombs . . ." Prescott thought for a few seconds. "The perpetrators wanted us dead because we were about to discover the origin of the female genes. And the official explanation for the explosion was an old gas line, which we managed to ignite to save our butts." Prescott smirked. "Unfortunately, the fire melted the broken pipe, so there was no evidence to suggest foul play. It could have passed as a coincidence. But we know better."

"The round stone gate did not roll on its own and block itself in the closed position to trap us inside," agreed Travis.

"The would-be assassins were probably hired thugs, amateurs," said Claire. "The attempt was too sloppy, compared to the finesse used on the Pope."

"We were probably followed," said Travis. "How did we miss them trailing us?"

"They did not need to follow us. They knew where we were going," said Claire.

"Inside information," affirmed Prescott.

"Two people knew where we were going— the Dottore and the Monsignore," said Claire.

Prescott nodded. "And let's not forget the padlock key," said Prescott. "The would-be assassin dropped it when he came to sabotage the gas pipe. He knew that we were coming."

"And the box with the two skeletons had had a visitor in the recent past," said Claire. "But the visitor did not open the lid."

"We'd better stay vigilant. They'll try to kill us again," said Travis. The other two agreed. Each one of them initiated new countersurveillance from their sensors.

"Therefore, let's start with earthly desires as a motive," said Claire. "Who would personally benefit from the Pope's demise?"

"His successors," said Prescott. "That would mean the Pope's closest council, Cardinals Cellini, Bertrand, and Navarro." Prescott looked at his team members, but they didn't suspect any of them in particular.

"Or someone else waiting in the wings," said Claire. "Or—this may be farfetched—but they have killed popes in the past just for being popes. Remember the assassination attempt on Pope John Paul II last century, in 1981?"

"Yes, but there is a huge difference between one deranged man with a gun and what is being attempted here," said Travis.

"I don't believe killing the Pope is their motive," said Prescott. "This is way too sophisticated for a simple murder."

"You think they are attempting to destroy the Church?" asked Travis. "In that case, the cardinals should not be suspects."

"Perhaps, but then who else?" asked Prescott. "The Monsignore?"

"I don't think so," said Claire. "Besides, he was with us in the catacombs, with a flaming torch."

"What if he carried a gas mask under his cassock or his hat?" Prescott pointed to his head.

"Maybe," said Travis.

"How about our good Dottore?" Prescott proposed.

"Same objection I had for the Monsignore," said Claire. "Besides, isn't the Dottore the one who wants the fetus removed to save the Pope?"

"That's true," agreed Prescott. "But I still don't believe the villain is someone outside the Pope's circle."

"Why?" Claire asked.

"This is such an unorthodox and risky method of causing mayhem," said Prescott. "Many things could go haywire, including surgery and the removal of the fetus, and no one would know what happened. The Church would be saved. Besides, if I were the villain, I would want to keep a close eye on the Pope and his condition. I would want this baby to be born, not aborted."

"In that case, we still have five suspects—the three cardinals, the Monsignore, and the Dottore," said Claire. "But the Dottore is against the baby being born, so he seems to be the least likely candidate. And if he wants the Pope dead, he could do it easily, as His Holiness's private physician."

"What do the potential suspects have in common?" Travis wondered out loud. "They all work for the Vatican. All five are learned men, but only four are of a religious order. Three could have a chance to become the next Pope. All five have close access to the Pope and know about this."

"I still think that the least likely suspect is the doctor." Claire stopped, as if thinking about something bothersome. "Why don't we consider the Pope a suspect?" Claire proposed.

Travis and Prescott looked at one another, and each gasped in jest.

"Why would the Pope do this to himself?" Prescott asked.

"Perhaps not to destroy the Church but to give it a boost in a new direction," answered Claire.

"Like giving birth to a new Messiah," said Travis. "And it would be an immaculate conception, for sure."

"If only the believers would buy the idea of a man giving birth to a male child," speculated Prescott. "Even in today's age of the weird and unusual, this would be sensational, even scandalous."

"Now, Prescott. Would that be the most shocking thing people have done lately?" Travis put his hands on his hips in mockery. "There is a woman in San Francisco who is legally married to her python. At the end of her life and after her snake grows large enough, she wants to be swallowed by the beast. To be one with her snake." Travis clasped his hands and looked up.

"Or become snake excrement." Prescott shrugged. "Anyway, we're dealing with the Catholic Church here. As conservative as it gets."

"Let's take one motive at a time," said Claire. "Suppose the Pope is the mastermind behind this charade to pave a new future for the Church."

"Yes, if he can convince his flock that this was divine intervention," said Prescott.

"Then why did he hire us to investigate?" asked Travis. "We could unmask him, and disaster would follow."

"Unless we fail to resolve this mystery and give credence to the idea of divine intervention." Prescott looked at his teammates, but they didn't seemed convinced

"Or, as it seems now, the Pope is the unsuspecting victim," said Claire. "He will be retired to spare the Church embarrassment and clear the way for a new pope. Then the villains are the three cardinals, the potential successors."

"Why only the cardinals?" asked Prescott. "You forget the Monsignore, although he's a very long shot."

"Or another candidate who we don't know about," said Travis. "Even the Dottore could become the next pope, if the cardinal conclave deems him fit for the job."

"Five suspects who could want to become the next pope," said Prescott. "But why not just kill the Pope and be done with it?"

"In the case of an assassination, even if it's done very well, the aspiring pope may not control the outcome," said Travis. "There is a risk of the perpetrator not getting what he wants after all that hard work."

"Or this could just be pure revenge," said Claire. "The villain could have no ulterior motive of becoming the next pope."

"In that case, we continue to have five suspects—the cardinals, the Monsignore, and the Dottore," said Prescott.

"But if plain murder is their motive, then why set up such a complex and sophisticated plan to get the Pope pregnant?" said Travis.

"True," agreed Prescott.

Claire stopped and looked at her partners. "The Pope has control over his body and the fetus. He is the only one who can put an end to this and hush it up, or continue with it to its full fruition."

"Indeed," agreed Travis, as Prescott nodded. "However, why the assassination attempt against us? In what way did we complicate matters by discovering the source of the woman's genes?"

"The situation has become fluid because of our investigation," said Prescott.

"We've started to upset their plans," concluded Claire. "One more thing—I had the distinct impression the first time we met with the Pope and the cardinals that someone else knew about the fetus. But the Pope did not want to divulge his identity."

Chapter 16. The Pope and the Cardinals

"I think they're looking for us." Claire opened the communication on her PAV with the Monsignore.

"*Signori*," he said. "The Holy Father and the cardinals would like to see you, *per favore*."

"We'll be over right away," answered Claire.

They followed the tracker set by the Monsignore to the Pope's quarters. The Monsignore opened the door to let them in and then stepped outside, closing the door behind him. There was an austere and somber mood in the room. The Pope, his face tranquil, sat in his chair. Cardinal Navarro was present, seated on the side sofa. Cardinal Cellini stood by the window, looking down on St. Peter's Square. Cardinal Bertrand paced around the room, fingering his prayer beads. With his hand, the Pope silently invited the CTT to sit down.

Cardinal Cellini stood back from the window and spoke for the Pope. "We reviewed again the hologram of the fetus's evolution. Those are disturbing realities. It seems that the Holy Father's body was subject to the devil's desecration. A sad time for all of us." He sighed and clasped his hands as in prayer. "Therefore, we concluded that the fetus, which is not a human fetus, is a malcreation, and it must be removed surgically and immediately from His Holiness."

Claire noted that the cardinal did not use the word abortion. The fetus was not a fetus but a mutation, and, soon after the operation, it would be incinerated.

"We thank you for your assistance and help," continued Cardinal Cellini. "You have really unveiled the truth and shed light on this incident. We consider this case closed."

"That's unfortunate," said Claire. "We've further investigated the fetus's evolution, and we found some surprising developments."

Cardinal Cellini started to object about any more explanations when the Pope raised his hand. "Please, tell us what you found out."

"In our assessment, the fetus started as an intervention by an evil agent," said Claire. "We don't know the motive, although we can speculate on a few. The satanic fetus was not to be discovered until after it was born, and, by then, it would have evolved to resemble a human being. It was conceived on March 6 at 2 pm, and it matured at a very fast rate, until—" Claire stopped to catch her breath and emphasize what she was going to say next. "Until April 11, at 10 am, when the genes of a woman who died a thousand years ago were introduced into your body, Your Holiness. Those genes corrected the anomaly."

The Pope sat up straight. The cardinals gathered closer, with renewed attention.

"Those female genes destroyed Satan's two genes that were responsible for the appearance of the early fetus. Within an extremely short period of time, your DNA and the woman's DNA combined and reconfigured the entire genetic makeup of the fetus into what it appears to be today. The fetus is maturing very quickly, perhaps a leftover effect from the original satanic seed, and it will be ready to be born by surgical means on June 6."

The Pope and his cardinals looked at each other, astounded.

"We believe that you are carrying a perfectly normal human fetus, and it was divine intervention that rectified the original blasphemy," concluded Claire.

"That's incredible," said Cardinal Navarro.

"A miracle, after all," said Cardinal Bertrand.

"And do you have proof?" Cardinal Cellini asked, narrowing his eyes. "Real, solid proof that the devil hasn't tricked us to make sure his child will be born?"

"Magdalena, I mean the Dottore's computer, has all the information," said Claire. "We are certain that the child is a normal human child."

The Pope smiled and spread his arms. "Divine intervention. When did you say this happened?"

"April 11 at 10 am, Your Holiness," said Claire.

"That's what I thought you said," said the Pope. He turned to face his cardinals with a knowing look. "Easter Sunday."

"Blessed be our Lord, our Father, and His Son, Jesus Christ." Cardinal Navarro made the sign of the cross several times. The other two cardinals did the same.

"A miracle on Easter Sunday, right before the mass," said the Pope, with a contented and serene look on his face.

"Were you all present?" Prescott asked.

"Not at ten o'clock on that Sunday," said Cardinal Cellini. "Each one of us was serving mass in his respective parish."

Cardinals Navarro and Bertrand nodded in acknowledgement.

"Do you remember what happened on March 6?" asked Prescott.

Cardinal Navarro removed a small electronic calendar from his pocket. After examining it, he said, "That was a Saturday. I was in Valencia, Spain."

"I was here in the Vatican, and I don't remember anything unusual," said Cardinal Cellini.

"As a matter of fact, I was with you, Cardinal Cellini, discussing the situation in Buenos Aires," said Cardinal Bertrand.

The Pope rang an electronic bell, and Monsignore Giuseppe came in. "*Sì*, Your Holiness, at your service."

"What was I doing on March 6 at two o'clock in the afternoon?"

The Monsignore produced a similar personal electronic calendar and, after examining it, he said, "You met with and blessed a group of sisters from several convents who had recently taken their perpetual vows as nuns."

"Oh, yes," said the Pope.

"Isn't that when a sister fainted?" Cardinal Bertrand wondered.

"It sure is," agreed Cardinal Navarro. "I am still treating Sister Terina at the convent of the Suore Mantellate Serve di Sofia. Tragic, very tragic how she lost her mind." Cardinal Navarro made the sign of the cross and said a quick prayer.

The Pope said a prayer as well for the sister's well-being. After a short moment of silence, he said, "Monsignore Giuseppe, please inform the Dottore that I will not be having the surgery after all."

"Certainly, Your Holiness." The Monsignore left the papal quarters with a satisfied smile on his face.

"There is the matter of the perpetrators," said Travis.

The cardinals gave him a puzzled look. Cardinal Cellini spoke: "You intend to make a case against Satan?"

"No, not him. Although he's guilty as hell," clarified Travis. "His minions could strike again. We must find them."

"Yes, you must find them," agreed the Pope. "Take whatever actions are necessary to bring them to justice."

"We will, Your Holiness," said Travis.

"We would like to talk with each one of you for a while longer, Your Eminences," said Claire to the cardinals. "Time permitting, of course."

She smiled at them. The cardinals looked at her with stony faces for a split second, but then they softened and nodded their heads. "Wonderful. We will contact your secretaries," concluded Claire.

Once they were out of the papal quarters, Travis said, "We need to do parallel investigations."

"I'll take the Dottore," said Claire. "And I want to talk to Cellini. He looks like a hard ass."

"I'm puzzled about that nun and what kind of treatment Cardinal Navarro is giving her," said Prescott. "I'll inquire with him. I feel a tingling sensation about this situation."

"Then I'll have a chat with the Monsignore," said Travis. "Bertrand intrigues me. I'll talk to him."

"But right now, let them churn," said Claire. "We may have upset a few plans. Killing the fetus was the easy way out, and we prevented it today."

"Indeed," agreed Travis. "Let them make the next move."

Chapter 17. The Secret Holy See Emergency Council

Cardinal Cellini was a man of action. This latest development was most upsetting, and he needed to get in touch with the members of the Secret Holy See Emergency Council at once. They were standing by for him to contact them. He entered his office and initiated the holopresence at once.

"What tidings do you have for us, Cardinal Cellini?" asked Cardinal Le Pere, this time present at the Secret Holy See Emergency Council holo-meeting.

Cardinal Cellini looked gravely at his twelve council members. "It was as I suspected. The fetus is the devil. That idiot Dottore Pietro did not do his due diligence to find out the nature of the fetus. It was the CTT that discovered the truth. But let me explain what happened." He proceeded to reveal the latest news.

"It was obvious from the CTT's trans-axiom-paranormal assessment and the genetic regression reconstruction that we are dealing with the devil's offspring. But then the CTT reverses its opinion and convinces the Holy Father that the fetus is human and that the devil was defeated by God, who supposedly used Papessa Giovanna's DNA to correct Satan's evil work." The cardinal slammed his fist on his desk.

"Papessa Giovanna?" asked Cardinal Molino.

"There is no proof of that, thank God," assured Cardinal Cellini. "Even the CTT won't confirm if the genes belong to Pope Joan."

"If word gets out that our Holy Father is carrying Satan's son, who has the genes of Papessa Giovanna, the Church is finished!" shouted Cardinal Tobutu Goba.

"Do you see the predicament we're in?" Cardinal Cellini glared at each one of them.

The twelve cardinals in the holopresence nodded. Some sighed.

"Where does Dottore Pietro stand on this?" asked Cardinal Le Pere.

"Fortunately, the Dottore is on our side. He considers the fetus a malignancy," answered Cardinal Cellini. "He was preparing to remove the fetus surgically this very evening, until our Holy Father changed his mind, believing that he carries the immaculate conception." The cardinals' expressions showed their disgust, all except for Cardinal Le Pere's.

"It seems to me that our Holy Father has full control over this situation," said Cardinal Le Pere.

"Unfortunately, with catastrophic consequences," said Cardinal Broninsky.

"The only uncontrollable factor in this situation is the CTT," Cardinal O'Connor spoke softly.

"Elaborate, please, Cardinal O'Connor," said Cardinal Le Pere.

"The CTT discovered some revealing facts, and our Holy Father has confidence in their findings. Even if they are misguided."

"The Trinity Investigation Organization and its teams are incorruptible," said Cardinal Le Pere.

"But what if they are misguided?" Cardinal O'Connor insisted.

"Are you saying that Satan has corrupted their minds?" asked Cardinal Cellini.

"They are mortals and prone to be seduced by the Unholy One, like all men and women," replied Cardinal O'Connor.

"This council, the Secret Holy See Emergency Council, is our Church's last defense," said Cardinal Cellini.

"What would you suggest we do?" asked Cardinal Le Pere.

"I agree with Cardinal O'Connor. The CTT is not helping our cause," said Cardinal Cellini. "We need to remove them. And I've tried, but they convinced our Holy Father that justice needs to be served, and they are continuing their investigation." The cardinal said as an afterthought, "I wish the gas explosion on Via Labicana had killed them."

"What?" several cardinals asked as one.

"It seems that while they were nosing around in the catacombs under the Basilica di San Clemente al Laterano, searching for the illusory Papessa Giovanna, a gas leak caused an explosion, cracking a section of the pavement under Via Labicana, close to the Basilica."

"What are the chances of that happening?" asked Cardinal Molino.

"I'd say that there are other entities at work here to prevent the CTT from discovering the true nature of this fetus," said Cardinal Cellini.

"However, according to the CTT, the fetus is normal," said Cardinal Le Pere.

"I'm sorry." Cardinal Cellini shook his head. "The fetus looked like a demon. Then it transformed itself into a human fetus—not because of any holy intervention but as a deception used by Satan to convince us otherwise and to let his son be born into our world."

"And be born of a man, our Holy Father himself," concluded Cardinal Tobutu Goba.

"I'm not sure why we need to end the CTT's investigation," said Cardinal Le Pere.

Cardinal Cellini pierced the air with his finger. "Because they convinced the Holy Father to continue with the fetus and therefore carry out Satan's wishes. As long as they are involved, the Holy Father has the illusion that he is doing the right thing. God help me, but I believe that the CTT is controlled by the Unholy One."

It was quiet. The cardinals were considering Cardinal Cellini's troubling words.

"There are other persuasive ways to derail the CTT," said Cardinal Gondolini after a while.

"Nothing illegal, I pray," said Cardinal Le Pere.

"Well, not exactly, but this woman has been very effective against men in the past," said the cardinal. "If we want results, we must rely on her decision of what course of action needs to be taken."

"Including murder?" asked Cardinal Le Pere, his eyes widening.

"I am concerned about that, too, just like the rest of you. I could ask her to just weaken them."

"Weakening them is acceptable," said Cardinal Cellini. "Any objections?"

No one in the council objected, nor did they voice their approval, but their silence meant, "Go ahead."

Except for one. "If she is who I think she is, God help her," said Cardinal Le Pere.

"She has never failed us."

Cardinal Le Pere sighed. "She's as good as dead if she attempts anything against the CTT."

Chapter 18. Il Dottore

The following morning at 9 am, Claire went to the medical quarters to have a chat with the doctor. She found him putting away the laser surgical instruments that he would have used to perform the surgery on the Pope. Perhaps he was still hopeful that he might get his chance to remove the fetus.

"Are you disappointed, Dottore?" Claire asked.

"Disappointed? About what?" the doctor asked.

"About not operating?"

"I'm concerned about our Holy Father's health." The doctor waved his hands. "God knows what medical complications this may entail. Besides, as you discovered, the fetus is not normal. It started as an evil seed. In my medical opinion, the fetus must be removed."

"You did not have those feelings when we first saw you," Claire said casually.

The doctor cleared his throat. "What makes you think so?"

"As a doctor, shouldn't you have aggressively recommended the surgery once you discovered the anomaly?"

"As you know, I did not know about the fetus until a week ago, when His Holiness did not feel well. I was shocked and surprised by what I discovered in his belly. After I revealed the matter to His Holiness, he involved the cardinals, and they decided not to come to a hasty decision but to consider this matter in depth."

"But you are the doctor. His Holiness's health is your responsibility."

"Of course it is my responsibility. However, His Holiness's life was not in immediate jeopardy."

Claire gave a half smile. "You mean to tell me that the decision to operate is made by a committee?"

"Not necessarily." The doctor smoothed his sleek hair. "I have the power to take action when His Holiness's life is at stake."

"Even if it would mean an abortion?" Claire asked

"I know. Catholics abhor abortions. But this fetus is not a human being. It is a mutation. It is a malignancy." He stressed the last word. "It's not an abortion, just a necessary surgery."

"All the tests showed a human being," said Claire.

"And so it was when I first discovered the fetus. But based on what we know now, thanks to you, the situation is completely different."

"But that was before. Now it corrected itself."

"I'm surprised that you say that. You and your team assessed the fetus with your TAP and found that his mind is connected to two different realms—heaven and hell."

Claire lifted her head slightly. "Most minds are connected to the Mind Realm of the White Energy Universe. Occasionally a mind is connected to the Dark Energy—hell, as you say. That doesn't mean that the fetuses connected to the light are angels and the ones connected to the dark are demons. Bad can come from the realm of light as well. As a matter of fact, by far, most evil minds are connected to the realm of light."

"So this boy is going to be a schizophrenic," argued the doctor. "A Dr. Jekyll and Mr. Hyde."

Claire sensed his anger. Which aspect was he most interested in: the Pope's well-being or killing the fetus? "So you'd rather kill this fetus than have a schizophrenic?" Claire watched him intently.

"Kill?" he shouted. "I'm a doctor. I have no desire to kill anyone, even if they deserve it, like those bastards who killed my sons!" His face turned red with fury.

Claire couldn't help but raise her eyebrows. "I'm sorry to hear that your sons were killed." Claire walked over to him and placed her hands on his arm to comfort him. "Would you care to tell me about them?"

"What's to tell?" said the doctor with a sad voice, pulling his arm away. "We had two sons, our only children. Two grown sons, and they're dead now. You'd think that because I work for the Vatican I would get a special dispensation and God would have protected them. But no, God took them away, and the killers lived on."

Claire sensed the bitterness in his voice. "Please, tell me what happened."

The doctor exhaled and his shoulders slumped, as if he were about to unload a great burden. "My sons raced automobiles. Not the ones with hydro-engines, but those antiques, the gasoline-powered automobiles. They crashed, and the gasoline tank ruptured and caught on fire. They were burned alive." The doctor covered his eyes with one hand as if to prevent his tears from escaping.

Claire waited for the doctor to calm down. "That's awful. I'm so sorry." Claire paused. "You said they were killed?"

"The other two boys they were racing against, they caused the crash," said the doctor. "They bragged afterward, when they collected their winnings, how they had maneuvered my sons into an outside curve to force them to crash. Later, when I confronted them, they laughed. For them, it was all part of the sport and the glory of winning, while my sons died."

"Did the police investigate? Were they able to do anything?" Claire asked.

"No, there was not enough evidence. As far as they were concerned, it was a fair race that went bad, and my sons were at fault."

"I'm sorry," Claire said again. She spotted the doctor's wedding ring. "How's your wife taking this?"

"She left me," said the doctor curtly, as if he didn't want to talk about it anymore. "How did we end up talking about my sons?" The doctor gave a small, nervous laugh. "We must protect the Holy Father's life."

"That's true. And the unborn child."

"This has never happened before," the doctor said. "God knows what complications could occur when we remove the full-grown fetus. It could be as serious as separating conjoined twins."

Claire knew that this was nothing like an operation on conjoined twins. The amniotic sac was self-contained. Only the placenta had blood vessels connected to the Pope's vascular system. "Are you afraid that the Holy Father may be at risk during the Caesarean section?"

"Yes! Very much so!" said the doctor.

Mit Sandru

Chapter 19. Il Monsignore

Travis found Monsignore Giuseppe in the corridor leading to the papal quarters. "Monsignore! Just the man I was looking for."

The Monsignore smiled curtly.

"Could we find a private place to talk, if you don't mind?" Travis asked.

"Of course, in my office. Right this way."

After Travis was seated, the Monsignore sat behind his desk, clasping his hands and leaning forward.

"What a day we had in the catacombs!" Travis exclaimed. "Even for me it was unusual."

"God was watching over us." The Monsignore made the sign of the cross.

"Indeed," agreed Travis. "How long have you been the Holy Father's personal secretary?"

"Seventeen glorious years." He raised his eyes as if thanking heaven.

"That's a long time," said Travis. "Have you made any plans for the future?"

"Plans for the future?"

"His Holiness is an old man, and in the current situation . . ." Travis shrugged and his voice trailed away.

The Monsignore's eyebrows jumped up his forehead. "Pardon me, but you are being rather blunt."

"Sorry to upset you."

"No need to apologize. I suspect that is part of your profession, to ask direct questions. It is true that His Holiness is old and the current situation is precarious, however, I don't think about it. With the help of God, I pray and I take one day at a time." The Monsignore interlaced his fingers and smiled again.

Travis smiled back. "What do you make of the Dottore's objection about the fetus?"

"It's a complicated matter." The Monsignore thought for a moment. "The Dottore is doing his job and wants to make sure that His Holiness is not harmed." He raised a hand. "However, the fetus has a right to life. He must be born. God has commanded so."

"God? Commanded?"

"We get explicit commands directly from God. Haven't you?"

"At times, yes," said Travis, observing the verve with which the Monsignore spoke. "Did God tell you that the fetus must be born?"

"Let's say that it is divine intervention when God sends you to find a saint to help the Holy Father in his hour of need."

"A saint? Were you contacted by a saint? Who?"

"No, no. I haven't been contacted by a saint." The Monsignore shook his head. "I meant to say that it must have been an angel who came down from heaven while I was asleep and asked me to help the Holy Father in his hour of need."

Travis noted that the Monsignore was sincere in his belief. "And did you do as instructed?"

"Yes. In my heart, I feel I carried out our Lord's command." The Monsignore placed his palms together as if in prayer.

"What did you do?"

"Frankly, I don't remember doing anything special. Just by being I was helping our Holy Father."

"When did this happen?"

"It was not at a specific time, just a knowing when you wake up, and it's happened a few times since the beginning of spring."

"Wow, that's incredible," said Travis. "But what exactly did the voice tell you to do?"

"'Find a saint, my son. Our Holy Father needs your help'," Monsignore Giuseppe intoned.

"That's powerful." Travis leaned forward. "And did you find a saint?"

"I think I did. But, then again, Rome is full of saints, and it was not a difficult task. All I had to do was pray at the site of a worthy saint."

"Fascinating—ask for a saint to help the Holy Father in his hour of need." Travis faked enchantment at what he heard. "Through your prayer, you might have saved the fetus."

"Maybe. I didn't know that, until your team unraveled the fetus's development," said the Monsignore modestly. "But now we have proof that the fetus has been touched by heaven."

"I gather you'd like the baby to be born at any cost," said Travis.

"He's a creation of God, and we cannot and should not end it," he said in a serious tone of voice.

"How true." Travis bobbed his head as if in approval, to keep the Monsignore on his side.

"Is this what you wanted to discuss with me?" the Monsignore asked.

"Uh, no." Travis pretended to remember. "As the Holy Father's personal secretary, you must spend a lot of time with him."

"Most of his waking hours."

"Can you recollect in more detail what happened on March 6 at two in the afternoon?"

The Monsignore caressed his chin. "I could, but I have a better record than my recollection."

Travis nodded, inviting him to go on.

"Whenever the Holy Father is in public, we record the events." The Monsignore smiled as if to say, "How about that?"

"Fabulous," said Travis, pleased about that news.

"Of course, only the public appearances," the Monsignore clarified.

"Let's watch what happened five minutes before two o'clock and five minutes after," said Travis.

"Giovanna." The Monsignore addressed his computer. "Display papal events from 13:55 to 14:05 on March 6."

Did he name his computer after Pope Joan? Interesting, thought Travis.

A hologram unfolded above the desk, showing a ceremony taking place in the basilica. Gregorian chants could be heard in the background. The Pope was seated, surrounded by an entourage of cardinals. A long line of nuns approached him, and each nun, one at a time, genuflected and kissed the Pope's ring. The Pope blessed each one of them.

Travis watched the gathering intently, trying to identify any unusual occurrence. He did not know what he was looking for, but he was sure he would spot it when it happened. The whole procession was monotonous, downright boring. Travis's eyes were about to glaze over when the nun who had just kissed the Pope's ring collapsed at his feet. That got Travis's attention.

"Stop, please," Travis said. "And go back to before that nun approached."

"Yes, that's when the sister fainted," said the Monsignore. "It happens from time to time."

The computer reversed the ceremony by a couple of nuns. Travis focused on the nun who would collapse. She looked pious, holding her rosary and praying as she got closer to the Pope. After genuflecting, she bent down and kissed his ring. She fainted for no apparent reason.

"Stop, please," Travis commanded. "Giovanna, magnify the scene from when she genuflects until she collapses."

Giovanna the computer enlarged the frame, which included only the nun and the Pope. Although it gave better detail, Travis could not detect anything unusual other than the nun fainting.

"Giovanna," said Travis, "please replay from the time the nun bends down to kiss the ring—zoom in on her face and reduce the speed by half."

The close-up showed the nun's profile. She bent her head down with a serene face to kiss the ring. When her lips were near the ring, she opened them wider and took the whole ring into her mouth, as if she were sucking on a plump cherry. Her lips covered the Pope's finger.

"Stop!" shouted Travis. "Is this normal?" Travis turned toward the Monsignore.

"*Madonna*, no," he said in shock. "I never saw that detail before."

"Were you present when it happened?"

"I was there, but I did not witness this ring kiss, only now on the recording."

"OK. Giovanna, continue playing from here at quarter speed," said Travis.

The nun removed her lips from the ring and raised her head slowly. Instead of the serene face she had when she approached the Pope, the nun's face now was contorted in a malicious and evil appearance. She was almost grinning, as if satisfied at what she had done. Just as fast, though, her eyes rolled up in their sockets and she lost consciousness.

"Normal speed, Giovanna," Travis asked.

Nuns from behind rushed to her aid. The Pope stood up, showing concern for the nun's condition. The nuns were patting her hands and fanning her. Unable to rouse her, they took her aside into the aisle, and she disappeared from the hologram.

"Thank you, Giovanna, you may stop now," said Travis. The hologram closed.

The Monsignore was frozen in place with his mouth wide open. Travis thought for a moment about the ring, the finger kissing, and the contorted face of the nun.

"I believe that is Sister Terina, isn't it?" Travis asked.

"Yes, Sister Terina," acknowledged the Monsignore, recovering from his temporary shock. "How do you know that?"

"Cardinal Navarro mentioned her name."

"Oh, yes. Poor soul. What could have happened to her?"

"Isn't she interned?"

"Not per se. She was taken to Suore Mantellate Serve di Sofia for treatment. She lost her mind and has not improved since. His Holiness was considering going to see her, to give her his blessings." The Monsignore made the sign of the cross.

"And she never showed any symptoms before kissing His Holiness's ring?" Travis asked.

"No, none at all, from what the mother superior said about Sister Terina. She was well," said the Monsignore.

"Hmm." Travis gathered his thoughts for a moment. Strange how she kissed the Pope's ring and then collapsed and lost her mind. Or maybe she lost her mind just before kissing the ring?

"Is there anything else?" the Monsignore asked, straightening.

"Oh yes," said Travis. "The second date, April 11, Easter Sunday, at 10 am. You wouldn't happen to have images from that date and time, would you?"

The Monsignore raised his finger as if to say, "Let's see." He turned his eyes toward the hologram location and said, "Giovanna, display papal events on April 11, at the ten o'clock hour, please."

A new hologram appeared, showing the Pope surrounded by his entourage. The Pope was getting ready to perform Easter Mass. Then the procession began at 10:01, a minute late. Travis and the Monsignore watched for another minute as the procession walked toward the altar.

"Giovanna, stop the hologram, and go back to 9:59. From there, proceed at half speed," said Travis.

The hologram restarted at 9:59 and showed the same fuss, with the retinue of cardinals and bishops jockeying for their positions in the procession. It took twice as long to observe this new hologram, but nothing unusual could be discerned.

"Giovanna, restart the hologram at 9:59 at half the speed and zoom-frame around the Pope," Travis ordered.

A much larger image of the Pope was displayed now. But nothing out of the ordinary happened. The Pope was not touched by anyone between 9:59 and 10:01, as Travis had expected.

"Giovanna, go backward at normal speed," said Travis. He watched and then he noticed what he wanted to see. "Stop. Play from this point on at half speed forward."

The time signature showed 9:57:02 at the start of the hologram. The Pope made a gesture as if to ask, "Is everyone ready?" Then, as an afterthought, at 9:57:48, he turned halfway and extended his ring hand. Monsignore Giuseppe genuflected and kissed the papal ring at 9:58:00.

"Giovanna, freeze frame!" shouted Travis.

His shout startled the Monsignore. "What is the matter?"

"You kissed the Pope's ring." Travis pointed to the Monsignore's head retreating from kissing the ring. "But the time was 9:58:00."

"But of course," said the Monsignore. "I kiss His Holiness's ring before all ceremonies."

"Giovanna, play back and stop at 9:58:00," said Travis.

The hologram froze as the Monsignore kissed the ring at exactly 9:58:00.

"What does it mean?" whispered the Monsignore.

"It seems, Monsignore, that no miracle happened at 10:00:00, as we expected."

"No?"

"Although you are the last person to touch the Holy Father before 10:00:00, when supposedly the miracle happened."

"No miracle?" The Monsignore shook his head disbelievingly. "How do you know?"

"The miracle happened all right," said Travis. "However, not at 10:00, and not what I had in mind."

"I don't understand." The Monsignore looked dumbfounded, holding his palms up.

"I'm baffled, too," said Travis. "I thought that you may have been the one bringing the saintly essence to the Pope." Travis paced around. "Do you have images of what happened before the ring kiss?" Travis asked.

The Monsignore did not seem disappointed. "No, we record visuals only when his Holy Father is in public or there is a ceremony. And this recording started at 9:57."

"Do you recall what happened before the ceremony?" Travis asked.

The Monsignore stood still, as if thinking about that day.

"Start from when you woke up and go forward," proposed Travis.

"I woke up at six o'clock in the morning. I'm an early riser. His Holiness sleeps until eight o'clock, so I usually have two hours for myself. That morning, being Easter Sunday, I decided to go and visit the tomb of my friend, Brother Luca, early in the morning and not in the afternoon as I had planned. He's buried at the

Basilica di San Clemente al Laterano, as I mentioned."

"Oh yes," said Travis. "Next to your friend's vault is where we found the rusted gate that led to the catacombs. What made you change your mind and go visit him early in the morning?"

"Another dream, perhaps." The Monsignore raised his eyes to the heavens. He continued, "At his vault I lit a candle, then I knelt and prayed for him and all the saints for a good, long time." The Monsignore's eyes filled with tears.

"Brother Luca was a good friend of yours," said Travis.

"We were like brothers, almost like blood brothers," said the Monsignore.

"Do you miss him?" Travis asked.

"I do, very much." He retrieved a handkerchief from his pocket and blew his nose. "I—we entombed him on April 6, just five days before Easter."

"When you prayed that Sunday, did you touch his vault?" Travis asked.

"*Sì*. I placed my hands and my forehead on the marble lid and prayed. I felt good afterward. I felt at peace. I knew he is in heaven, and that gave me a sense of well-being." The Monsignore lifted his eyes again.

"Where did you go from there?"

"I returned to the Vatican to prepare for the Easter Mass ceremony."

"Do you realize, Monsignore, that Brother Luca's tomb is close to the tomb of the woman where the genes were found? The remains of the alleged Pope Joan?"

"Well, maybe it was divine guidance." The Monsignore beamed.

Chapter 20. The Cardinals

Claire wasted no time and arrived at Cardinal Cellini's office a half-hour early. She took a seat, waiting for their appointment. His Eminence's secretary was kind enough to offer her an espresso, and she sipped it slowly while she waited. Cardinal Cellini's waiting chamber was ornate and full of exquisite oil paintings of past popes, statuettes of saints, and Holy See flags and insignias. It would all be impressive and overwhelming to anyone having an appointment with Cardinal Cellini, the Secretary of State of the Holy See.

Claire formulated her strategy on the approach to use with this powerful man, an alpha male. She would let him take charge and lead the discussion, and, in the process, he would say enough for Claire to understand his motives and possible involvement.

At the appointed time, the secretary took her into Cardinal's Cellini's sumptuously appointed office. The cardinal rose from behind his desk and offered his hand to her with a cold smile. "Ms. Claire German, it's a pleasure. Please be seated."

"Good afternoon, Your Eminence. Thank you for taking time from your busy schedule to see me."

The credenza behind his chair held pictures of Cardinal Cellini with just about all the important leaders of the time. On the wall behind him, between the two tall windows of his office, a large gilded crucifix of Jesus Christ was an overpowering presence.

"What is on your mind?" asked the cardinal.

Her PAV's sensors indicated that she was being monitored for any probing sensors she might have pointed at the cardinal. "This must be a trying time for your Eminence and for the Curia."

"Yes, it is. The Curia has not yet been informed of the Holy Father's situation. We hope that we can resolve this without earthshattering repercussions."

"Is there anything more my team and I can do for the Holy See?" asked Claire with a supplicant's smile.

"Oh, I think you're doing wonderfully. In such a short time, you have discovered so much and shed light on this situation. However, I was wondering if the genes you discovered were those of Pope Joan?"

"No, we cannot say with any certainty. They could belong to any woman from a thousand years ago."

Cardinal Cellini lowered his head and placed a crooked index finger over his chin, thinking. "In spite of what people may think, we are an open-minded church. If there were a real Papessa Giovanna, and it could be proven, we would rectify such an injustice at once."

"I'm sure the Holy See would." Claire smiled. "However, we don't have any proof, nor are we chartered to uncover the mystery of Pope Joan."

"An excellent point. However, the question remains: Who was this woman? What was she doing with an infant in a burial box covered with heaps of stones? What drove the people of that time to do such a thing? What were they afraid of?"

"There was great anguish and suffering at the time of her death. We simply don't know what happened, what caused the uproar."

"Since this woman was not Pope Joan, and, from what you and your team have told us, the reaction of those people toward her was so violent, one may think that she was of the evil kind. Hmm?" Cardinal Cellini looked pointedly at Claire.

"I wish we could answer your questions, but we cannot. We don't have enough information."

"This is of great concern to us and the Holy Father. Once our Curia hears of this, they will be very troubled about the intricate twists of how this fetus came to be. Don't you think?"

Claire nodded and noted with certainty that Cellini was not enthusiastic about the fetus. "We only provide you with the facts. It is your decision on what course of action must be taken."

"That is so true. However, you must admit that there were only two unknown genes in the original embryo, and these two genes disappeared after the DNA from the mysterious woman appeared. Ergo, we really don't know what we have here." Cardinal Cellini raised an eyebrow.

"We have a healthy male fetus," answered Claire.

"Healthy now, but a monster recently, and a monster after he will be born, perhaps?" The Cardinal's stare fixed on her.

"That is the miracle of life." Claire smiled. "Cardinal Cellini, what outcome would you wish?"

He raised his hands up to his shoulders as if surrendering. "I wish the best for our Holy Father and the Holy See." He paused. "Would the birth of a male child from the belly of a man, from genes of questionable origins, be the best for us?" He sighed. "I don't think so, and probing deeper into this mystery will not bode well. Frankly, I believe you have done all you can, and you should stop searching further, before tragedy strikes." His face hardened.

"You are disagreeing with the His Holiness about finding the culprits?" Claire tilted her head in feigned surprise.

"Not at all. Quite the contrary." The Cardinal smiled coldly. "This is the work of the Unholy One. Finding his minions won't change what has already happened. Your continuing investigation resembles a vendetta."

"I'm sorry that you see it that way," Claire said evenly. "However, we must fulfill His Holiness's orders."

Cardinal Cellini stood up, indicating that their discussion was over. "You are meddling with powerful forces, Ms. German."

"That's what we do, Your Eminence."

Travis contemplated what the video recordings had divulged. Some metaphysical infecting agent was released twice into the Pope: The first time to cause the procreation of the fetus, and the second time to correct two evil genes of that fetus and introduce new ones. Members of the Church had performed both these acts. Did Satan initiate the first one, and if he did, how did he get to Sister Terina? There is an aura of God surrounding the religious, protecting them from the Unholy One, unless he or she lets him in. Again, Travis thought, were there one or two masterminds at work here? Depending on how this situation evolves, there are people who will benefit and others who will suffer.

Cardinal Bertrand could benefit. He's the youngest of the three cardinals, French, and capable enough to have been elevated to the position of Camerlengo. He would handle the Vatican's affairs after the Pope dies and the new pope is in the process of being elected. Travis spotted him crossing the courtyard, just as his secretary had informed Travis on where to find him.

"Hello, Your Eminence!" said Travis, catching up with him.

"Hello, Travis St. John! I must admit that it is not common to talk to a saint." The cardinal laughed heartily.

"Indeed, I feel as if I'm outranking you." Travis laughed as well.

"My son, everyone outranks me. I am here to serve God and His people."

"Very well said, Your Eminence," said Travis.

"I hope you don't mind our informal meeting place, walking around the Vatican. But we can talk and exercise and accomplish—at least I will accomplish—a few small tasks at the same time."

"No problem," answered Travis.

"What's on your mind, my son?"

Travis made a note of the patronizing word "son." It was time to throw the cardinal a curveball question. "I was wondering. Would you want to become the next pope?"

Cardinal Bertrand stopped on the spot. "That is a very unorthodox question, don't you think?"

"Yes, it is," said Travis with a smile.

The Cardinal resumed walking. "Let's not beat around the bush. Every priest dreams of becoming the next Holy Father. But, like everything in life, each one of us eventually finds the highest level we can aspire to in serving God. Some of us will not progress beyond priesthood. Still a fulfilling life, I have to say. A few will become bishops, a job that requires good administrative abilities. Cardinals, however, well, that requires good political skills, the ability to please humanity and all their earthly desires while staying true to the Church. Beyond that, there are the special tasks that the Holy Father assigns to certain cardinals possessing practical skills to carry out the business of the Church, or, for lack of a better word, the business of everyday life here on Earth. Am I boring you?"

"No, not at all. It's quite fascinating."

"Very well! And then there are the positions that some cardinals are called to perform for the Holy See to function as a state. Not just any state, but the State of God!"

"Very well said."

"The ultimate post in pleasing and helping God is to become the Holy Father, the Pope. It is a job for a genius and a saint to balance the wants of men with those of heaven. Our Holy Father is the link from humanity to God." They walked for a few moments in silence. "So the question is not if I want to become the next pope, but am I worthy?"

"Are you worthy?" Travis asked.

"It is not for me to decide, but for my brother cardinals, for whom I have the utmost respect and trust."

"Let's say, for simplicity's sake, that, unlike in politics, where a candidate announces his candidacy for a political office, at the Vatican a cardinal has to be endorsed for the position of pope by one or more cardinals. Is that correct?" Travis asked.

"That is correct," said Cardinal Bertrand. "And, for simplicity's sake, as you say, if a group of my brother cardinals were to advance my name, I should humbly acknowledge their consideration, but not outright campaign for the position, as would be the case in politics."

"Forgive me, Your Eminence." Travis took an official tone. "Aren't politics practiced anyway in the Sistine Chapel when the new pope is elected?"

"Not really. There are no political maneuverings of factions among the conclave of cardinals. The ultimate candidate must convince two-thirds of the conclave that he is the best choice to become the next Holy Father by showing temerity, foresight, humbleness, and piety."

"Indeed," said Travis. "And these characteristics have to be demonstrated over the candidate's life in the clergy?"

"Or even before joining the clergy," said Cardinal Bertrand.

"I can see how these qualities are tried and true in stable times, but not for what is just about to happen very soon." Travis folded his arms to indicate his concern.

Cardinal Bertrand stopped. "Mr. St. John, what exactly are you alluding to?"

"Well, from my point of view, stable times favor the elder, proven candidate," said Travis. "Tumultuous times favor the younger, more forward-thinking candidate."

Cardinal Bertrand turned red as a beet. "How dare you accuse me of such, such things?" He shook with indignation.

"Pardon me, Your Eminence. I do not accuse you of anything. I made a comment based on the reality of the moment. The situation with the Holy Father would wreak extensive havoc if the fetus became a newborn. Who would be most able to hold the Church together? The humble and the pious, or the bold and the visionary?"

"Hmm. My apologies, Travis," said Cardinal Bertrand, regaining his composure. "Your reasoning is correct. We need to be prepared for all alternatives—business as usual or a new direction for the Church of our Lord."

"Indeed," agreed Travis. "Your Eminence, do you have any suspicion about who could have done this?"

Cardinal Bertrand smoothed his hair behind his scarlet zucchetto. "God!"

"That's too simple," said Travis.

"Yes, I believe God did it," the cardinal said seriously. "The Church has been too reluctant to change, especially in the past one hundred years. God has caused his earthly son, the Holy Father of the Holy See, to procreate, and he will give birth to a boy. After this, the Church will have to change and adopt to modern times."

Prescott was informed through his PAV about what Claire and Travis had found out. He hadn't had his meeting yet, but saw Cardinal Navarro coming his way as he exited a small chapel. "Good afternoon, Cardinal Navarro. If I may, I'd like to have a word with you," said Prescott.

"Good afternoon, Mr. Alighieri." He stopped and placed his thumb and forefinger to his forehead, as if remembering that he should have asked his secretary to make an appointment for Prescott to see him. "I'm terribly sorry, but it slipped my mind. Would you mind having a late lunch with me? We can talk then."

"That's very kind of you."

After they had selected their food, they chose a private table in a corner of the eating hall. Cardinal Navarro prayed before starting his meal. "What would you like to discuss, Prescott?"

"Thank you for taking the time to talk to me, Your Eminence," started Prescott. "What is your assessment of this situation?"

Cardinal Navarro bit off a piece of bread and chewed thoughtfully. "It is such an incredible situation that, if this event comes to pass, it will be as historical as the procreation of Our Lord Jesus Christ."

"Surely you don't mean to say that the unborn baby will be the new Messiah?" wondered Prescott.

"Mary had an immaculate conception. Our science today cannot explain how a man, our Holy Father, had this conception. An immaculate conception for a woman is a miracle. An immaculate conception for a man is godly."

"Do you think that God caused the conception?" asked Prescott.

"Who else?"

"Satan?"

"God help us all if that is the case." Cardinal Navarro made the sign of the cross. "If Satan were involved in this affair, humanity would be finished." They ate quietly. "I believe that Satan had no hand in it," the cardinal spoke again. "And if he did cause this, I believe that God intervened and saved us."

"Why do you think Sister Terina lost her mind at the exact time when the conception took place?" Prescott asked.

Cardinal Navarro thought for a moment. "I think she lost her mind because she resisted Satan. I am treating Sister Terina for her affliction, and after this I'll be going to see her to perform another session of exorcism."

Mit Sandru

Chapter 21. Exorcism

"Your Eminence, if I may, I would like to accompany you to the Suore Mantellate Serve di Sofia," said Prescott.

"Yes, but what is your interest in her?" Cardinal Navarro looked quizzically at him.

"It's part of our investigation."

"I understand that. However, Sister Terina is in a condition of . . . how shall I put it?" He grasped his jaw between his thumb and forefinger, as if searching for the right words. "She is a total mess. She is not communicating, or, if she does, she communicates in tongues. She is not capable of following any instructions."

"Is her mental situation that dire?"

"I believe that by resisting him, she was possessed by the devil," said Cardinal Navarro. "I will be performing another exorcism on her. I don't see how that would help you with your investigation."

"You shouldn't be worried about her or my presence there," said Prescott.

"Oh, I'm not worried about her." Cardinal Navarro looked intently at Prescott. "I'm worried about you."

"Why would you be worried about me?"

"Have you ever experienced an exorcism?"

"No, but I've seen movies about such things." Prescott didn't know what the cardinal was hinting at.

"Ahh, cinema." Cardinal Navarro smirked. "Real exorcism and make-believe cinema are not the same thing. I know of relatives of victims who were afraid to enter the chamber where the exorcism was performed afterward. Some barred the doors or bricked the entrance for no one to enter there ever again."

"Your Eminence," protested Prescott. "I am a professional, a member of a Trinity Team. I have experienced extremely disturbing events and visions in my career."

"*Mi scusi*. You are right. Sometimes I'm overly cautious about these things." Cardinal Navarro bowed slightly. "You may accompany me, if you wish."

Prescott and Cardinal Navarro did not speak while riding toward the convent located on the outskirts of Rome, although the cardinal made some calls. Prescott used this time to monitor the temperature, blood pressure, and brain activities of the cardinal by using the sensors on his Roman collar, which were projected in his PAV. Everything was normal. The cardinal was very calm and composed, showing no signs of stress.

The convent of the Suore Mantellate Serve di Sofia was an old building. Judging by the style of its architecture, it could have been built during the Renaissance or even before. It was kept in reasonable condition from what could be seen on the outside. Their car approached the heavy wooden gates, which opened without delay, letting them inside the cobblestone courtyard.

The courtyard was surrounded by a two-story arched colonnade that enclosed the quad completely. The structure was built in the typical Romanesque style, with the colonnade corridors on the inside and the chamber doors exiting onto the corridors. The chambers' windows were recessed, with wrought iron bars located on the outside walls.

Cardinal Navarro walked to one of the corridor's entrances, where two nuns, one old and one young, were waiting for them. Both of them were dressed in gray frocks with black scarves around their heads. They exchanged a few quiet words with Cardinal Navarro, who then motioned with his hand to invite Prescott to join them.

"Prescott, allow me to introduce Mother Superior Giuseppina and her assistant, Sister Clemenza. Mother Superior and Sister, this is Prescott Alighieri."

The two stern-faced nuns bowed their heads slightly. They didn't seem to be pleased by his presence, Prescott observed. Nuns are like that sometimes.

"Prescott is conducting a delicate investigation, and he will be observing the session." Cardinal Navarro kept his eyes on Prescott, as if what he said was intended for Prescott's benefit rather than the nuns'.

Without saying a word, the sisters turned and led them down the stairs toward an underground corridor illuminated by dim lights. Prescott doubted that these underground chambers were used for living quarters at the present time, but then, where else would you keep a screaming, demon-possessed nun but in the dungeon?

They arrived at a heavy wooden door, barred with a hefty wrought iron latch. A small window, crossed by iron bars, allowed one to peek inside the chamber, which was like a jail cell. However, the opening was now blocked from the inside. There was a lamp up on the vaulted corridor's ceiling, weakly lighting the space in front of the door. Mother Superior slid the latch and glanced at Cardinal Navarro worriedly.

The Cardinal took in her concerned look. "I think we'd better wait for Mother Superior and Sister to enter first."

Sister Clemenza cracked the door open just enough to allow the mother superior and her to go inside. The door closed behind them quickly. There was no sound whatsoever coming from inside, although the door's heavy planks might have muffled any noise.

"Prescott, what you'll see in there is shocking," warned Cardinal Navarro. "As I said, Sister Terina is possessed by the devil. She almost killed two orderlies when she was interned in a mental sanatorium. The doctors ran out of options in sedating her, short of killing her with higher and higher dosages."

"Cardinal Navarro, nothing can shock me anymore," said Prescott. "As for the devil, well, I've encountered him on a few occasions."

Cardinal Navarro raised his eyebrows in surprise. Sister Clemenza opened the door for them a moment later, and they entered. Prescott activated his PAV to dark shades.

The chamber was not completely underground, but only halfway below the grade, judging by the recessed window close to the ceiling. However, barn-style wooden shutters, locked by a heavy latch, covered the window completely. No outside light could be seen from any cracks, and the only light came from a dim lamp on the right wall. In the middle of the room, a four-poster bed held a frail woman clad in a grayish hospital gown. The woman's hands and feet were tied to each post of the bed with leather manacles. There were no other blankets or pillows on the bed, just the mattress covered by a bed sheet. Despite the fact that, judging by appearances, the sisters must have done their best to keep the room and the bed clean, the stench of urine, excrement, and ammonia filled the chamber.

At the top of the chamber's vaulted ceiling, a large wooden cross was suspended horizontally, facing down, such that the woman lying in the bed—Sister Terina—could not avoid seeing it. Sister Terina had her black hair cropped short, and it was oily and limp. Dark circles surrounded her closed eyes, and she appeared to be sleeping. Judging by her skinny body and ashy complexion, she looked almost dead.

"How is she?" Cardinal Navarro asked.

From a dark corner, another sister stood up from her watch chair. "*Dorme, Sua Eminenza. Tutto bene.*" Prescott's PAV translated, "She is sleeping, Your Eminence. All is well." Sister Terina slept, apparently giving them no trouble lately.

The "all is well" seemed to contradict the warnings Cardinal Navarro had given Prescott. The contradiction did not last long. Prescott's PAV was set on paranormal sensory perception. Something dark and foreboding was awakening inside Sister Terina. A slight amount of evil energy was leaching into the chamber's air. Undeniably, she was possessed by the devil.

Sister Terina stirred and opened her eyes slightly. "*Cardinale Navarro, bastardo!*" she lurched up, screaming at the top of her lungs, but she was held back by the restraints. The bed rocked. Cardinal Navarro raised the silver crucifix from around his neck as if to warn her. The silver crucifix transfixed Sister Terina. Her gaze turned upward and, when she saw the large wooden crucifix hanging above her, she started laughing hysterically, interrupted at times by gurgles in her throat.

"*In nomine patris...*" Cardinal Navarro started praying.

Suddenly, Sister Terina stopped laughing. She saw Prescott standing behind the cardinal, and she narrowed her eyes in hatred. "What the fuck are you doing here?" She spoke English in a manly, gruff voice. Vapors came out of her mouth as she spoke.

Cardinal Navarro stopped in the middle of his prayer, eyes wide in disbelief at what Sister Terina had just said. The nuns around the chamber made the sign of the cross and prayed in earnest.

"What are you staring at, *Cardinale di merda*?" She insulted the cardinal by calling him Cardinal Shit. "And you, Prescott Alighieri, I asked you: What the fuck are you doing here?" She was able to recognize Prescott despite the dark shades of his PAV.

"Hello, Zepar," said Prescott in a calm voice, stepping out from behind the cardinal. "Haven't heard from you in a while."

"Go fuck a goat, you miserable ass sucker," she replied. Then she stuck her tongue out at him. It resembled a large and gross-looking purple penis, but it was just her tongue, which she somehow had rolled to resemble a penis.

Prescott sensed the full dark power of the devil inside Sister Terina. Definitely, none other than Zepar, the Grand Duke of infertility, possessed her. Her poor soul trembled in fear inside her body, as the devil's claws encased her soul.

"Do you fear me?" Prescott asked coldly.

"I fear no mortal. I fear no make-believe child of God, priest." She hacked phlegm from deep inside her throat and spat on Cardinal Navarro. Green mucus hit him in the chest. Sister Clemenza ran to the cardinal and cleaned him with a washcloth. "And I definitely do not fear you, you bag of puke." She stared evilly at Prescott.

"Do you fear me?" Prescott asked again.

"Are you deaf, or have you lost your wet noodle?" she replied. Dark shadows swirled in the room, and the bed vibrated as if a large truck had rolled by outside.

"Do you fear my love?" Prescott asked, undisturbed by the devil's display of evil power.

"Nooo! You bastard, lay off me!" Sister Terina contorted on the bed. "Lay off me, I command you!"

"If you feel my love, you should leave this poor soul at once," Prescott ordered.

Sister Terina began shaking as if she had the chills. She stopped and stared at Prescott from beneath her lowered eyebrows. "Not in a thousand years. Although this bitch will not last through the night."

"We chased you before, Zepar. We'll do it again," said Prescott.

"We? Who else is with you?"

"Worried?" asked Prescott in a sarcastic tone. "Why don't you take the easy way out and leave this poor soul? Now!" He shouted.

Sister Terina laughed convulsively. "Time for a lesson, Prescott Alighieri." She arched her back, causing her gown to slide to her waist, exposing her vagina surrounded by wet, black pubic hair. "You want some of this?" She stared lasciviously at Prescott while licking her lips, as if inviting him to succumb to this grotesque exposure of her genitals.

Cardinal Navarro and the sisters averted their faces. Prescott looked into her eyes, concentrating on her pupils through his PAV. He knew that this was a trick; something sinister was about to happen, and, devil or not, it was the body of Sister Terina—her pupils actually—that would give away the devil's next action. In a split second, he saw her pupils dilate, and he moved sideways to the left. He pushed Cardinal Navarro to the right while keeping his eyes on her at all times.

A stream of yellow urine exploded from Sister Terina, aiming for his face and eyes. The jet sprayed harmlessly onto the wall behind him, missing its mark. The urine must have been extremely acidic, as it started foaming when it reacted with the plaster wall. The acid dissolved the plaster, and long streaks of brown, bubbling liquid ran down the wall.

Sister Terina shrieked a long howl of disappointment about missing her target. That lethal dose of acid-urine would have blinded Prescott, but he had ducked and moved out of the way in time. Sister Terina bounced up and down on the bed, stretching her leather ties to the breaking point. The bed lifted off the floor, rocking and stomping on the stone floor. Then, suddenly, she stopped and went silent, lying limp on the bed.

"I've seen what I needed to see." Prescott nodded to Cardinal Navarro to follow him outside. As soon as he exited the room, he opened the aural channel to communicate with his Trinity Team. "Claire, Travis, I need you here ASAP, before sunset, at Suore Mantellate Serve di Sofia."

"We're on our way," responded Travis.

"What happened? What is the matter?" Cardinal Navarro asked agitatedly.

"I've asked my team members to join me," answered Prescott.

"But why?"

"To drive the devil Zepar out of Sister Terina."

"Are you going to perform an exorcism?"

"No, Your Eminence. The devil in Sister Terina will kill her soon if we don't intervene. He doesn't want her alive. No exorcism will drive him out of her, unless he leaves her dead."

"What are you going to do?"

"Our Trinity Team will meet the devil holding Sister Terina's soul, and we will chase him out."

Cardinal Navarro looked at Prescott, speechless. After a few moments he said, "That was what I was trying to do."

"Exorcism drives the devil out through external intervention, such as prayers. It works most of the time, but not this time," said Prescott. "We will confront him inside her Spiritual Realm, where he is entrapping and strangling her soul."

Mit Sandru

Chapter 22. The Devil in Sister Terina

Travis and Claire descended quickly into the corridor, led by a nun to Sister Terina's chamber. Cardinal Navarro was pacing nervously with his hands clasped behind his back, and his anxiety did not subside with the arrival of Claire and Travis.

"What's the situation?" asked Travis breathlessly.

"The Grand Duke Zepar is inside Sister Terina. He recognized me," said Prescott. "He will kill her. There is something very sinister he is trying to protect."

"Then we must act immediately after we enter the realm of her soul," said Claire.

Prescott nodded. "Cardinal Navarro, what we will do next requires some preparation."

"Whatever you need," Cardinal Navarro assured.

"The bed Sister Terina is held in faces the door. It must be turned to face the window."

The cardinal opened slightly the door and asked Mother Superior to join them. Once she was in their company, he asked, "*Madre Superiore*, could you see that the bed is rotated such that Sister Terina faces the window, please?"

"*Sì*," acknowledged Mother Superior.

"But that's not all," said Prescott. "After the bed is turned to face the window, the shutters must be opened and the sun allowed in. At this time it is near sunset, and the rays will fall on her face."

Cardinal Navarro and Mother Superior nodded in understanding.

"When the sun hits her face and she is blinded for that moment, you must give us the signal. We will enter. She will not be able to see us. I will position myself at the footboard to face Sister Terina, as Zepar knows I'm here, while Claire and Travis will approach the bed from the headboard, not giving Zepar a chance to recognize them."

"I think I understand," said Cardinal Navarro.

"It must happen quickly, to catch the devil by surprise," concluded Prescott.

"One more thing," added Claire. "It could be dangerous inside the chamber. I suggest you leave us after we enter."

"I will not leave my young sisters alone," said Mother Superior.

"Neither will I," said Cardinal Navarro. He turned toward Mother Superior and said, "Everyone else should leave the chamber."

"Very well," said Prescott.

"What would you like us to say to signal that she's ready?" asked the cardinal.

"Say, 'enter sun,' as you open the shutters," said Prescott.

"We will say, *'sole, entra,'* then." Cardinal Navarro and Mother Superior went into the chamber.

Prescott, Travis, and Claire positioned themselves near the heavy door. They could hear the screeching of the bed legs as the cardinal and the three sisters moved the bed containing Sister Terina. A howl of laughter resonated from inside, and it was quickly followed by a bestial scream, as if a vampire were being exposed to the sunlight. The shutters must have been cracked open.

Inside, Cardinal Navarro shouted, "*Sole, entra!*"

The Capuchin Trinity Team did not waste a moment. Prescott was first in, followed by Travis and Claire.

Mother Superior gave a quick order for the other two sisters to depart: "*Fuori, fuori!*" The sisters did not wait for another invitation and got out, shutting the door behind them.

Prescott took his position at the foot of the bed, with his arms folded across his chest. The setting sun washed Sister Terina's face in red light. She was breathing heavily, and her eyes were closed to avert the sunlight. Claire and Travis took the same stance and stood to the right and left behind the headboard.

Sister Terina sensed Prescott and opened her eyes. "*Bastardo!* Close those fucking shutters!"

Those were her last words as the Capuchin Trinity Team joined their souls and plunged into her soul's realm . . .

We enter in the white light fog of Sister Terina's Spiritual Realm. Occasional fuzzy images flicker in and out of the white obscurity. We advance deeper into this realm, and the white light fog turns gray and then into dark stormy clouds that swirl around the captured soul ahead of us. The devil pollutes the white light fog of Sister Terina's soul by his presence.

A flash of lightning illuminates a tormented environment of broken and twisted feelings. Her mind does not comprehend what is happening to her soul. The thunder that follows is deafening, but this is only inside her soul's realm. It is quiet after a moment. Then screams of anguish erupt all around us. We advance through even darker clouds interspersed with occasional partial feelings from Sister Terina's life.

Gut-wrenching laughter sounds ahead of us. A small voice implores, "*Aiuto*! Help!" Sobbing follows it, and then another bout of satanic laughter overpowers any other sound. Red, silky, spidery threads reach toward us. The threads grow into a cobweb with small filaments swaying in the ether, as if to taste our presence. We advance and dodge the spider matrix set up by Zepar to investigate the disturbance we created in the realm of Sister Terina's soul. It is important that we get as close as possible to her soul without being detected by Zepar the devil.

The devil senses that an intrusion has happened. This intrusion is not like the prayers the Cardinal lashed him with during the exorcism. This is different and yet familiar.

Love? That's what it is; love has entered this nun's soul. He feels irritated and annoyed by it. Who could possibly do this? It is quiet outside the nun's body. No prayer can be heard. Besides Prescott, who else is there?

"Prescott Alighieri?" Zepar shouts, demanding to know. "Where are you?"

We hear the cavernous voice. Then silence. We continue to advance and dodge the red webs that thrash around everywhere like fishing nets. Zepar hurls black-thorned red balls in our direction to detect us. Our essence is one, without form or color, but an essence that could be discovered by the devil before we get to Sister Terina's soul. We are closer now, and through the dark fog we can see her soul's faded light.

A red thunderbolt discharges toward us. We avoid it and advance. The devil has changed tactics and starts an electrical storm, blasting everything with jagged, twisted, red lightning rods. One unlucky blast would kick us out of Sister Terina's soul, and we would have to start all over but without the element of some surprise we have now. There is only one option: charge toward the entrapped soul.

We advance at full speed toward the core. As we get near it, the electrical storm stops. Being closer to the core, the lightning rods are dangerous even for Zepar. Even his red web evaporates. We orbit around the soul's core, getting closer and closer. Her white soul is caged in the devil's red spidery legs.

Zepar resembles a giant red spider with a black abdomen. With his red legs and black hairs he forms the cage that entraps Sister Terina's soul. Zepar's head resembles a fusion of reptile and locust. He fixes us with laser-red eyes. "The Capuchin Trinity Team! I should have known."

"Release the sister, we command you!"

"*Aiuto*, help!" Sister Terina's small voice comes from inside the cage.

The devil gives a thundering roar. "How dare you command me?"

"In the name of God, release the sister," we demand.

"Ahh, in the name of God. Well, why didn't you say so in the first place? I would have waited with cow pies and cups full of hot tar to celebrate."

"How cordial of you," we say. "Release Sister Terina."

"No! Do you think I invested all this dark energy to wrap myself around her soul just to slink out of here?"

"Unless you want us to discharge the white light upon you, release her."

"You know, that's such a poor choice of words," the devil says. "It is not white, it is the opposite of dark. The Undark!"

A common thought crosses our mind, "He's stalling. Attack now!" We evolve our essence into white light, the light of life, and engulf

Zepar and Sister Terina in our embrace. Tough as Zepar is, he cannot stand life's white light. In an instant, the devil's spider legs dissolve, releasing Sister Terina's soul.

Zepar appears as himself, in his red armor with leathery, opened wings, and his devil-locust head adorned with four sets of sharp horns. His bulbous black eyes contain penetrating, red laser-beam clusters. He has four arms, which he keeps close to his black chest. His legs and feet resemble those of a velociraptor, with three large claws on each foot sinking into the fabric of this realm. "You miserable humans!" he screams.

"Why did you abduct Sister Terina?"

Zepar looks around. He is fearful of our life light essence. He opens his wings wider.

"How did you penetrate her religious aura?"

Zepar squirms. He is not as cocky and confident now that we surround him.

He laughs nervously, turning his head around, observing us worriedly. "What's this soul to you?" He opens his four arms, which end in menacing, curved blades.

We do not answer. We let him squirm. He whirls his blades at us. They have no impact.

"Did your Lord Satan send you?" we ask. "Does it have to do with the fetus?"

Zepar stops and he seems to think. "It is none of your business. This is larger than you pitiful humans." He looks up and shrieks. Out of the dark clouds a black skeletal horse comes charging and bursts through our life ring.

Zepar is freed, and, without wasting a moment, he jumps on the horse's back and absconds in a red cloud, which soon evaporates without a trace.

We move toward Sister Terina and hold her soul in our warm life light. Sister Terina whispers, "*Grazie!*" We cannot linger anymore. We spent a tremendous amount of life energy to drive the devil out, and now we need to return to our bodies.

On our way out, a blast of white thoughts buffets us. It is disorienting, as if we are caught in a sand storm, and it takes us what seems like an eternity to exit this cloud of anguished thoughts. We make an extra effort and finally exit Sister Terina's soul . . .

Prescott opened his eyes and inhaled deeply. He was soaking wet from perspiration. Travis and Claire looked as drained and wet as he was. He walked to the other two and embraced them both, to rebalance their life energies. Fighting and chasing the devil away was exhausting to their bodies.

Sister Terina lay serenely on her bed, which was askew from its original position because of the confrontation that went on inside her soul between Zepar and the CTT. The color of life returned to her face. Cardinal Navarro and Mother Superior were kneeling and praying quietly. They made the sign of the cross and rose. Hope highlighted their faces, seeing Sister Terina in her calm, sleeping state.

"Did it work?" Cardinal Navarro asked with a trembling voice.

"Yes, it did," said Prescott. "Zepar is gone."

Cardinal Navarro and Mother Superior each interlaced their fingers in prayer and looked upward, thanking heaven for this miracle.

"I suggest taking Sister Terina to a medical ward and administering an IV," said Claire. "She is definitely dehydrated and malnourished."

"Right away." Mother Superior exited to get help.

"I don't know how to thank you," said Cardinal Navarro.

"Your blessing will be greatly appreciated, Your Eminence," said Travis.

Cardinal Navarro said a short prayer. Then he approached them and, with his thumb, he made the sign of the cross on their foreheads. This religious ritual had a beneficial effect on the three of them. It restored the energy they had lost fighting the devil. It was hard to prove scientifically, but Prescott and his team felt immediately refueled with life energy.

"I think our job is done here," said Prescott. "With your permission, Cardinal Navarro, we would like to return to the Vatican."

"Of course, of course. And thank you very, very much!"

As they were walking toward the robo-car to return to the Vatican, they passed by a woman in the courtyard. She was not a nun, but a layperson.

Chapter 23. The Dottore's Wife

"How is Sister Terina?" she asked in excellent English, with tears in her eyes.

"She's doing very well," said Claire, looking inquisitively at her. "May I ask who you are?"

"Oh, I'm sorry. I am Lucia Pietro, Dottore Pietro's wife." The woman looked to be in her forties, her dark hair kept tight in a bun.

Claire straightened up, surprised. It was a small world meeting the Dottore's wife here. Perhaps she found refuge in this convent. It seemed like a good place to find solace, to mourn, and to pray. "I'm very sorry for your loss."

"Thank you," she said sadly. "It is hard to lose your children, but they are in a better place."

Prescott and Travis glanced inquisitively at Claire, but then they remembered that Dottore Pietro and his wife had lost their two sons in a car racing accident.

"They were murdered," Lucia Pietro said with bitterness.

"We're very sorry," said Travis. "If you'll excuse us, we will wait in the car." Prescott and Travis left.

"I'm very sorry for your loss," Claire repeated to calm Lucia.

"That's life—cruel. But what is important is that not all setbacks end tragically. You said Sister Terina is doing well, right?" Lucia looked intently at Claire.

"Yes, she's resting now. She will be up and about in no time."

"Incredible what happened to her. Is it true that the devil possessed her?"

"Very true," acknowledged Claire.

"And you chased the devil away?"

"Yes, we did."

"Cardinal Navarro performed an exorcism several times and couldn't get rid of the devil."

"Eventually he would have chased the devil away. We took a more direct approach."

"So, Sister Terina is fine?"

"Yes, she's doing very well," said Claire.

"Thank God." Lucia bit her knuckles as if trying to keep from bursting into tears. "Did she say anything? Did she have any recollection about what happened?"

"No, she never woke up. She is asleep now and she'll be taken to a medical ward for further treatment."

"That's good, that's very good."

"Do you know Sister Terina?" asked Claire.

"Only from what I heard around the convent. It seemed so sad to have such a young life possessed by the devil."

"It is indeed, but it all ended well," said Claire. "So, how are you holding up?"

"Me? What do you mean?"

"After the loss of your sons and the separation from your husband," clarified Claire.

Lucia Pietro looked confused.

"Your husband, Dottore Pietro, told me what happened. I'm sorry about your separation."

"Oh, I see. He told you," said Lucia, looking down at the cobblestones. "Well, it is getting better. This is a place of solitude and peace. It is good for me here. I'm escaping the painful reality for a while."

"Time will heal everything," said Claire.

"Yes, and especially after justice was served."

"What kind of justice?" Claire asked. "You mean against the boys involved in your sons' accident?"

Lucia Pietro did not answer but looked coldly into Claire's eyes.

Mit Sandru

Chapter 24. Murders in the Night

"I have a bad feeling about leaving Sister Terina alone back there," said Claire as the robo-taxi headed for Rome.

"Your feelings are seldom wrong," agreed Travis. "I think we should have her guarded." He tapped on his aural-comm. "Albert Glauser, *per favore*. Travis St. John with the Capuchin Trinity Team."

"The Swiss Guard is a good choice," agreed Claire.

"Oberst Glauser," said Travis as he made contact with the Swiss Guard colonel. Travis switched to conf-com so Claire and Prescott could listen in.

"*Sì*, Travis St. John," acknowledged the colonel. "What may I do for you?"

"Are you aware of Sister Terina and the exorcism Cardinal Navarro was performing at Suore Mantellate Serve di Sofia?"

"Yes, I know a few things about that."

"Well, Sister Terina has been cured," said Travis.

"*Grazie a Dio e a Cardinale Navarro.*" The colonel thanked God and the cardinal.

"Indeed," said Travis without batting an eye. "However, we have a strong suspicion that she may still be in danger, and I'm requesting protection for her."

"Would you like me to call the *carabinieri*, the police?"

"Sister Terina is instrumental in the case we're investigating for the Holy Father. Your officers should guard her."

"I understand. I will send two officers immediately to guard her until further notice."

"Thank you, Oberst Glauser," said Travis.

"My pleasure, *signore* St. John," said Glauser. "Anything else I can do for you?"

"No, that will do." Travis interrupted the conf-com.

"This is better. I feel more at ease about Sister Terina," said Claire.

It was one o'clock in the morning when the Swiss Guards banged on the doors of the rooms Travis, Prescott, and Claire were in. "*Signori,* you are needed immediately at Suore Mantellate Serve di Sofia," the young guard informed them as they gathered outside.

"What happened?" asked Claire as she came out.

"We are instructed to take you there by air immediately," said the young guard. "There have been murders committed there."

As they were swiftly moved to the hover-pad, Travis contacted Glauser on conf-comm. "Oberst Glauser, what is the emergency?"

"It is not an emergency anymore," said the colonel in a tired but professional voice. "Three murders were committed at midnight."

"Is Sister Terina all right?" Claire asked.

There was a pause. "Sister Terina is one of the dead."

"Jesus," whispered Claire.

They boarded the hover-copter and strapped themselves in. The craft took off immediately.

"Who are the other two victims?" Prescott asked.

"My officers," responded Glauser.

"I'm sorry," said Travis. "Anything else we need to know before we arrive?"

"My men were shot by a sniper, and Sister Terina was stabbed with a pair of scissors while asleep in her bed. You're five minutes away—you'll see for yourselves."

Travis, Claire, and Prescott looked at each other with grim faces.

"We're dealing with cold-blooded murderers," said Claire.

"Satan's agents, no doubt," said Prescott. "Sister Terina needed to be silenced. And she was."

The hover-copter landed on the street in front of the convent's gates. Many police cars, with their lights flashing, blocked the street. Ambulances and a van that seemed to belong to the Italian CSI division were there as well. Plainclothes officers met them and escorted them inside. Makeshift bright lights bathed the upper corridor, where many police and Swiss Guard officers were in the process of investigating the murders.

After their departure, Sister Terina had been moved to a second-floor chamber. At the scene, Glauser was talking to a police officer in uniform. She was an attractive brunette of medium height. In front of Sister Terina's chamber door lay the two dead Swiss Guard officers, face down, with their heads blown off. A diluted string of blood flowed from each man's head. Their hands were empty; there were no drawn weapons. They must have been caught by surprise by the sniper bullets. The walls were splattered with blood and brain matter.

Glauser concluded his conversation with the officer and viewed the Capuchin Trinity Team with steely eyes. "This is Ispettore Carlotta Romano. She will be leading this crime investigation."

"*Piacere di conoscerli*," said Ispettore Romano. "Nice to meet you. I finally get to meet one of those mysterious Trinity Teams."

"Nice to meet you, too. This is Claire and Travis, and I am Prescott." They shook hands. "What happened?"

"It was a clean professional hit," Ispettore Romano told them. "The Swiss Guard officers were shot by snipers from that tower." She pointed to a church tower a street away from the convent. "They were shot concurrently, and my officers inspecting the tower confirmed the presence of three men at that location based on footprints on the dusty floor. Two snipers and one spotter."

"Why were they shot in the back of their heads?" Claire asked.

"It seems they were distracted by Sister Terina's murderer," said Ispettore Romano. "They must have heard something inside the chamber. They turned and looked at the door, and the snipers shot them at that moment."

"Hmm, that doesn't make sense," said Travis, eyeing the church tower. "They could have shot the guards at any time. Why wait until they turned their backs?"

"My men were equipped with laser-sighting detection ware," said Glauser. "They could have detected and recorded the wavelength signature, taken evasive action, and the police could have traced them."

"How about the bullets used?" Travis asked.

"The killers used titanium tip, frozen mercury bullets," said Ispettore Romano. "The tips exited their heads, but the mercury disintegrated in the officers' skulls. No possible way to trace the guns."

"That is rare," commented Travis. "Only professional killers hired to assassinate high-profile political targets use those. Even the guns are special. But there are only a handful of frozen mercury ammunition suppliers."

"We've informed Interpol about the ammo," said Ispettore Romano. "But if they were supplied from China or Russia, we will get nothing."

"Did you perform an infrared scan of the footprints around here?" asked Prescott.

"We arrived here too late," said Ispettore Romano. "No thermal traces."

"How about a molecular disturbance analysis?" Travis asked.

"It drizzled tonight," said Ispettore Romano, pointing to the wet pavement and a few wet spots on the open corridor floor. "The evidence was compromised."

"GeneID?" asked Claire.

"That we will do, just as we will analyze the tower, too. Let us show you inside."

They followed Ispettore Romano and Glauser inside Sister Terina's chamber. As they entered, two police officers concluded examining the crime scene and exited. Sister Terina was lying on her back on the tall bed, dressed in a white nightgown. The scissors handle stuck out of her solar plexus. A round spot of blood encircled the murder weapon, and probably more blood soaked the mattress underneath her. Her left arm was attached to the IV bag that had fed and hydrated her.

Claire went to the side of the bed and placed a hand on Sister Terina's forehead. The warmth of life had drained from her, but Claire sensed a tingling sensation in her arm. It was coming from the body, but she did not know why. She kept her hand on the nun's forehead, although Ispettore Romano made a face of disapproval. Claire could be contaminating the crime scene, but she doubted there was anything to be found on the nun's forehead. It seemed that Sister Terina was killed instantly, without a struggle. The murderer came in and stabbed her. Quick and simple. Sister Terina was sedated, and most likely she died in her sleep without suffering.

Prescott walked around the chamber, inspecting the floor and the ceiling. He searched for a hidden entrance but found nothing. The chamber had only one door, leading into the corridor; the window was the only other possible access. He opened the wooden shutters and checked the window. It was latched from the inside and barred on the outside. He peered through the bars into the street. They were two-and-a-half stories above the street. Only a spider could have climbed up here, and spiders don't use scissors. The murderer came through the front door. How could he have passed the guards posted at the door?

Travis circled the bed, which was positioned in the middle of the room. It was a high bed of dark wood, the old-fashioned kind standing on four spindly legs. Someone could have hidden under the bed, but not a large person. He bent down and examined the wood-plank floor under the bed. It was clean, but not hospital clean. Through his PAV, he detected slight smudges in the thin layer of dust.

"Ispettore Romano," said Travis. "Did you do a thermal scan under the bed?"

Ispettore Romano called someone to bring a scanner immediately.

"Someone was under this bed," Travis said to Prescott. "And if it was tonight, the wood floor probably has some residual heat left in it."

Prescott bent down and examined the floor under the bed from the opposite side. "Someone was there." He continued to walk, half-squatting, around the bed when he stopped at the footboard and looked at the scissors' handle. "The scissors have a slight angle to the right."

Travis joined him. "Yes, the murderer stabbed her from her right side, and it was a person of medium height. This bed is rather tall."

"A nun?" wondered Prescott.

"Or a man of less than average height," replied Travis.

Ispettore Romano took the handheld scanner from an officer who had just entered the room, and she bent down and scanned the floor. The imaging screen showed the faint infrared form of someone lying down in a fetal position. Probably he or she tried to be as inconspicuous as possible, lying in wait. Ispettore Romano pushed a few buttons and examined the results. "Whoever was here, a small person, came out from under the bed about three and a half hours ago. Most likely a woman, I would say. She came out on the right side, stood on the balls of her feet, and plunged the scissors into the nun's solar plexus. The thermal imaging is very clear here." Ispettore Romano pointed the scanner at the location of the murderer's feet, and the thermal marks showed distinctly on the scanner.

"Considering the slight tilt of the scissors to the right, the murderer had to almost go up on her toes to reach and stab the sister because the bed is so high," commented Travis.

"A nun," Prescott wondered.

"A nun?" Glauser's eyebrows sprang up, but then he fell silent, turned, and looked at the door. "If the murderer was here all along, after she killed Sister Terina, then . . ." He pointed out the path from the bed to the door. "She opened the door and came out. My officers turned to see who was coming out, and the snipers shot them."

"It seems that way," agreed Prescott. "The officers may not have known the murderer, as we thought originally." He put a finger to his lips and added, "The murderer was a nun, or someone impersonating a nun, and your officers were not alarmed when she came out."

"Yes, that explains why the officers did not draw their weapons," said Travis.

"*Certamente*," agreed Ispettore Romano. "A nun who kept watch on the Sister, who decided to come out of the room. She probably exchanged a few words with the officers to put them at ease and to cause them to turn their backs to the courtyard, to the church tower. I need a sniffer." She spoke into her communication device. "By the way, the scissors handle had no fingerprints or any organic traces on it."

"Let's see how far she went," said Travis. "I bet she is from here, from this convent."

"I don't think they're going to find her," said Prescott, shaking his head.

As he said that, a police officer from the CSI team came in and placed the sniffer under the bed. The device was the size of a plump mouse and had a sensing capacity one thousand times that of a dog. It sniffed under the bed and followed the trail of the murderer through the door and outside, followed by Ispettore Romano, the CSI officer, and Glauser.

"Travis, Prescott," said Claire, who all this time had stood quietly. "We need to do a TAP on her."

Chapter 25. Sister Terina

"But she's dead, her mind is gone," objected Prescott.

"Claire, you know that for living people like us it is extremely dangerous to enter the Mind Realm when people are dead," said Travis.

"I know," said Claire. "I don't think we have to go there. She left a message for us in her dead mind."

"Are you sure?" Travis asked.

"Almost certain," said Claire.

"And the secret is in there?" said Prescott, pointing with a finger to the nun's head.

"If it's in there," doubted Travis. "Besides, the sniffer will track the murderer." Travis pointed toward the door.

"I doubt it. The murderer is too canny," repeated Prescott, glancing in the direction of the sniffer.

"The murderer may not know what she left behind in Sister Terina's mind," said Claire. "Let's agree that if we don't find the memory, we will not pursue it in the Mind Realm."

"Fair enough," agreed Prescott.

"All right," Travis accepted reluctantly.

They took their positions around the dead nun's bed: Claire behind the headboard, Travis and Prescott on either side. They closed their eyes and their minds became one.

We see the corpse of Sister Terina as a void of life. Her soul has already departed. There is little life energy of any kind left behind, just some small flickering of electrical energy in the cells, the nervous system, and the brain. The postmortem decaying has started, and the bacteria invading the body glows with its own life energy.

As we agreed, we enter the void where once her mind existed, the empty nebula that once was the memory. It is a desolate landscape, dreary and bare. No flashes of energy, no memories flying by, and no caches of stored remembrances.

We press on, as if traveling through an immense, abandoned warehouse. Wisps of gray vapors flutter by now and then. We see no light or darkness whatsoever, just a bland lunar landscape lit as if by the Earth's sun reflection. In the far distance, the link to the Mind Realm is disintegrating slowly. There are two reasons why that is a deadly path for us.

First, we could get lost in the Mind Realm, which contains infinite amounts of information, memories, and so many things to see, feelings to experience, music to hear, and worlds to discover that we would lose track of time. The Mind Realm is the Library of God, where everything that happened, will happen, or might happen is stored.

Second, the link between what was once Sister Terina's mind and the Mind Realm is disintegrating. Once broken, there is no way for us to return to our bodies. We would end up in comas, vegetables. Our souls would linger on until our bodies died, our common mind forever lost in the infinite Library of God. For all practical purposes, we would cease to exist.

Sister Terina's mind has been emptied. All her knowledge and experiences are no longer here. We are about to give up and return when we spot a whitish puff, tumbling around raggedly. It requires investigation, and we approach. It is a fluff of nothing, although the closer we get, the denser it becomes. The white puff is the center of a memory, and it comes toward us. Unlike living memories in a living person's mind, this dead memory is attracted to us, as if it were waiting for our arrival. It is coming straight at us, and it penetrates our joined minds . . .

Claire, Prescott, and Travis opened their eyes. It took a millisecond to encounter this experience, but they knew they captured it, and it lodged itself in each of their minds. They inhaled deeply. The memory of Sister Terina's experience, which she left behind for them to find, was theirs now. They could not make sense of it immediately, but it was theirs to decipher and discover who implanted the devil's agent in her and why, because that's what the memory was about.

"I think we acquired the right memory," said Prescott.

"Yes, her soul left that behind for us to rescue," agreed Claire. "It is just a matter of time until we will be able to decipher the memory in our dreams."

"Remember after we drove the devil out of her soul?" Travis hesitated for a moment and then added, "That white cloud that buffeted our common entity? That was the memory. Her fear cocooned it long ago, and it was left behind."

"That makes sense. Zepar couldn't find that memory and destroy it," said Claire. "That's why he couldn't kill her until he was sure the memory was destroyed. He fled and left it behind."

"The murderer thought that, by killing Sister Terina, she was being silenced forever," said Travis.

"And now that memory is ours," said Prescott.

"We must decipher her memory faster than relying on our dreams," said Travis.

"We must have a séance among ourselves," agreed Claire.

Chapter 26. Whodunnit?

Glauser and Ispettore Romano returned with gloomy faces.

"We found a nun's habit outside one of the first-story windows," said Ispettore Romano.

"She couldn't have exited through the barred window," said Travis.

"No, the trail ends at the window and with the habit," said Ispettore Romano. "If she wore a no-residue plastic suit under the habit, she is within the convent but untraceable."

"You mentioned that you found no traces on the scissors," said Travis. "That explains it."

"The habit had a hood, and it would have given the murderer complete anonymity," said Ispettore Romano. "No worries about being captured by some hidden camera, either."

"We need to talk to everyone here," said Glauser.

"My officers have rounded up everyone in the assembly room, and they've already started interrogating them," said Ispettore Romano.

"May we?" asked Travis, pointing toward the assembly room.

"Of course, please follow me," said Ispettore Romano.

The assembly room of the convent served as the mess hall as well. About thirty nuns sat on the wooden benches around the tables. Some were speaking quietly with their neighbors, some were praying, and a few were crying.

There was one man in the room. He was a large man, probably the gatekeeper, the guard, and the heavy-objects mover. He couldn't have squeezed under Sister Terina's bed.

Among the nuns sat a plain-clad woman. She was Lucia Pietro, Dottore Pietro's wife, with whom Claire had spoken earlier. Her eyes were red from crying. Claire approached and sat next to her.

"How are you doing?" Claire asked.

"I'm alright," Lucia Pietro answered, though she was jittery. "This is horrible. I came here for solace and peace, but murder seems to follow me." She dabbed the corners of her eyes with a handkerchief.

"Don't take the blame for what happened here," said Claire, patting her arm.

"I know I shouldn't." Lucia blew her nose into the handkerchief.

"You said, you didn't know Sister Terina?" Claire asked.

"No, I didn't. I came here while she was in a psychiatric institution, I was told. Then she was brought here. Some of the sisters talked about her poor state of mental health and about how the devil possessed her soul. They talked about exorcism. I didn't believe that such a thing could be until you told me that it was true. How could the devil possess anyone?"

"Well, in this case it is true. She was possessed by the devil," said Claire.

"And you were able to chase it away!"

"Our team entered her Spiritual Realm, and we met the devil there."

"Incredible," Lucia shook her head, amazed and curious at the same time. "Isn't that deadly? How did you survive?"

"We have our methods of encountering and fighting the devil."

"Wow!" Lucia's expression conveyed admiration tinged by some jealousy. "I don't understand something."

"What's that?"

"Isn't the devil supposed to hold the soul hostage?"

"Yes. But souls are as powerful as the devil himself," said Claire. "In the case of religious people, like priests or nuns like Sister Terina, the devil is almost powerless."

"Oh my God," whispered Lucia. "And the devil got her nonetheless?"

Claire nodded. "He had help from someone else to overpower her. Someone she trusted."

"Why would the devil want Sister Terina's soul?" Lucia wondered.

"A soul is a precious commodity for the devil," said Claire. "Who knows? In this case, a certain memory could have been all he wanted."

"A memory?" Lucia flinched and bent closer. "What memory?"

"That's all I can tell you." Claire realized that she had said too much, as she observed some of the nuns eavesdropping.

"But I'm sure you prevented him from destroying that memory."

"God was on our side," said Claire with a small smile. "But tell me, what did you do tonight?"

"Me? Well, I was asleep." Lucia sat up straight.

"Did you see or hear anything out of the ordinary?"

"No. Like what?"

"Gunfire shortly after midnight, or anyone walking the corridor in a hurry?"

Lucia shook her head. "I went to the evening mass and then retreated to my chamber. I was awakened by Madre Superiore, pounding on my door and on the others, and ordering us to the mess hall."

"Have the police talked to you yet?"

"Yes. Unfortunately, I saw and heard nothing." Lucia Pietro folded her hands on her lap, looking calm.

From the opposite side of the hall, Travis gestured to Claire to join him.

"Take care, Lucia," said Claire.

She walked toward Travis. "Any news?"

"Yes, the habit belongs to a Sister Clemenza," said Travis, and he gestured for her to follow him. "Ispettore Romano is interrogating her right now. Prescott is there."

In an adjacent room, a young, scared nun, pale as the white walls around her, sat on a wooden stool, holding her crucifix necklace with both hands. A bandage on her left temple indicated some sort of recent injury. Ispettore Romano sat in front of her, leaning toward her. With a stern face, she looked into the nun's eyes as she drilled her in Italian. The nun shook her head in denial. Albert Glauser stood behind the nun. He leaned close to her ear and asked her a loud question, causing the nun to jump. Sister Clemenza began crying.

Claire approached Prescott, who was leaning against the wall observing the interrogation, and asked in a low voice, "What's going on?"

"They found Sister Clemenza in her nightgown and bare feet in the bathroom, not in her chamber," said Prescott. "She was the sister I first met with Mother Superior."

"And?" wondered Claire.

"She had no robe on over her nightgown. It looked like she was in a hurry to clean some blood from her head. Then the habit they found in the street is hers."

"Someone could have hit her and stolen the habit from her wardrobe," assessed Claire.

"That's what they're trying to determine," said Prescott. "The blow to her head was on her temple. It could have been accidental or self-inflicted."

Travis came close and asked Prescott, "What do your feelings tell you about her?"

"She is genuinely panic-stricken, and I think she has no idea what happened," said Prescott. "To make matters worse, she was in Sister Terina's chamber tonight, helping."

"The bio-scans picked up her DNA, I gather," said Travis.

"Yeah, along with the DNA of other nuns," said Prescott. "Technically she's guilty, but I don't sense that."

"Did they interrogate all the sisters?" Claire asked.

"Just about," said Prescott. "Several officers are using other rooms to conduct concurrent interrogations. This is the first promising suspect they've found."

"I share your feelings about her," said Claire. "She's not the culprit."

Ispettore Romano signaled to two female officers to approach. They picked Sister Clemenza up by the arms and escorted her out of the room.

"We're taking Sister Clemenza into custody," said Ispettore Romano.

"What evidence do you have against her?" Claire asked.

"Other than the habit, it is her head injury. We found Sister Clemenza's blood on the bedpost of her bed. That's how she got the head injury. She doesn't remember what happened or how she banged her head while in bed."

"But what if someone hit her?" asked Claire.

"Not unless that someone removed the un-removable bed post and hit her on the front temple area," said Ispettore Romano. "It looks highly suspicious, and she could have self-inflicted that injury as a cover up for her missing habit."

"There was blood around the bedpost, the pillow, and a few drops trailing from her bed to the bathroom," added Albert Glauser. "After the injury, she walked on her own to the bathroom to clean up. Her first recollection about this evening's events was when she saw herself in the bathroom mirror with a bloody face."

"Wasn't her nightgown soaked in blood?" Claire asked.

Ispettore Romano looked quizzically at Claire. "Like I said, the blood was around the bedpost and most of it was on the pillow. Very little was on her nightgown."

"It doesn't make sense for her to injure herself and stay in bed without hurrying to the bathroom to stop the bleeding," said Claire. "Unless someone lifted her head and slammed it into the bedpost. She could have fainted and, when she woke up, she was disoriented from the contusion. Then she got up to go to the bathroom to clean the blood off her head and face."

Ispettore Romano nodded. "It could be. But nevertheless we'll take her into custody until we investigate further."

"How about the other nuns who assisted Sister Terina last night?" asked Travis.

"We sequestered them in their rooms. All the nuns who visited Sister Terina tonight will have guards posted at their doors, until we get to the bottom of this."

"What time was it when the last attending nun left Sister Terina's chamber, and who was that nun?" asked Travis.

"Sister Clemenza was the last one who left the room, with Madre Superiore. My men arrived after the sisters left," said Oberst Glauser. "There was a half-hour between the time the sisters left and when my men arrived and positioned themselves at the door. That might have been when the assassin entered Sister Terina's room. Madre Superiore, who showed my officers to the door, told them that Sister Terina was alone inside."

"And imagine their surprise when the assassin, a nun, comes out later," said Travis.

"Yes. They turned to see who was coming out, and the snipers shot them, allowing the assassin to get away," agreed Glauser.

"You know, something bothers me about the frozen mercury bullets used," said Travis. They all looked at him. "If those bullets were shot through the door, the mercury would have atomized in the chamber and killed Sister Terina anyway. Why didn't they do that?"

"Are you saying that the bullets were not intended for my men but for Sister Terina?" Albert Glauser asked.

"Maybe," said Travis.

"Either the killers wanted Sister Terina absolutely dead, or the plan was upset by someone or something and they had to improvise," conjectured Ispettore Romano. "We have one inside suspect and three on the outside. What secrets was Sister Terina keeping to have such a professional assassination team come after her?" She looked penetratingly at Travis.

Travis shrugged.

"That's what we would like to find out, Ispettore Romano," said Prescott.

She looked at him as if deciding whether to believe him or not.

"Really," Prescott assured her.

After a short while, she seemed to be convinced that Prescott might be telling the truth, and she smiled thinly at him.

"Well, then," said Travis. "I don't think there is anything else for us to do here." He exchanged glances with his teammates, who agreed. "We'll return to the Vatican. Perhaps someone can call a robo-taxi to take us back?"

"One more thing, Claire," said Ispettore Romano. "I saw you speaking to that lay woman, Lucia Pietro."

"Yes, she's Dottore Pietro's estranged wife," said Claire, and then added, "Her husband is the Pope's personal doctor. She said one of your officers spoke to her."

"Yes, we did," said the Ispettore. "And now that you mentioned who her husband is, it reminds me of an open case we have regarding the murders of two young men who were accused by the Pietros of killing their sons."

"The other two drivers? What happened to them?" Claire asked. Travis and Prescott got closer.

The Ispettore widened her eyes as if divulging a secret. "Months ago, they were found burned alive in an industrial oven."

"Did you find the culprits? Are the Pietros suspects?"

"They had a solid alibi. They were in the Vatican when the crime was committed," said the Ispettore. "Did she say anything about this matter to you?"

"Only that justice was served," said Claire, exchanging suspicious glances with Travis and Prescott inside her PAV.

Chapter 27. The Ambush

Claire, Travis, and Prescott boarded a robo-taxi to return to the Vatican.

"The Pietros got their revenge after all," commented Travis.

"That's something to keep in mind," said Prescott.

"I found the Dottore not to be thankful to God anymore," said Claire.

The taxi took the highway route on Via Pontino toward Rome. The traffic was light in the predawn hours. They passed the Circonvallazione Meridionale and entered the periphery of Rome. Eventually they crossed the Tiber River on Viale Guglielmo Marconi heading for the Vatican. The divided boulevard of Piazza della Radio converged into Via Portuense, heading under the light train overpass of the Roma Trastevere line.

The railway overpass was wide, and the lights were out underneath it, giving the impression that they were entering into a tunnel.

Travis had an eerie feeling about this place. "Activate your PAVs for night vision."

Claire and Prescott sensed trouble as well. With their PAVs on, they were able to see every detail in the underpass. It didn't look right. Midway in the dark underpass, two vans were stopped in the middle of the road, both at an angle to each other as if they were fixing a

Mit Sandru

mechanical problem or, perhaps, intentionally barring the road. The vans' rears were facing them.

"Do you think that we're about to be stopped by a gang of hooligans?" cautioned Claire.

Travis looked back and didn't like what he saw. Another van with its reverse tail lights out was rearing toward them. "It's an ambush," shouted Travis. "EPB!"

All three touched their wrist devices and released an Electromagnetic Pulse Burst, frying the taxi's electronics and disabling the vehicle, thereby unlatching its doors. In an instant, the three of them kicked the doors open and rolled out of the dead robo-taxi.

High beams of light coming from the roof of each van flooded the robo-taxi. The rear doors of the vans burst open, and men armed with automatic weapons jumped out, spraying the robo-taxi with gunfire. The taxi's windows burst in showers of sparkles as the bullets hit them. The body of the vehicle became a colander, and all its tires popped. The gunmen had no intention to stop shooting as long as they had bullets in their magazines. They were in a perfect triangulation position, and no one or nothing would come out of the taxi alive. It just took seconds, but the amount of bullets hitting the robo-taxi must have filled the car with lead.

Three smoke mini-bombs, the size of lipstick cartridges, burst almost concurrently around each group of gunmen. The bombs spun like tops from the velocity of the effused gases, engulfing the entire area in thick smoke. Before some of the gunmen could empty their magazines, the powerful lights from their vans were reflected and diffused by the smoke, blinding them. It seemed as if they were in a thick fog at high noon.

"*Cessare il fuoco!*" someone shouted, ordering the men to cease firing. They did so while shouting obscenities not limited only to mothers, saints, or devils.

"*Spegnere le luci!*" Someone else ordered them to turn the blinding lights off. Shortly after, the lights went out.

The smoke bombs kept emitting gasses, and the smoke became so thick in the dark underpass that no light could penetrate the site. No one could see even their hands in front of their faces, except for Claire, Travis, and Prescott, who could see perfectly well through their microwave-radar PAVs.

There were six men, two from each van. They wore dark clothes, ski masks, and at least two of them had red bandannas around their necks.

They raised their automatic weapons that were still smoking from the gunfire, but the men seemed unsure about what to do in the dense smoke surrounding them. Some were turning slowly, trying to guide themselves by any noise they could hear. However, their gunfire had woken up the neighborhood, and dogs were barking relentlessly. The ambient sounds were soon overpowered by loud and sharp ringing coming from the smoke mini-bombs canisters. The sound emitted exceeded one hundred decibels. No man could shout over that noise.

The assailants dropped their weapons and covered their ears. Some ran every which way to escape the infernal noise. Without their weapons and thus no risk that one of those fools could start blindly shooting, they became easy pickings for the Trinity Team.

A man, half-bent, ran by Travis and received a karate chop behind his neck, throwing him headfirst into a nearby van. He sat up and for his effort received a kick in the head that decommissioned him. Travis grabbed a second one and spun him around, bouncing him into yet another assailant. The two assailants grabbed each other's arms, not sure if they were friends or foes. Travis wasted no time in placing one hand behind each man's head, grabbed them by their hair and pulled them back. They resisted and Travis reversed direction slamming their heads together. It sounded, in spite of the ringing, as if two pottery steins had collided. The two fell to the ground, unconscious.

Prescott squatted and kicked the legs out from under one of the assailants, toppling him. This one seemed to be no novice fighter; he rolled over and came up on his feet effortlessly. He ignored the ringing noise and pulled a knife from each sleeve. He spun around quickly, using the knives in his hands as killing blades. Prescott concentrated on the knife-spinning maniac, ran toward him, and, with a swift kung-fu jump, kicked the man in the temple. The man collapsed like a rag doll.

Claire was in the path of two of the gunmen walking side by side in her direction. She jumped and simultaneously kicked each man in his respective manhood while grabbing each one's head by their hair to keep her balance. The two unfortunate saps clutched their smashed jewels and bent over in agony. Claire showed no mercy; she jumped up and kicked their foreheads with her low heels. They jerked back and fell onto their backs like two bugs, side by side, holding their hands to their groins. Claire walked between them and placed her feet on each one's neck, pinning them down. "OK, *ragazzi, fermi.*" The two thugs under Claire's shoes might not have heard her command not to move with all the noise, but a hard shoe sole on each of their throats convinced them to stop squirming.

The high-pitched ringing ceased. The smoke started clearing, helped by a light breeze. In the distance, police sirens screamed as they approached the ambush site.

"Not bad for predown work," said Travis. "Six thugs lying on the ground like slugs."

Prescott spoke into his aural-comm, "Ispettore Romano, *per favore.*"

He and the others surveyed the site. Six men on the ground, a bullet-riddled taxi with all its windows smashed and its tires flat, and three vans with their back doors open.

"Yes, Ispettore Romano? This is Prescott. We've been ambushed."

Claire and Travis could hear the conversation through their inner-com as well. "*Madonna!*" exclaimed Ispettore Romano. "Are you OK?"

"Yes, we're OK. We were ambushed on Via Portuense under the overpass of the Roma Trastevere line. We've apprehended six assailants. The local police are coming toward us. Would you please tell them to approach without their guns blazing? The situation is under control."

"Look what I found here." Travis held something that he just retrieved from the back of the van that drove in reverse: a sniper rifle equipped with a laser and a night scope.

"Travis found a sniper rifle in one of the vans," Prescott informed the Ispettore.

"It's getting better," added Travis. "I found a second one. What are the chances that these babies belong to the snipers who killed Colonel Glauser's men?" Travis placed one rifle back into the van and unloaded the other one, catching the expelled cartridge in one hand. "Yep, titanium tip, frozen mercury bullet. We've found the snipers."

"Did you hear that, Ispettore Romano?" Prescott asked.

"Oberst Glauser and I will be right over in a hover-copter," said Ispettore Romano.

The police sirens were getting closer. "What should we do until the officials are here?" Claire pressed down on the neck of one of the men who was getting frisky. He stopped.

"I think we should beat the truth out of them," said Travis with a smirk.

"Yes, they are ready for a full confession," agreed Prescott. "We'll need to gas them to make sure they stay asleep."

Without a word, Claire bent down and pushed a button on her wrist device. The eyes of the two assailants bulged, but seconds after they inhaled the gas Claire had released, they were sound asleep. Travis and Prescott dragged the others, after they gassed them, near Claire's two.

Travis, Prescott, and Claire encircled the six sleeping assailants. "Let's find out what they know," said Prescott. The Trinity Team lowered their heads and joined their minds.

The first police car arrived at the ambush scene with flashing lights but silent sirens. Two officers came out of the patrol car, guns drawn, approaching cautiously. It seemed that they had gotten the message not to shoot before asking questions. The Capuchin Trinity Team had finished their trans-axiom-paranormal mind penetration and waited for the officers to approach. Two more patrol cars and a van arrived, disgorging more armed officers who converged onto the shooting scene. Farther away, two trucks belonging to the *vigili del fuoco*, the fire department, and several ambulances waited with their emergency lights flashing.

Italians are not the quiet types, but they were silent now as they surveyed the bullet-ridden car, the guns lying on the ground, and the neat pile made by the six unconscious assailants. The hover-copter landed outside the underpass, and Ispettore Romano, Albert Glauser, and two other officers came running to the scene.

Breaking from his usual cool demeanor, Oberst Glauser couldn't help but whistle when he saw the mayhem. "I've never seen anything like this in my entire life."

"The two sniper rifles are in that van." Travis pointed it out.

"Are you OK?" Ispettore Romano asked Prescott with concern.

"Yes, we're doing fine, not a scratch," said Prescott on behalf of his teammates and himself.

"I gather you were not in the taxi when they opened fire," said Ispettore Romano.

"No, we got suspicious and jumped out in the nick of time," said Prescott.

"How did you manage to, to . . ." Ispettore Romano scratched her head, trying to find the right words. "To kick the shit out of them?" The words were right out of an American movie.

"Well," said Prescott, approaching her with a swagger. "We have our ways."

Ispettore Romano smiled slightly. "Impressive ways."

"Nothing to boast about, but they were only six, and we were three." Prescott reached under his jacket and pulled his pants up.

The Ispettore's smile widened. "Six of them with automatic weapons against the three of you, empty-handed. Sounds like a fair fight."

Claire glanced at Travis, pointing at Prescott with a sideways thumb as if saying, "Get a load of that."

Another officer who had arrived with the Ispettore bent down and picked up one of the smoke mini-bombs and gave it to her. She analyzed the lipstick-size metallic container for a moment, smelled it, and asked, "What's this?"

"Oh, that's one of the smoke mini-bombs we used," replied Prescott. "It created lots of smoke and lots of noise to disorient the assailants. Then we did what we do best."

"You don't say." Ispettore Romano shook her head in disbelief, but she was impressed. She turned to her assistant and gave quick orders. The rest of the police officers broke out of their silent amazement and begin to work around the crime scene. Paramedics approached with stretchers.

Prescott took the cartridge from her and picked up the other two from the ground. "We have to turn these in. You know, rules," he explained.

"Ispettore Romano, you may want to isolate each suspect," said Claire.

"Why?" she wondered. "You mean before they get their story together."

"You may want to hear what we found out about each one of them," answered Claire.

Chapter 28. Confessions

"You interrogated them?" Ispettore Romano asked sharply.

"In a manner of speaking," said Claire.

"They told us everything they know," said Travis, who had returned from the van with Glauser.

"How did you manage to do that?" Ispettore Romano asked.

"After we kicked the shit out of them, then we beat the shit out of them for good measure, and they spilled their guts," said Travis, glancing at Prescott.

"I did not hear that," said Ispettore Romano. "Violence against perpetrators is not allowed, and we cannot use any evidence obtained in that manner."

"We understand," said Claire. "We did not torture them. But we penetrated their minds and extracted a lot of information. Would you like to hear it?"

"Certainly." Ispettore Romano looked at Oberst Glauser to make sure that he was listening as well. He nodded eagerly, as if acknowledging that serving the Vatican and not the Italian state made him somehow less encumbered by legalities.

"The snipers are these two," said Travis, pointing to two dark-skinned men dressed in fatigues. "They are professional assassins and brothers. Their names are Mohamed and Ahmed Abadi, Tunisians. They served time in prison in Germany, and Interpol has their dossiers. The sniper rifles have their bio-traces, and you'll have no problem convicting them. Their last job before this one was the assassination of someone called Bartolini."

"Franco Bartolini, the Lega Nord deputy?" Ispettore Romano asked quickly. Travis shrugged, not knowing.

Glauser squatted to take a better look at the two Tunisians and searched for their IDs. They had none.

"The politician Bartolini was in their thoughts," said Travis. "Now, this scumbag over here." He kicked a large, rugged man in the ribs. "This is the leader of today's ambush and of the murders of the officers back at the convent. An unknown woman, who never had direct contact with him, hired him and gave the orders. He was the spotter for the snipers in the church tower. His name is Gino Serpe, and he is a low-level leader in an extreme leftist group."

"The Bandiera Rossa extremist group," said Ispettore, shaking her head.

Travis nodded. "What's interesting about this thug is that he moonlights as an assassin. He was the spotter as well when they shot Bartolini." Travis kicked a fat man, unshaven and reeking of alcohol. "His cohort over here is his sidekick. His name is Ilario Bruzzi. Gino and Ilario are also union enforcers. Ilario was the driver when they assassinated Bartolini."

"How did you really get this information out of them?" Ispettore Romano asked incredulously.

"As Claire said, we penetrated their minds, and they sang like castrati," said Prescott.

"You can do that to anyone?" Ispettore Romano asked, as if troubled by the idea.

"Not if they are awake and aware," said Prescott. "Then they can resist us—in their minds, that is—and we wouldn't be able to learn any more than we would by regular interrogation. However, if they are unconscious or drunk or drugged, we can learn anything we want from them. And, as you see, they're unconscious and completely unaware that we visited their minds and extracted all these secrets from each one of them."

"Incredible," whispered the Ispettore.

"These last two hooligans." Travis pointed to two young men. "Claire smashed their family jewels and . . . well, I'd better let Claire tell you about them."

Claire was slightly amused with Travis's remark. "Their names are Luigi Meola and Quirino Sirianni. These two guidos are aspiring to become members of the Bandiera Rossa. They seem to be very proud of that, even wearing red scarves around their necks tonight. Like any young, ignorant idealists, they couldn't tell the political differences represented by a red scarf or a black one. Ilario Bruzzi hired them for tonight's ambush. These two are serial rapists, working together as a team. I got three of their victims' names: Francesca Salvati, Arianna Zicaro, and Paola Di Fusco."

"Di Fusco? That poor woman is still in a coma," said Ispettore Romano, visibly angry.

Ahmed, or Mohamed, and Ilario started squirming as they awakened. Ispettore Romano gave a quick snap of her fingers, and police officers approached and begun cuffing them. Although they were incapacitated and needed medical attention, they were still dangerous.

"This is great information. Unfortunately, it is not admissible as evidence," said Ispettore Romano. "Except for the Tunisians, because of the guns. The others we can charge with possession of weapons and intent to kill."

"There is another way, you know," said Prescott.

"Don't tell me that you put the fear of the devil in their souls and they will give us full confessions." Ispettore Romano smiled at Prescott.

"It can be arranged. We can do that," said Prescott with a straight face.

Ispettore Romano's smile vanished.

"Something totally benign," said Prescott, and he smiled.

"*Bene*, good. What do you suggest?"

"Keep them isolated from each other, and—"

Ispettore Romano almost laughed. "You are a devious creature. Of course, we were going to play them off against each other with the knowledge we obtained from you. For the first eight hours, we can interrogate them without their lawyers. If they don't have lawyers, we've got twenty-four hours until they get public defenders."

"That's a good procedure, but what I had in mind was different," said Prescott with a mischievous smile.

"Like what? More of your specialty stuff?"

"You see, Claire could pay them a short visit each before you whisk them away," said Prescott mysteriously. Seeing the Ispettore's puzzled look, he clarified, "Claire seems to scare the living daylights out of men, especially after she beats them up." Prescott smiled at Claire. Claire made an innocent face.

Ispettore Romano gave Claire a quick look. "But she wasn't alone. You two helped."

"Yes, but they don't know that," said Prescott. "It was dark, with dense smoke and ear-splitting noise. And she knows how we each incapacitated them. With a few words from her, those men will...well, you get the picture."

"You can do that?" Ispettore Romano asked Claire, and, without waiting for an answer, she continued, "What are you going to do to them?"

"We will both do something to them," answered Claire. "We will play good-cop, bad-cop. You will tell them that I am a mercenary and that they are lucky to be alive and in your custody. You brought me along to identify them. I, in turn, will implant a thought in their minds on how I took them down and that, as soon as they get out on the streets, I will kill them."

Ispettore Romano stood still, digesting what she heard. "Unbelievable! A good incentive for them to want to stay in prison. Let's do it," she said mischievously.

She gave quick orders, and each assailant was removed, one by one, to different vans to get medical attention and later to be transported for booking and individual interrogation. The two young rapists walked half-crouched, with their thighs squeezed tight. The Tunisians were cool as ice. Little did they know what they had already divulged. Ilario was wobbly, being drunk and dizzy from the encounter. Gino shouted orders in Italian, informing his crew to keep their mouths shut.

Claire and Ispettore Romano visited each perpetrator's van. The six criminals reacted differently: The rapists cried, drunken Ilario screamed in horror and then he pissed himself, Gino erupted in a fusillade of vulgarities, and one of the Tunisians began praying to Allah.

"I've never seen grown men scared like that," said the Ispettore, as she and Claire returned.

"It works every time," said Prescott, overhearing them.

"Yes, Prescott, you and your team did well today. I'm impressed," Ispettore Romano said. "Do you like Chianti?"

"I love Chianti, Ispettore Romano," said Prescott with a big smile.

"Please, call me Carlota. And if you don't, I'll have to call you Special Agent Alighieri."

"Carlota. Such a romantic name," said Prescott, feeling like a teenager.

"Good. Maybe before you leave Rome I can share with you a well-aged bottle of Chianti I've kept for a special occasion."

Claire turned to Travis and placed her finger in her mouth to mimic vomiting.

"We would be glad to join you, Carlota," Travis said eagerly.

"Ispettore," she corrected him. "Well, it is a small bottle, you know, only for two," she replied, without much regret. "I'm sure Oberst Glauser will be more than happy to treat you to some fine Vatican wine. Isn't that so, Glauser?"

Glauser was caught by surprise. The Ispettore gave him an elbow in the ribs as a hint. "Of course, of course, it will be my pleasure," Glauser said, recovering.

"I see." Travis stroked the back of his head and neck, somehow deflated. "We'd better be going. We need to catch up with some sleep and hopefully we will dream about Sister Terina's nightmare and the mastermind, the unknown woman behind all this."

Ispettore Romano looked intently at them. "Besides the woman who hired the assassins, what nightmare are you talking about?"

"Vatican work," interjected Glauser. He gave her a leave-it-at-that look.

"Can we get a ride back to the Vatican, Ispettore?" Claire asked.

"Certainly." The Ispettore signaled to an officer to retrieve a vehicle. "Stay out of trouble," she said. "And *ciao*, Prescott. I'll see you soon?"

"*Ciao*, Carlota." Prescott blushed.

Claire took him by the elbow, escorting him toward their ride. "C'mon, lover boy."

"Don't forget to take your vitamins," Travis added.

"What, why?" Prescott asked.

"These Italian women are ferocious in bed," said Travis. "Isn't that so, Claire?"

"Oh yes, especially the ispettori," agreed Claire, with a sly smile.

"Stop yanking my chain," Prescott protested.

Chapter 29. Oberst Glauser

Prescott, Claire, and Travis met in the mess hall for their breakfast at ten o'clock. Outside it looked like rain, and it was cooler than the day before. Claire had a cup of hot tea to warm up. They were quiet, contemplating the events of the past few days.

A plainclothes Swiss Guard officer approached their table. *"Buongiorno, signori.* Oberst Glauser would like to have a meeting with you at your earliest convenience."

They looked up at the young man—Travis with his cup of cappuccino near his lips, Claire holding her steamy cup in both hands, and Prescott about to spread butter on a roll. They must not have been completely awake, because, at first, it didn't seem to register why Glauser would want to see them.

"Did something else happen while we were asleep?" Travis asked.

"No, nothing happened since early this morning. Oberst Glauser wants to have a meeting with you. In his office."

"Where is his office?" Travis inquired.

"I will escort you there."

"Right away, or can we can finish our breakfast first?" Claire asked.

"Please finish your breakfast. I will wait by the door." The officer bowed slightly and left, taking his position near the door.

Claire glanced inquisitively at her colleagues. Prescott shrugged and continued spreading butter on his roll. Travis took a sip of his cappuccino and said, "He must have questions on his mind."

"I would," said Prescott.

After they finished eating, they followed the officer to Glauser's office. Oberst Glauser sat behind his desk, reading e-reports with the door open. The officer knocked on the doorjamb and cleared his throat to indicate their presence. Glauser looked up. "*Grazie*, Murner. Good morning, please come in." Glauser invited them to take a seat in front of his desk. "Murner, please close the door behind you."

Claire, Prescott, and Travis sat down and assessed Glauser's office. The Pope's picture hung on one wall, flanked by the Vatican, Swiss Guard, and Italian flags. The window behind Glauser's desk opened up to an interior courtyard that served as a parking lot. On another wall there was a large crucifix and many memento photos of the Pope and other highly placed dignitaries.

"You may wonder why I asked you here for a meeting." Without waiting for a reply, Glauser continued, "Well, let's cut through the formalities. Who are you and what are you doing here?"

"I agree. Let's cut through the formalities," said Travis. "Albert—may I call you Albert?" Glauser nodded. "First, we would like to know what you know about us and why we are here."

Glauser seemed to be taken aback by the question. After all, he was the one who was supposed to be asking the questions.

Travis spoke, "We were invited by the Holy Father on a highly confidential mission. We need to know first what you were told about this."

Glauser recovered his demeanor. "I was told that a special team from the Trinity Investigation Organization was to come to the Vatican to help the Holy Father with a delicate situation. And that I should assist you as needed."

The Capuchin Trinity Team remained motionless, waiting for Glauser to continue.

"However, in light of what happened last night, I need some answers. I'll have to deal with the Rome police. Besides, I have two dead officers, and it is my duty to conclude this investigation."

"Of course," agreed Travis. "We are the Capuchin Trinity Team, a criminal, paranormal, and supernatural investigation team. Not many people, even from law enforcement agencies, know about us."

"I certainly did not know much about you," said Glauser.

"We're not a secret team. Just not well-known," clarified Claire. "Even the Vatican has one such Trinity Team. Did you know that?"

"No, but then I don't get involved with the clergy," replied Glauser.

"They're not clergy, just like we're not clergy," said Prescott. "We are investigators of unusual crimes or potential crimes that involve paranormal and supernatural agents."

"Why isn't our Trinity Team helping out?" Glauser asked.

"That was the Holy Father's decision," said Claire.

"I see," said Glauser. "Can you tell me why Sister Terina was murdered along with two of my men?"

"Whoever killed her wanted her silenced," said Claire. "We cannot tell you what secrets she was harboring. Unfortunately, your men were in the way, and they were killed as well."

"As we discussed last night, the snipers could have easily killed Sister Terina with the mercury bullets and not touched your officers," added Travis. "But with the other assassin inside the chamber, they couldn't shoot through the door. It would have killed the assassin inside as well. I think they improvised at the last minute."

"You could have warned me of the dangers involved," said Glauser gloomily.

"We did not know how dangerous it would be, just as we didn't know what was waiting for us in the underpass," said Claire.

"Is the Holy Father in any danger?" Glauser asked.

"He is in as much danger as he usually is," said Prescott.

"Three people are dead, you could have been dead as well, and you tell me it's business as usual?" Glauser argued.

"What I meant to say is, he is in no more danger than usual," said Prescott. "Other people around him may be in danger as well. Including us."

"Those criminals, what do they want from you?" Glauser asked.

"The criminals want us out of the way. They are afraid that we may discover who they are," said Travis.

"Did you have any idea before this morning that you were targets as well?" Glauser asked.

"We did," affirmed Travis. "Remember the explosion near the Basilica di San Clemente?"

"Yes, a gas explosion."

"We were underground when that explosion happened, and, yes, it was a gas explosion, but not an accident," said Travis.

"You were the targets?" Glauser blanched. "Since you've arrived here, you've been subject to two assassination attempts?"

"Yes," said Travis. "It's part of the job. However, Sister Terina was our main concern. She was the real target. Whoever the perpetrator is, she is very dangerous."

"Are the thugs from last night involved?" Glauser asked.

"Yes, but they are just minions. Hired guns to kill Sister Terina and then us," said Travis. "They don't know any more than they've already told us."

"Why do they want you dead?" wondered Glauser.

"Because we extracted a certain thought—knowledge, if you will—from Sister Terina's mind," said Travis. "We cannot discuss the content."

"Uh, the delicate matter," said Glauser.

"Yes," said Travis. "Anyway, the brain behind this seems to be a woman. It could be the same woman who stabbed Sister Terina."

"Do you have any idea who this femme fatale is?"

"No, unfortunately," said Travis. "Perhaps someone who belongs to a satanic cult."

"Do you need any help to search for such a woman?"

"We initiated a search with our organization, and, so far, all potentially dangerous Satanist women are either in jail or elsewhere, away from Rome."

"In that case, I was right to raise the level of security at the Vatican. Do you need any security as well?"

"Do as you deem fit," said Prescott. "As for us, we don't need anyone to protect us. Any security may be an encumbrance."

"Anything else I need to be aware of?" Glauser asked.

"The mystery woman," said Travis. "If she has free passage in the Vatican, then there is imminent danger."

"No one is allowed in the Vatican without permission," said Glauser.

"She may have permission," said Travis.

"Can you check for all females who have access to the Vatican and who are less than 160 centimeters in height and less than fifty years old?" asked Prescott.

Glauser pressed a button on the desk console. A hologram appeared above his desk showing 299 women. Glauser pressed another button. "Ninety-two are here as employees. The others have passes to enter as needed. We'll investigate them all."

"Do you have any information on visitors who have legal access?" Claire asked.

"No, visitors are given temporary passes, and we keep video records for three months after they pass through security," said Glauser. "We could review past records. But who are we looking for?"

"I wish we knew," said Claire. "What we told you is all we could deduce from Sister Terina's deathbed."

"The female mastermind and the woman assassin could be two different women," said Glauser.

"They could be," agreed Claire. "Could you keep track and alert us of any suspicious women entering the Vatican, Albert?" Claire asked.

"Sure." Glauser pressed a few more buttons. "Meanwhile, you'll see more guards posted around the Vatican and the Holy Father." Glauser thought for a moment. "The gas explosion. Was the same woman involved?"

"We don't know that, either," said Prescott. "The assailants in the ambush were unaware of that attempt. They were not involved. And only the Monsignore, you, and we know that the explosion was not an accident. We'd appreciate it if you didn't disclose this information to anyone for the time being."

Chapter 30. Revelation

"The mystery woman, the mastermind, wants us out of the way," said Prescott as they were walking away from Glauser's office.

"I think she's afraid that we can foil her plans," said Travis. "Let's walk this way and talk fully cloaked." They passed two security guards armed with automatic weapons as they walked toward Viale del Giardino Quatrado. "She wanted us removed when we were in the catacombs. We were not supposed to discover Pope Joan's tomb."

"And last night," said Claire, "did she want to finish the job from the crypt, or did she know that we found Terina's memory?"

"How could she have known that we captured Terina's memory?" wondered Prescott.

"Glauser knows," said Travis. "He knows that now. Early in the morning after the ambush, he might have had a suspicion. And Ispettore Romano got a hint of it at the same time with Glauser. But it all happened after the ambush."

"But there were two different motives," said Prescott. "In the crypt we were about to discover the female genes, and I can see why someone would kill us to keep it a secret. But after we discovered it, I don't see a reason for anyone to pursue our deaths. The second motive is the memory from the sister. We have it and, if we unveil it, we could discover another secret."

"That makes sense," agreed Travis. "We hold the secret, although we don't know what it is yet. She wants us eliminated. We'd better switch our gear to full-alert condition."

The three of them initiated the full alert. That meant their monitoring devices were switched to a continuous observation of their surroundings. Their suits became bullet-proof-ready.

"Back to this memory," said Travis. "We need to unveil it. It has to do with why the Pope became pregnant and/or who's behind it."

Claire suddenly stopped and clutched her forehead with one hand.

"What's the matter? A headache?" asked Prescott.

"I know who knew about the memory before the ambush," said Claire.

"Who?" Travis and Prescott asked.

"Lucia Pietro."

"The doctor's wife?" Travis asked incredulously.

"Yes, I hinted about it last night in the assembly room. How stupid of me."

"I'd say lucky stupid," said Prescott.

"She must have told someone else," said Travis. "I didn't get the feeling that she had a mastermind brain."

"But we have a suspect now," said Prescott. "She was in the convent when all this happened."

"And she is under fifty and under 160 centimeters in height," added Travis.

Claire exhaled. "I'm sorry to have put you in danger."

"Hey, this is when we make lemonade from lemons." Travis gave Claire a hug.

"Don't give it a second thought," said Prescott. "And stop hugging her," he admonished Travis. Claire gave Prescott a hug, too, so he wouldn't feel left out.

"The doctor's wife." Travis narrowed his eyes, thinking.

"What does she really want?" Claire asked rhetorically. "There could be three answers: The Pope dead, the Pope giving birth to the boy, or preventing the birth and killing the fetus. Can you think of anything else?"

"Or she's trying to save her ass," said Prescott.

"I think she wants to discredit the Pope, one way or another," said Travis.

"Then what could we discover that would jeopardize that?" Prescott restarted the walk.

"Wait a minute, let's analyze this in a different way," said Claire. Prescott and Travis stopped, all ears. "In the first place, the suspects used Sister Terina to contaminate the Pope and cause him to bear a child. Then their plans were thwarted by the spirit of Pope Joan, reversing Satan's genes and replacing them with those of a human. So now, the suspects have no use for this fetus."

"Other than embarrassing the Pope and the Church," said Prescott.

"Maybe the embarrassment was never a motive," said Travis. "The child is the real motive."

"As Satan's child from the body of the Holy Father," said Claire.

"But not as God's child from the body of the Holy Father," said Prescott.

Travis folded his arms and looked at the tips of his shoes. "Do you realize that this is the strongest suspicion that there are two culprits? One pro-Satan and another pro-God?"

"Yes, it makes sense," said Claire, eyes wide. "Satan's agent causes the Pope to carry his son. But the fetus is altered, which is not good. Then Satan's agent wants the fetus destroyed, while God's agent wants the fetus to be born."

"I think the attempts on our lives were carried out by these two suspect groups," said Travis. "Separately from each other."

"Yes," said Prescott. "Two different motives. And somehow they're afraid that we will prevent the killing of the fetus.

"The most expedient way to kill the fetus is to kill the Pope," said Travis. "And who else but the doctor has the best access to him?"

"Doctor Angelo and Lucia Pietro, a husband-and-wife team," said Claire.

Travis made contact with Glauser. "Albert, the Holy Father is in danger. Don't let anyone get near him, especially Dottore Pietro. Place round-the-clock surveillance on Dottore Pietro and his wife, Lucia."

"Yes, understood," acknowledged Glauser. "Lucia from the convent? Oh, how interesting."

"Indeed." Travis ended the call.

"From the people who know about this, only Dottore Pietro wants the fetus dead," said Prescott.

"And Cardinal Cellini," said Claire. "Maybe he's the one who is holding back Dottore Pietro from killing the Pope outright."

Travis made contact at once with Monsignore Giuseppe. "Monsignore, we need to speak with the Holy Father right away. Alone."

"Yes, may I tell him the nature of your visit?" asked the Monsignore in a businesslike tone.

"It is very urgent and confidential." Travis had to restrain himself from shouting.

"Please come over," said the Monsignore.

"On our way," Travis said, and they changed their direction to the Pope's quarters.

"This is Oberst Glauser." The CTT's aural-comm opened. "Lucia Pietro is not at the convent. No one is sure when she left. Also, she had a permanent visitor badge for the Vatican, which I've suspended. We have her GeneID. If she enters the Vatican, we will know and arrest her. Shall I arrest Dottore Pietro?"

"Thanks, Albert," said Travis. "Please do not arrest him yet, but do not leave him alone with the Holy Father, either."

"Understood," said Glauser.

"This is Monsignore Giuseppe," he said through the CTT's aural-comm. "His Holy Father will see you at four this afternoon."

"What? Did you explain to him what I just told you?" shouted Travis. "It is imperative that we see him immediately."

"I certainly did, Mr. St. John," answered the Monsignore coolly. "Our Holy Father is praying and does not want to be disturbed until four o'clock. Afterward, His Holiness will see you. Good-bye!"

"Hold it!" shouted Travis. "Is he alone?"

"Yes. The Swiss Guards have doubled their presence here. I must go. Good-bye!"

Travis was furious. "What the hell!"

Prescott contacted Glauser. "Albert, do you know the whereabouts of Dottore Pietro?"

"Yes, Prescott. The Dottore left Vatican City, and we are trailing him. At this time his destination is unknown."

"Thanks! And one more thing, Albert—do you have access to Cardinal Cellini's whereabouts?"

"We sure do. We track all our high-level officials for security reasons. And he is out of the Vatican, at Suore Mantellate Serve di Sofia with Cardinal Navarro."

"Thanks, Albert," interjected Claire. "Talking about security, would you know if the Holy Father is feeling well? Right now?"

"What's the matter, Claire?" asked Glauser in a worried voice.

"Maybe we are a little jumpy, but we were told he is alone and praying. We want to make sure that the Holy Father is well."

"Thank you for your concern," said Albert Glauser. "He is with Cardinal Le Pere. We monitor our Holy Father 24/7, and all his vital signs are stable. I would not worry about his safety for now."

"What do you know about Cardinal Le Pere?" Travis asked.

"He is our Holy Father's confidant."

Travis and Prescott raised their eyebrows.

"He is safe with Cardinal Le Pere," added Albert.

"Thanks, Albert, that's a relief." Claire disconnected.

"Cardinal Le Pere is a new element," said Travis.

"Could Cardinal Le Pere be the ace in the hole for the Pope?" wondered Prescott. "Or his accomplice?"

"We need to have our séance and find out what's in Sister Terina's memory," said Claire.

"We need to be more clear-headed than we are right now," said Prescott, rubbing his temples. "I didn't get enough sleep. Maybe tomorrow?"

"Let's hope that another attempt on our lives doesn't take place," said Travis.

"Today is Thursday, June 3. We have three days until the birth," said Claire. "The fetus, the Pope, or both are at grave risk."

Mit Sandru

Chapter 31. The Chianti Lunch

Prescott's aural-comm indicated a private call from Ispettore Romano. "Hello, Carlota!" Prescott turned around to avert his teammates' startled looks. "Such a surprise to hear from you so soon."

"*Ciao*! How are you, Prescott? This week I have the night shift at the police station—you Americans call it the graveyard shift, no?—and I was thinking that we could have lunch together. Are you busy right now?"

Prescott cleared his throat. "As luck would have it, we are in a lull, and lunch sounds good. Hold on a second." He placed her on hold. "Carlota would like to have lunch with me. I don't think we have anything pressing until four o'clock, right?"

Claire and Travis looked each other without saying a word. They joined hands and departed to have lunch on their own, feeling left out.

"Where shall I meet you, Carlota?" Prescott answered, watching his teammates walk away.

"Over at my apartment. That's where I keep my aged Chianti."

"Sure, send me directions, and I'll see you soon."

Prescott stopped to get a bouquet of flowers, not roses—they might send the wrong signals—but only a simple arrangement of natural flowers. The robo-taxi took him to his destination, a modern, multi-story apartment building. The computerized security gate let him in and directed him to the elevator.

Carlota was waiting for Prescott at the door. She was dressed beyond casually. She was wearing a long white silk gown that was semitransparent, which just hinted at enough of her sexy, white-underwear-clad body underneath. Prescott liked what he saw. He felt his blood rushing to a part of his body below his navel. He had to remind himself that this was just a simple lunch invitation, and if Carlota dressed this way when she had company, presumably adult company, then so much the better.

"*Ciao*, Prescott!"

"*Ciao*, Carlota! I brought you fresh flowers." Prescott handed her the bouquet. She held it with one hand to her bosom, inviting him with the other hand to enter. Prescott took a quick look at the modern and airy apartment. Through his PAV he detected no hidden sensors or any other maldevices. "Beautiful apartment. Look at that view!" Prescott admired the view of Rome through the glass wall leading onto her balcony-terrace. He could see the dome of Saint Peter's Basilica, the Coliseum, and the Tiber snaking through the city.

"Yes, it is beautiful. A gift from my sugar daddy." She winked at him.

Good for her, Prescott thought. She went to the kitchen and brought back the flowers in a vase. As she bent down to place the vase on a low glass table, her well-rounded posterior could be seen through the gown in its entire splendor. Prescott had to remind himself again that this was just a lunch date.

"Only one sugar daddy?" Prescott asked, as if asking whether she had only one pair of shoes—which she wasn't wearing at the moment.

"Maybe," she giggled, taking no offense at his question. "Prescott, I am a well-to-do woman, but people think that if I work for the police, even as an ispettore, I couldn't afford this place on my salary and, therefore, that I must take bribes. To dispel that suspicion, if they ask, I tell them about my sugar daddy. Especially the women. Let them eat their hearts out." She giggled again. "And when they hear that I even have a housemaid, they turn green."

"I didn't ask any of that stuff," said Prescott.

"I know, but I told you about my sugar daddy to see your reaction." She smiled at him. "No. You are not a prude."

"I hope that's good," said Prescott, looking some more around the room. No cleaning robots—a human maid cleaned and maintained this place.

"Not being a prude depends on the situation. Like our get-together. I prepared a table outside on the terrace for our lunch. I hope you like prosciutto."

They sat down at a wicker table, which held appetizers, glasses, and the uncorked bottle of

Chianti Classico. Judging by the patina of dust on the bottle, it seemed well-aged.

Carlota opened a bottle of mineral water and filled their glasses. "Your PAV is set on dark and full alert."

"After what's happened in the past few days, we've assessed that we continue to be targeted by that mystery woman. We are on full alert. And we are almost sure that the woman is Lucia Pietro." Prescott took a sip of his mineral water and disabled his PAV. Carlota could see his eyes now, which were light brown compared to her own dark brown eyes.

"Yes, Lucia Pietro," commented Carlota. "Who would have thought? She escaped through a back door at the convent during the time of your ambush. We haven't been able to locate her yet."

Prescott listened to his aural-comm. "What's up, Travis?"

"Sorry to interrupt your depraved lunch, but I thought that you would like to know the doctor's whereabouts. He's at the cemetery, visiting his sons' graves."

"Anything on Lucia Pietro?"

Carlota's attention turned to Prescott.

"No, nothing yet," said Travis. "Well, I'd better let you return to your *amoroso* Chianti."

"Thanks, Travis! Enjoy your lunch with our sister." Prescott disconnected and looked at Carlota. "Dottore Pietro is a suspect as well."

"I figured that much. You must have something big on him." She looked suspiciously at Prescott, who did not flinch. "But let's not talk shop." She smiled.

"Good idea," said Prescott, smiling back. "Carlota, I'm flattered that you've invited me for lunch, but what's the real reason?"

"To share with you a good bottle of Chianti Classico from Tuscany." She took the bottle and poured wine into the glasses. "And because you are cute and an Italian." She raised her glass. "*Salute!*"

"Yes, but I'm only half-Italian," Prescott said, raising his glass. "*Salute!*"

Carlota raised her wine glass to her lips and took a small sip when her aural-comm beeped. She lowered her glass and answered, "*Pronto.*"

Prescott took a sip as well. The Chianti was good, but it had an underlying bitter taste. Maybe it had peaked. He took small sips, watching Carlota converse in Italian with someone. She was animated and trying to end the conversation, but it dragged on and on.

Before he realized it, he had finished his wine. He placed the empty glass back on the table and wondered if he should refill it. He felt dizzy, and his breath was shallow. His vision was hazy. Carlota was looking into the distance as she was talking. Her voice trailed off.

Carlota finished the conversation, reached for her wine glass, and took a sip.

Chapter 32. Poisoned

Claire and Travis jumped when they were notified by their PAVs that Prescott's vital signs were erratic. Their security protocol during an investigation was set up such that they were in contact with each other's whereabouts and vital signs in case of danger, injury, or—God forbid—death.

"Albert, we have an emergency with Prescott!" Travis shouted into his aural-comm.

"What's the emergency?"

"Prescott is dying. And the Ispettore is not answering, either. Do you have a hover-copter to take us to Ispettore Romano's apartment immediately?"

"Right away," answered Oberst Glauser. "One of my officers will be taking you to the copter."

It took four minutes for the hover-copter to arrive over Ispettore Romano's balcony. Glauser notified the paramedics, but they would arrive via the streets. Claire monitored Prescott's vital signs continuously.

"He has been poisoned," said Claire. "From the symptoms, it appears it was belladonna or hemlock."

"I need to land on top of the roof," the pilot informed them.

"How close can you get to the balcony?" Travis asked.

"You're not planning to jump, are you?" asked the pilot.

"How close can you get?" Travis repeated his question.

"Two meters, maybe closer," said the pilot.

"Swing the copter in, so you can give me momentum for the jump."

"OK, but you're crazy. We're twenty stories high."

Travis opened the door and leaned out. The copter moved in close, above the balcony rail. When Travis judged it was close enough, he jumped, and landed on the balcony without any difficulty.

"Do the same thing for me!" demanded Claire.

"OK, but you're crazy, too, lady." The pilot repeated the approach and, just as the copter was at its closest to the balcony, a gust of wind jerked it away.

Claire jumped, but because of the loss of momentum from the wind gust, she was off the mark. She was too low, and her fingertips just brushed the balcony's rail. Her fingers slid along the balcony's glass panel, but there was nothing to grab. Time slowed down. It was terrible to end up this way, she thought, falling to the ground below.

Below the balcony floor level, the window-washer rail protruded away from the balcony's glass panels. Claire grabbed it with both hands, praying that she would be able to hold onto the round tubing. Her right hand slipped off, but the left hand clutched the rail. She steadied her swing, reached with her other hand and grabbed the rail. She looked up. Travis was leaning over to help her. The copter was hovering above.

She swung sideways and placed one foot above the rail. Slowly she raised her other foot onto the rail. Now she was holding on with all four of her limbs. She pulled up and managed to climb up on the window-washer rail. She felt Travis's hand clutch her back collar and pull her up over the balcony's banister onto safe ground.

"Crap!" she said, once on the balcony. "And thanks, Travis!"

"I can't afford to lose both my partners."

"How's Prescott?" asked Claire.

"Didn't have time to check on him," said Travis.

They both rushed to Prescott, who was lying motionless and blue.

"Asphyxia." Claire opened Prescott's jacket and began CPR.

Travis checked the sensors in his PAV. "He was poisoned with hemlock. Albert, we're on the balcony. Relay that the poison is hemlock."

"The police are on their way," said Glauser. "How is Prescott? How is Ispettore Romano?"

"Prescott is in bad shape. He needs artificial resuscitation. Didn't see Romano yet. We'll check on her."

"Be careful, the perpetrators may be in the apartment," cautioned Albert Glauser.

"Thanks. Point well taken." Travis took out his gun. "I'll go see where Romano is." Travis went to the door and called for her. There was no response. Either she and the others were waiting in ambush, or she was poisoned, too. He moved stealthily, using his PAV to detect motion, heat, or chemical abnormalities emanating from a possible bomb. There were no signs of her or others until he reached her bedroom, where he found her on the floor, gasping for air. She was semiconscious.

"Romano is poisoned as well. In slightly better shape than Prescott, but she's suffering from the same symptoms. Hurry!" Travis announced on the open comm, which was connected with the emergency units and the police now. He moved cautiously to the closet and checked inside. Nothing. Same situation in the bathroom. He checked the other rooms, but found no one. "All clear."

Near were Carlota lay he saw a first-aid bag. It seemed that Carlota was trying to retrieve it to help Prescott. Unfortunately, she was in no position to help anyone. Travis couldn't help her, other than performing CPR to keep her alive, but it was not necessary yet. He ran to the panel near the main door to deactivate the emergency protocol and allow the paramedics in. But the door was wide open.

"Glauser here. A medi-copter was dispatched to the roof to transport the two victims. The paramedics have respirators with them."

Travis returned to Carlota. She had problems breathing. "Travis, how's Prescott?" she asked between gasps.

"In the same bad shape," Travis replied and listened to his aural-comm. "The paramedics have arrived. Hang in there." He then told the emergency team, "Dispatch one team to the balcony, the other to the bedroom for Carlota."

After they arrived, the paramedics attached respirators connected to oxygen bottles to both Prescott and Carlota. Without delay, they took them on stretchers to the roof where the medi-copter was waiting for them. The Rome Police and their CSI unit soon arrived and started their investigation at the crime scene in Carlota's apartment.

On the roof, Claire and Travis waited for the medi-copter to depart. After it left, their hover-copter landed on the pad. "Where to?" asked the pilot.

"Take us to the hospital," said Travis. "Follow them."

The hover-copter lifted up and followed the medi-copter in the distance.

"I'm so sorry about the mishap," the pilot apologized to Claire. "That gust of wind came out of nowhere."

"That's all right," said Claire. "These things can happen in the air."

"Where did the air gust come from?" Travis asked. "Which direction?"

"It came from the apartment," replied the pilot.

"I found the front door open," said Travis. "That might have caused the draft from the interior out."

"Did you find anyone at the door?" asked Claire.

"No, the door was wide open, and no one was nearby," said Travis.

"I've just confirmed the air vector with the onboard computer," said the pilot. "It came from the apartment."

"Do you have any idea what could have caused that?" asked Travis.

"No, not particularly. A window could have been opened somewhere else, or . . ." The pilot paused, thinking. "The elevator moving in its shaft could have pushed the current of air outward."

"I see what you mean," said Travis. "While the front door was open and the elevator moved, the increased air pressure burst out through the balcony."

"Yes, but only if the elevator door was open, too," said the pilot.

"Good point," admitted Travis, and he opened his aural comm with Glauser. "Albert, please get in touch with the police team at the apartment and see if the elevator door was tampered with."

"Yes, I will," acknowledged Glauser.

"A coincidence?" wondered Claire.

"I doubt it," said Travis. "Front doors and elevator doors don't open simultaneously of their own volition." Travis resumed contact with Glauser. "Albert, have the police check on the front door. How was it opened? And any bio-traces?"

"Will do," answered Glauser.

Their hover-copter approached the hospital's roof landing pad, where the medi-copter had already unloaded the two patients and was taking off again. Their hover-copter landed, and Claire and Travis jumped out and ran to the elevator.

"Glauser here. The police determined that the poison in the wine bottle was hemlock extract. The corridor elevator doors were opened with a bypass electronic key approximately 10 seconds after the front door was opened. And the front door was opened from inside."

"Thanks, Albert," acknowledged Travis. "How about the bio-traces?"

"They are working on those. I'll get back to you."

"An inside job?" wondered Claire as they were exiting the elevator.

"It seems that way," said Travis. "After seeing that I can jump off the hover-copter safely, why not sabotage your jump by opening the front door, opening the elevator corridor doors, and then calling the elevator up? The rush of air was enough to destabilize the hover-copter. Once the elevator arrived at the floor, the perpetrator rode it down and disappeared."

"Who the hell are these people?" Claire bit her lower lip in frustration.

They approached the nurse's station.

"*Prego, infermiera,*" Travis asked a nurse. "Do you know the status of Prescott Alighieri and Carlota Romano?"

"*Un momento.*" The nurse checked on her panel. "Dr. Virgilio will be with you shortly."

A tall policeman in uniform approached them. "Hello, I am Ispettore Del Favero with the Rome city police. You must be Prescott Alighieri's partners."

Claire and Travis introduced themselves. In their PAVs, they verified the credentials of Ispettore Del Favero.

"Do you have any information on Prescott and Ispettore Romano?" asked Claire.

"No, just like you, I'm waiting for Dottore Virgilio," he answered. "It's a terrible thing to be poisoned."

"Do you know where someone could have acquired hemlock?" asked Claire.

"Anywhere outside Rome, in the fields." Ispettore Del Favero made a motion as he listened to his aural-comm. "The bio-sensors have identified traces of Carlota, Prescott, and Carlota's maid, Edda Passarelli, within an hour before the poisoning."

"Were they able to locate Edda Passarelli?" asked Claire.

Ispettore Del Favero turned his attention to his aural-comm. "*Cosa?*" He paled. "*Dio mio!*"

He wiped sweat off his forehead and addressed Claire and Travis. "Yes, they found her with her throat slashed in the dumbwaiter."

Mit Sandru

Chapter 33. What Happened?

Travis and Claire exchanged troubled glances through their PAVs. Murder? There were powerful forces out there that wanted them and anyone else who interfered dead.

Two uniformed police officers approached Ispettore Del Favero, and they exchanged a few words, after which the two officers departed toward the ER.

"I'm sorry to tell you, but we've just opened a murder investigation," said the Ispettore. "Both Prescott Alighieri and Ispettore Carlota Romano are suspects. They will be under police guard."

"What?" Claire asked. "Prescott is a victim."

"That's what we need to determine," said the Ispettore.

"Ispettore Del Favero, you should be aware of what we just discovered on our way to the hospital," said Travis. The Ispettore raised his eyebrows inquisitively. Travis continued, "Claire German here had a near-deadly accident as she jumped from the hover-copter to Ispettore Romano's balcony to help her and Prescott. The front door of the apartment was open, the elevator corridor door was forced open, and the elevator was called up. The rush of air destabilized the copter, causing her to nearly miss the balcony. You can verify that with your officers at the scene."

Ispettore Del Favero contacted the officers at Romano's apartment, and a few seconds later he said, "That is correct about the doors. But we don't have proof about the air outflow. It cannot be verified."

"Yes, it can. The Vatican pilot has the data. But the point I'm trying to make is that I was on the balcony when this happened and Prescott was unconscious on the balcony's floor. He could not have opened the doors or killed the maid or poisoned himself and Ispettore Romano afterward."

Ispettore contacted his colleagues again. After listening intently, he let out a few curses in Italian to no one in particular. "I just verified the timing of the maid's murder. The maid was killed soon after you landed on the balcony, at about 13:20. It seems you are correct. Three people in the apartment—two are poisoned and one has her throat slashed. Prescott Alighieri seems to be the least of our suspects. Also, the cameras and recordings in the elevator and all other entrances were disabled. We have no recorded data about who came in or went out of the apartment, or the building, for that matter." He frowned and paced around, and, as if remembering something, he stopped and said, "The maid, Edda Passarelli, was murdered with her hands tied behind her back."

Claire put a hand on Travis's shoulder so as to prompt him to take the lead.

"Let's work on this together," said Travis. "We know that Carlota Romano invited Prescott for lunch and an old bottle of Chianti. The bottle in question was mentioned early this morning after we were ambushed. We know that at 12:37 Prescott was in Carlota's apartment and possibly had not drunk the wine yet. At 12:43, the first symptoms of distress were recorded. It did not become a full alert until 12:49, when we were notified of the emergency in our PAVs.

"By the time we jumped on Carlota's balcony, it was 12:58. Prescott was poisoned for 15 minutes by then. We don't know when Carlota drank her wine, but it must have been from the time Prescott drunk his to the time we arrived. Therefore, after I jumped and landed safely, Claire jumped at 13:01 but, because of the air gust, she missed, almost taking a fatal fall. It took her until 13:04 to get back with me on the balcony."

"I presume your sensors recorded all these times?" asked Ispettore Del Favero.

"Yes, our PAVs. Subject to verification by your department," said Travis. "By the time I swept the apartment for security and found Carlota in her bedroom, it was 13:21. The paramedics arrived at 13:26. I checked every room and closet, except the dumbwaiter in the kitchen. There was no one else in the apartment. But the maid was killed at 13:20 or just before I found Carlota gasping for air on the floor."

Ispettore Del Favero nodded.

Travis continued, "Possible scenarios: Prescott is out of commission and, if he's a suspect, he couldn't have done anything else other than poison the wine. Carlota and her maid are in the apartment. Probably at the same time I landed on the balcony, the apartment's door is opened, and the perpetrator commenced work on the elevator. It is 13:01, just in time for Claire to jump. The perpetrator could have taken the elevator to a lower or higher floor or to the lobby, but the cameras and recorders are on the fritz.

"But the maid is still alive," Travis went on. "Who killed her twenty minutes later? Maybe the suspect did not leave with the elevator. Maybe the suspect killed the maid, escaped down the dumbwaiter, and then disappeared. Where was the maid found?"

"The maid was found at the bottom," said Ispettore Del Favero. "So even if the surveillance cameras in the building were working, the suspect did not leave through the front door."

Travis rubbed his forehead. "Maybe there are two suspects: One took care of the copter with the front door and the other killed the maid. And then there is the more gruesome explanation—Carlota Romano is the killer."

Claire flinched. The Ispettore raised his eyebrows in shock.

"This is how it would work. We are involved in a very delicate and classified investigation, and very early this morning there was an ambush to kill us. They failed. Ispettore Romano takes a liking to Prescott and suggests getting together with him later for a bottle of Chianti. The motive could be to dispose of Prescott. As a Trinity Team, we are not effective without one of our partners. Why kill all three, when one will do?"

The Ispettore held his chin on the knuckles of one hand and listened intently.

"She invites Prescott to her apartment, poisons him, and, to cover up, she takes a sip of the poisoned wine as well. Before being able to call the emergency services, she finds out that we are on our way to her apartment. She retreats inside, where it occurs to her that she could kill Claire by causing the air current, and she almost succeeds. Her maid gets in the way, so she binds her, slashes her throat, sends her down the dumbwaiter, and then Carlota fakes her own dying in her bedroom."

"I have to admit. It fits the timing. It is possible," said Ispettore Del Favero, rubbing the back of his neck. "What would be the motive?"

"Maybe she is our mystery woman who ordered the ambush," said Claire. "The motive: she wants us dead or disabled."

"I read the transcript about last night's murder," said Ispettore. "Do you think that Ispettore Romano is the same woman who killed Sister Terina and then ordered your assassination?"

Travis shook his head slowly. "Not Sister Terina. Lucia Pietro killed her."

"Who really is this bitch?" said Claire under her breath, clearly pissed off.

"Ispettore, do you have a record of Ispettore Romano's whereabouts at the time Sister Terina was murdered?" asked Travis.

Ispettore Del Favero relayed the question and listened intently. "Her duty started at midnight, but she left her apartment at 21:00. We'll have to inquire about her whereabouts before her arrival."

A doctor in scrubs approached them. "Good afternoon, I am Dottore Virgilio."

"Good to see you, Doctor," said Claire. "How are Prescott and Carlota?"

"I was informed that this is police business, therefore I will be able to discuss their conditions," said Dottore Virgilio. "Let me start by telling you that your quick intervention was very helpful. The hemlock emulsion used as the poison would have killed them within an hour. The good news is that Ispettore Carlota Romano is in fair condition. She is sedated and on a respirator. By tonight, she should be able to talk to you."

Travis and Claire waited with abated breaths.

"As for Mr. Prescott Alighieri, the next twenty-four hours will be perilous. He is in critical condition."

"No!" Claire screamed, and tears ran down her cheeks.

"I'm very sorry, *Signorina*," said the doctor.

"Travis, what do we do?" Claire seemed desperate.

"Dottore Virgilio, we will stay on duty with Prescott tonight," said Travis. "Please make accommodations."

"But for what purpose?" the doctor asked.

"To rescue him from death," said Travis in a firm voice.

"But—" objected the doctor.

"I suggest you grant them what they ask you, Dottore," said Ispettore Del Favero, who added, "Police business. I will triple the security in and around the hospital."

"Very well." The doctor left.

"I'm afraid for Ispettore Romano's own life," said Ispettore Del Favero. "If she were just a pawn in this whole affair, she would be next to be disposed of. On the other hand, if she did it, she might try to escape."

Mit Sandru

Chapter 34. Help Is Needed

"You'll have to excuse us, Ispettore Del Favero. We have a meeting with the Holy Father at four o'clock," said Claire, and they departed.

She and Travis exited the hospital and took a robo-taxi to the Vatican. In the cab, they initiated full cloak status on their conversation.

"We need help," said Claire. Travis nodded, and both of them made contact with TIO.

Maximus appeared in their PAVs. "It's getting hot over there for you," Maximus said. "Prescott OK?"

"We'll spend the night with him to help him," said Claire.

"That will be good. What do you need?" asked Maximus.

"We need a medical team for the Pope," said Claire.

"That bad?" Maximus's computer-generated lips tightened. "Request submitted. Why?"

"We believe the Pope is in danger from his doctor performing surgery on him," said Claire. "We need a complete team: two surgeons, an anesthesiologist, and a nurse."

"You realize you're asking for a four-person team. This is highly confidential. Four more people will need to keep silent after the surgery."

"Please try to put a team together consisting of four people who don't know each other or about each other. Is Dr. Stark available?" asked Claire.

"He is in Switzerland. How fortunate, wouldn't you say?" said Maximus. "I'll contact him and check his availability. If he's available, there will be one less doctor to locate. "

"We will need a technical team to analyze if the Pope's medical quarters are safe to perform the surgery in: the equipment, the anesthesiologist robot, and the medical assistant robot," demanded Travis. "They don't need to know what will happen in the medical quarters. And we need their help fast."

"Understood." Maximus paused, verifying the availability of such experts. "You're in luck. There is just such a team in Rome doing routine diagnostics at Nuovo Concordia Roma Hospital. I'll dispatch agents from AISI, the Italian Internal Information and Security Agency, to escort them to the Vatican as soon as they are available."

"Good," said Travis. "If they find everything in order, maybe, just maybe, we will need a smaller medical team. We'll have to consult with Dr. Stark."

"I hope so. It will mean fewer security complications. If there are no other issues, good luck!" Maximus disconnected.

"I'll inform Glauser about the technical team," Travis said to Claire. He opened his comm to speak with him.

"Glauser here. How's Prescott?"

"In critical condition. Albert, we need your help." Without waiting for his response, Travis continued. "A technical team will arrive at the Vatican soon, and they will need access to the Pope's medical quarters."

"Why? Do you expect the Holy Father will require medical attention?"

"In case there is such a need, we want to make sure that everything is in working condition, and for other medical eventualities that may arise."

"Very well, I will take the necessary steps." Oberst Glauser did not inquire about what other eventualities entailed.

"Also, please take Dottore Pietro into custody," said Travis.

"Very well," said Glauser, nonplussed. "But, in case of emergency, who will take care of the Holy Father?"

"We have an external medical team being assembled as we speak," said Travis.

"It sounds like trouble," said Glauser darkly. "It seems you expect an emergency."

"Yes, we do," said Claire. "One more thing, Albert—please investigate Dottore Pietro's staff, especially those who would be assisting him in any emergency and especially any females."

"There are no females on his staff," responded Glauser. "But I understand what you need, and I'll have my men investigate the medical staff. By the way, do the Monsignore and the Holy Father know about this?"

"We have a private meeting with the Holy Father at four o'clock," said Claire. "We will explain the situation then."

"As for the Monsignore, please don't divulge any information to him," said Travis.

"Is he a suspect?"

Chapter 35. The Holy Father

At the doors of the papal apartment, two Swiss Guards saluted when they saw Claire and Travis approach. Their Oberst had informed them of the visit, and one of them opened the door. Monsignore Giuseppe raised his head from his writing tablet and looked at them with surprise, seeing just the two of them.

"We're here for our appointment with the Holy Father, Monsignore," said Claire.

Without a word, the Monsignore activated his comm device. "Your Holiness, Travis and Claire are here to see you." He nodded and bowed slightly. "Right away, Your Holiness." He straightened up. "This way, please."

Instead of entering the Pope's living quarters, the Monsignore took them to another door and let them into the Pope's private office. He did not join them inside. The high-back, white armchair behind the large mahogany desk was empty at the moment. The desk was lustrous and clean, except for the typical electronic devices needed to communicate and review documents. Behind the desk, two tall windows with long sheer draperies flanked a painting of the Pietà. Ornate, shaded floor lamps occupied each corner of the room, dispersing soft light on the tapestry-laden walls. It was quiet in here. In front of the desk, four gold-and-white upholstered fauteuil chairs were lined up and awaiting visitors.

Claire and Travis sat down and waited. A side door on the left side of the office opened. The Monsignore allowed the Pope to enter and then closed the door behind him. They stood up, waiting for the Pope to sit down on his armchair behind the desk, but instead he approached them with a serene smile. The gold crucifix bounced on his large belly.

"Oberst Glauser informed me of the troubles you have encountered. How is Prescott? I pray for him." The Pope sat down sideways on a chair next to them.

"Thank you for seeing us, Your Holiness," said Claire. "Prescott is in critical condition, but after our meeting we will return to the hospital and help him recover more quickly."

The Pope smiled hopefully at her and nodded a few times.

"First of all, how do you feel, Your Holiness?" Claire asked.

"Considering my situation, fairly well. However, I don't know what kind of symptoms I should experience. I asked Dottore Pietro to prognosticate what I should feel by the time the fetus is mature and ready to be born. He told me that I should not expect to have any cramps, which women usually have when they enter labor, but I should feel increased pressure and movement in my belly."

"We are glad you feel well, Your Holiness. There are important matters that we must inform you of regarding your situation," said

Claire. "We need to take additional precautionary measures."

The Pope gestured for them to continue.

"We asked Oberst Glauser to take Dottore Pietro in custody. We have reasons to believe that your Dottore may bring harm to you and the fetus."

The Pope leaned back in his chair, but he did not show any emotion.

"Also, we requested a technical team to inspect the reliability of the equipment in your medical quarters," continued Claire.

"You foresee sabotage of the equipment," said the Pope.

"We want to make sure that there will be no harm brought to you by the equipment or the people operating it."

"Since my Dottore is detained, who will perform the surgery on me?"

"We requested a new medical team to stand by and take action as needed," said Claire.

"This is a very grave matter for our Church," said the Pope. "I'll ask my Camerlengo, Cardinal Bertrand, to find a trusted doctor and small staff from one of our Catholic hospitals."

"We understand, Your Holiness," said Travis. "We've asked Dr. Stark, who knows about your case, to be the surgeon or assisting surgeon, as the case may be."

"That's prudent." The Pope glanced sideways as if in thought. "I haven't had a complete report from you, so please tell me what you found out and what suspicions you have."

"Certainly, Your Holiness," said Travis. He cleared his throat. "Satan's minions intended to have his son born from his essence and from the flesh of a holy man, such as yourself. In order to do that, they needed a woman of the church to, for lack of a better word, inseminate you. This occurred on March 6, when Sister Terina kissed your ring and, intentionally, your finger. That was the touch of the evil."

"Are you saying that a sister of the Church was the agent of Satan?" The Pope's eyes were wide open with surprise.

"No, Your Holiness, she was an unwilling participant," answered Travis quickly. "Someone she trusted entrapped her and enabled the devil's access to her soul. At the time of the kiss, Sister Terina was possessed by the devil. We don't know yet who carried out the deed of entrapping her in Satan's web. We suspect a woman was involved in this, and we believe it was Lucia Pietro, the Dottore's wife. She murdered Sister Terina and had two Swiss Guards shot by snipers."

The Pope bowed his head, said a prayer, and made the sign of the cross. "Please continue," he said with sadness in his voice.

"The same woman, Lucia perhaps, was behind an attempted assassination on us after Sister Terina was murdered. We were able to extract an important memory from Sister Terina's mind that might contain the identity of who carried out Satan's plan. Unfortunately, we haven't been able to understand Sister

Terina's memory yet. As soon as Prescott's health is restored and he is back on his feet with us, we will decipher her memory."

"Why are you suspicious of Dottore Pietro? He is my doctor and has served me well for many, many years."

"We suspect that Dottore Pietro has fallen for Satan," said Claire this time. "He and his wife were devastated by the deaths of their two sons. They lost their faith in God, while Satan gave them hope for revenge and a reunion with their sons. The two young men who caused their sons' deaths were killed. They were burned alive in an industrial oven."

The Pope gasped.

"Probably, Dr. Pietro and his wife, or their accomplices, committed the murders. But they have solid alibis. In their minds, that act may be Satan's compensation for what they did or will do on his behalf."

The Pope sighed heavily.

"After you were contaminated with the evil essence, Dr. Pietro was in a perfect position to take care of you and make sure you gave birth to Satan's son," said Claire. "Even if you decided to abort the fetus, he probably had plans to place that fetus in an incubator and bring him to maturity. He didn't know that God had thwarted Satan's plan when Monsignore Giuseppe introduced the DNA of a thousand-year-old woman into your body on April 11, reversing the genes of the fetus to those of a normal male fetus.

"At first, when we discovered the female genes, Dr. Pietro thought that Satan used Pope Joan's DNA—a perfect exploit, he thought. At that time, he was the champion and future guardian of Satan's son. But then, when we discovered through our investigation that the woman's DNA, brought by the Monsignore, had reversed Satan's doing, he changed his mind. Dr. Pietro wants to kill the fetus, or both of you, whichever assures the destruction of the fetus."

"Well, thank God and Monsignore Giuseppe for bringing the good DNA," said the Pope.

"It is good." Travis looked the Pope straight in the eyes. "However, Monsignore Giuseppe is the second perpetrator, although he served God."

"I don't understand how that could be. He did a good deed," said the Pope.

"He had a choice, Your Holiness," said Travis.

"A choice, what choice?"

"He was commanded by God to use the essence of a saint, but he chose what he believed to be Pope Joan's essence."

The Pope looked intently at Travis in disbelief and in alarm. "Are you sure the DNA belongs to Pope Joan?"

"No, we don't know if the dead woman was Pope Joan, Your Holiness," said Travis. "However, Monsignore Giuseppe believes it to be true. That's why he was willing to die and kill us with him in the catacombs when he caused the gas pipe breakage, to keep Pope Joan's genes a secret."

"*Dio mio*," whispered the Pope. "Why then is Monsignore Giuseppe a threat?"

"He wants to see the fetus born at all costs. Even if it means killing you, if you decide to abort."

The Pope leaned his head in his hands, overwhelmed by what he had heard. "Those are grave accusations."

"They are, Your Holiness," said Travis. "Within your inner circle there are people who want the fetus born, some who want the fetus dead, and others who want you dead."

The Pope raised his head and looked somber. "There is always someone who wants me dead. That doesn't frighten me. What saddens me is that people I know, who are close to me, are using this situation to further their goals."

Claire and Travis exchanged quick glances. The Pope was well aware of what was going on at the Vatican.

"You have discovered much, and I thank you," said the Pope. "What I wanted most was to be sure that the fetus is good, God's gift. You've done well." The Pope paused as if gathering his thoughts. "You might like to know what my wishes in this matter are. I want to see this baby born, even if my life is at risk. I believe this child will be special."

"We understand, Your Holiness," said Claire. "That's why we've taken these precautions. I am sure your life is not in jeopardy with the new medical team."

"God will guide us all." The Pope made the sign of the cross. "Now, the woman who killed so many innocent people: Are you sure she is the Dottore's wife?"

"We have strong suspicions," said Travis. "Although there is a slight chance that there may be another suspect, another woman."

The Pope startled and then shook his head. "Another woman suspect."

"One such suspect is Ispettore Romano of the Rome police," said Travis. "We will be sure after we talk to her and decipher Sister Terina's memory. In the meantime, we need to remain at high alert, Your Holiness."

The Pope winced as if in pain.

"Your Holiness, are you all right?" asked Claire.

"I felt a pressure here." The Pope pointed to the area of his stomach where the fetus was located. "But I'm better now."

"Shall we summon medical help?" asked Claire.

"I'm better, I'm better. I'll contact Cardinal Bertrand for the medical help." He stood and walked to his desk, where he sat, clasping his hands together. "There is a matter you need to know about."

Claire and Travis were all ears.

"There is a select group of thirteen cardinals, headed by Cardinal Cellini," said the Pope. "Just like Jesus and his apostles. They are very dedicated to the Church, and, as such, sometimes they are too eager to step outside boundaries. Cardinal Cellini told them about my situation, and they fear the consequences of giving birth to the baby."

"Your Holiness, are you in danger from them?" Claire asked.

"No, not at all. They want to persuade me to give up the fetus. They even concocted an action against you, believing that you gave me unwise advice."

"You don't mean to say that they were involved in the ambush against us?" Travis asked.

"No, they were not. They wanted to use a woman with paranormal abilities to dissuade you from continuing this investigation. Cardinal Le Pere is part of that group. He contacted that woman and informed her who she would be dealing with. At the name of the Capuchin Trinity Team, she almost ran for the hills. Cardinal Le Pere is a persuasive man of faith and convinced the woman to give the impression to the cardinals that she is doing her best to get rid of you."

Travis smiled widely. "We know who this woman is. I bet she didn't want anything to do with us. She is just a pretend witch."

"We're not worried about her." Claire smiled, too.

"Your Holiness, are you sure you'll not be at risk from this zealous group of cardinals?" Travis asked.

"I fear nothing from them. I have Cardinal Le Pere among them, and he will keep them in check," said the Pope. He looked thoughtful. "What shall we do about Monsignore Giuseppe?"

Chapter 36. Monsignore Giuseppe's Confession

"I will ask Monsignore Giuseppe to give me his confession," the Pope said, straightening up. He turned to the intercom and asked Monsignore to come in. "Please stay and witness his confession," he told Claire and Travis.

The door opened and Monsignore Giuseppe came in. "How may I be of assistance, Your Holiness?"

"Monsignore Giuseppe, please take a seat." The Pope indicated one of the two unoccupied chairs. The Monsignore did as he was instructed, sitting straight up with his hands folded in his lap. The Holy Father interlaced his fingers and rested his hands on the desk.

"Monsignore Giuseppe, you have been with me for a long time, and I value the dedication and excellent service you have provided me and the Holy See." The Pope paused. "The Capuchin Trinity Team brought to my attention disheartening news about the matter they were hired to investigate."

Monsignore Giuseppe bowed slightly and smiled, as if concurring with what the Pope said.

The Pope looked into the Monsignore's eyes. "Monsignore Giuseppe, Claire and Travis will remain here in my office to hear your confession about your sin."

Monsignore Giuseppe's eyes widened in surprise and shock. "My, my sin, Your Holiness?"

"Yes. Please tell us all you know about your intervention on behalf of the fetus."

Monsignore Giuseppe buried his face in his hands and started crying. They waited until he calmed down. After wiping his tears with his handkerchief, he collected himself. "I only did what I did as instructed by God," he said calmly.

"Then tell us so we can understand, Monsignore Giuseppe," said the Pope.

"The night before Easter, I saw an apparition as I was praying. A bright light appeared on the wall in front of me. It was warm and calming. I felt so happy seeing it. It flooded my soul with love and acceptance. I knew God was present. I had heard about such apparitions, but this was the first time it had happened to me.

"Tears of joy ran down my cheeks. I was speechless, although I continued praying to Him quietly. Singing angels surrounded me, and the entire room seemed to have disappeared among white clouds. I was in a welcoming place, in a state of bliss.

"God spoke to me in a warm, fatherly voice. 'Giuseppe, my son, I need your help.' I nodded, accepting whatever God wanted of me, and then He continued, 'A great harm has been done by Satan against the Holy Father. Of the harm, you will soon learn. In the meanwhile, I need you to bring the essence of Santa

Francesca Romana to the Holy Father and deliver it to him tomorrow on Easter Sunday.'

"I left early on Easter Sunday to go to the Church of Santa Francesca Romana, however, I decided first to go and pray for Brother Luca at the Basilica di San Clemente, after which I was to stop at the Church of Santa Francesca Romana.

"As I was praying for Brother Luca's soul, I heard a woman's voice say, 'Papessa Giovanna.' I stopped my prayers and looked around, but I was alone. I prayed, and again I heard, 'Papessa Giovanna.' I knew about the name and the myth of Pope Joan, but I never thought I would hear it so clearly, right there, in the Basilica di San Clemente. And why now, while I was praying for Brother Luca?

"I sat down against the cold wall, and a thought crossed my mind: What if Pope Joan had lived once? She dedicated her whole life to the Church, and, because of her knowledge and good deeds, she was elected to be the pope. And did she sin by bringing a baby to life? No. I thought she was saintly. I felt that she was castigated to oblivion by the fear of having a woman pope. She should have been a saint.

"Yes. I felt reassured by the realization that Pope Joan is an unacknowledged saint. I kneeled and prayed again for her soul, and I heard the woman's voice say, 'You chose right.' I asked in a loud voice, 'What do you mean, what did I do?' The voice answered back, 'You chose Papessa Giovanna, you chose right. Follow the path of light to obtain her essence.'

"The path ahead of me glowed, and I followed it. It took me through drainage tunnels several levels below ground. There I found a wooden gate, which I opened and entered into the underground catacombs. The illuminated path took me to the stone burial box, which later the Capuchin Trinity Team discovered. I kneeled and prayed there. The woman's voice told me, 'You've done well. Go in peace back to the Holy City.' I returned to the Vatican for the Easter Sunday mass."

"Those were your foot prints in the catacombs, near the burial box," said Travis. "We detected your knee marks where you prayed as well. It was you who placed the padlock on the wooden gate. Later, when we sought shelter from the gas, you lost the key when we lifted you to place you in the box."

"Yes, I did all that."

"And then?" asked Travis.

"The next thing I remember, I was kissing the Holy Father's ring, and I was so overwhelmed by his aura that I kissed his hand. The Easter liturgy followed, and all was well. I forgot about the whole affair until we found out about the fetus the Holy Father was carrying. I remember the words of God, 'A great harm has been done by Satan against the Holy Father. Of the harm, you will soon learn.' And now I know about the harm. My God!" Monsignore Giuseppe looked upward toward heaven.

"Why did you alter the visual record by two minutes when you kissed His Holiness's hand?" asked Travis.

"I didn't do that."

"Are you sure?"

"Well. Maybe."

"Indeed," said Travis. "You were not the only one who had public visual recordings," said Travis. "Oberst Glauser had another recording. And that wasn't altered."

The Monsignore stared at Travis as if someone had pulled the rug out from under him and he was about to topple. "But, but, Your Holiness, I was instrumental in stopping Satan, as God instructed me. I don't understand even now why I chose Pope Joan, but I was told to do so. I felt certain that I did the right thing. Later, when the Trinity Team came to investigate and soon after they suspected Pope Joan's DNA, I was worried about what would happen if the truth were discovered. The fetus, undoubtedly, would be harmed. That's why I went back to the catacombs before taking them there and rigged the gas pipe to start a gas leak."

"That's why your hand was bandaged and why the worker in the Basilica's courtyard asked you if the plumbing tools were useful," said Travis coldly.

"I didn't know you understood Italian," said the Monsignore in surprise.

"Even if we don't, our PAVs are able to translate. Later, when we reviewed the conversation, we realized that you were the one who wanted us dead. You closed the round stone and opened the gas pipe while we were digging the rocks out of the burial box."

The Monsignore nodded.

"You were willing to kill yourself along with us?" asked Claire.

Monsignore Giuseppe looked at Claire with sad eyes. "I would rather die than allow harm to the fetus. The boy must be born. He will do great things for mankind. You were quick to find out what happened, and I was afraid that the Holy Father would allow the Dottore to kill the fetus. And why not? Pope Joan discredited the Church. She was erased from history. But she is a saint. Her essence came to life again to defeat Satan.

"You three of the Capuchin Trinity Team are either the biggest villains in this world or angels. I think you are angels, and for all you've uncovered and for convincing the Holy Father to keep the baby, I thank you and ask forgiveness for attempting to kill you. Holy Father, please forgive me for what I have done." Monsignore Giuseppe began weeping quietly again.

"What did you do with the gas mask under your hat?" asked Travis.

Monsignore Giuseppe recoiled. "Wha-wha-what gas mask?"

"Don't play games with us. You were not so willing to die after all." Travis narrowed his eyes.

"How did you know about the gas mask?" Monsignore Giuseppe looked defeated.

"We didn't, until now. But thank you for telling us."

The Monsignore slid down from his chair onto his knees. He was red as his sash. He lowered his head to the floor, as if in deep prayer.

Claire cleared her throat. "Monsignore Giuseppe, do you have anything to say about Dottore Pietro?"

Monsignore Giuseppe raised his head, surprised. "You suspect him, too?"

"What do you suspect him of?" Claire asked.

"He wants the baby dead." Monsignore Giuseppe started crying again. "Forgive me, Your Holiness, but I made plans to kill the Dottore tonight."

The Pope was taken aback, hearing the murderous thoughts expressed by the Monsignore. "Well, as it happens, thank God, you won't have to commit murder and enter hell. Oberst Glauser will have Dottore Pietro soon in custody, thanks to the Capuchin Trinity Team."

"That's a revelation, Monsignore," said Claire. "Originally we thought you were in cahoots with the Dottore, but since you didn't tell him that the gas explosion was an attempt on our lives, you cleared yourself on that suspicion. However, what else can you tell us about the Dottore?"

"He has a dark soul."

"Where were you going to kill him?" Claire asked.

"I was planning to stab him, tonight, at the medical quarters."

"What can you tell us about Lucia Pietro, the Dottore's wife?" asked Claire.

"Hmm?" The Monsignore wondered dumbly, looking from Claire to Travis.

"Who do you think caused the evil essence to contaminate the Holy Father on March 6?" Travis asked.

"Sister Terina." The Monsignore stared with wide, watery eyes at him.

"Sister Terina is a victim," said Travis. "Who unknowingly helped the devil breach her religious aura?"

The Monsignore shrugged and shook his head. "What religious aura?"

Claire and Travis exchanged glances in their PAVs. He had no idea. This was a dead end.

Monsignore Giuseppe turned on his knees to face the Pope. "My Holy Father, please forgive me. I have sinned. I have sinned gravely."

"You are lucky that no one has been killed," said the Pope. "The Vatican will have to pay for the damage caused by your explosion." The Pope looked at him with pity, shaking his head slowly. "You are forgiven, my son. In the name of the Father, the Son, and the Holy Spirit, amen." The Pope blessed Monsignore Giuseppe.

Hearing that, Monsignore Giuseppe bowed his head to the floor and started praying.

"You should ask forgiveness from Claire and Travis, and from Prescott, who is in the hospital in critical condition, poisoned," said the Pope sternly.

The Monsignore turned on his knees to Claire and Travis. "Please forgive me, Claire, Travis, and especially Prescott. God bless you, God bless you." He buried his hands in his palms and started sobbing.

Claire felt sorry for him. Travis felt an urge to slap him for breaking the gas pipe in the underground. Then he came to his senses; kicking him would be better. But it would not be proper to kick the shit out of him in front of the Pope.

"Monsignore Giuseppe, please rise," asked the Pope. "If you want to be with God, I suggest you select a secluded monastery, where you should spend the rest of your life praying and asking for forgiveness from God."

Chapter 37. Ispettore Carlota Romano

Claire and Travis were on their way to the hospital. Their PAVs had a message from Oberst Glauser; he had arrested the Dottore and had him within the Vatican's walls.

"Well, two out of the way, and one or—maybe two—more to go," said Travis.

"Except the Monsignore is small potatoes and an accidental villain," replied Claire. "At least with the Dottore behind bars, he won't be able to hurt the Pope. I wonder if Lucia Pietro is hiding, running away, or plotting to finish the job."

"She is very resourceful," said Travis. "I think she will do everything possible to kill the unborn child. And the only way to do that is to get inside the Vatican and get near the Pope."

"What if she stays in hiding and kills the boy after he's born?" wondered Claire.

"Maybe." A thought crossed his mind. "What if the baby is born at night and must be killed before sunrise?"

As they were going through the lobby of the hospital, Lucia Pietro's face appeared on the holodisplays, asking people to call the Rome police if they knew of her whereabouts. At least the fact that the public knew her now would make her movements more difficult.

Ispettore Del Favero was sipping from a disposable cup of coffee, chatting with another policeman outside Carlota's room. "I hope everything went well with the Holy Father," said the Ispettore, a trace of respect and envy in his voice. He probably had never met anyone before who had access to the Pope like they did.

"Actually, not bad," said Claire. "But the danger is not over yet."

"Would you care to explain what the danger is and how the Holy Father is involved?" asked Ispettore Del Favero.

"The danger is Lucia Pietro, who killed three people, almost killed us, and now Prescott is in grave condition," said Claire, omitting to include the Pope's involvement. "How are Carlota and Prescott?"

"Ispettore Romano is doing well," said Ispettore Del Favero. "Prescott is in critical but stable condition, according to the latest report from the doctor."

Claire inhaled deeply to calm her anxiety.

"Did you talk to Ispettore Romano?" asked Travis.

"Not yet. We are waiting for the doctor to give us permission," replied Ispettore Del Favero. As he finished saying that, the door opened and Dottore Virgilio came out of Carlota Romano's room.

"*Tutto va bene.* Ispettore Romano is fine," said the doctor. "She wants to talk to you as soon as possible."

"How's Prescott?" asked Claire.

"Prescott is still in critical but stable condition. I've had two lounges set up near his bed, as you requested."

"Thank you, Dottore Virgilio, we appreciate your help," replied Claire. They walked to Carlota's room. "Because they removed Prescott's PAV, I feel uncomfortable not knowing his situation, minute by minute." Travis acknowledged Claire's concern with a slight nod.

Ispettore Del Favero was waiting at the open door, expecting Claire and Travis to join him.

"*Ciao*, Carlota!" he said, smiling, as he entered in the room. "*Come ti senti*? How do you feel?"

Carlota Romano lay in the hospital bed without any hookups to assist her recovery and most life support equipment turned off. A slight odor of medication lingered in the air. She looked pale, but otherwise fine.

"Very well, considering," she said in a hoarse voice. "How is Prescott?"

"Fair, but not out of the woods yet."

"I hoped you had better news," she said. "Claire and Travis, I'm so sorry for what happened. My poor Edda was killed." Tears streamed down her face. She dabbed her face with a tissue and said, "What's going on?"

"That's what we would like to know," said Ispettore Del Favero. "Please tell us what happened."

Carlota scooted up to sit in a better position. "Before Prescott arrived, Edda set up the table on the terrace, and she opened the bottle of

Chianti to breathe. Prescott arrived and brought me flowers, and we sat at the table outside and chatted. I believe he received a call from you, Travis."

Travis nodded.

"After that, we decided not to talk police business, and I poured some wine into our glasses. We toasted, and both of us took a sip. I received a call—a woman started talking to me about some interior design ideas that I was researching. She went on and on, until I finally ended the conversation. I took another sip of my wine, and then I saw Prescott lying on the floor, unconscious.

"I checked his vital signs and then I ran to my bedroom where I kept the first-aid kit. I felt dizzy, and after I removed the bag from the closet, I blacked out. I remember talking to you Travis, and after that I woke up here in the hospital to find out that we were poisoned with hemlock. How Greek!" She chuckled bitterly at her allusion to Socrates' death.

"I'm glad you feel better," said Ispettore Del Favero. "We have questions. Did you know that the wine was poisoned?"

"No, it was an unopened bottle, at least until Edda opened it."

"Do you have any reason to suspect that Edda poisoned the wine?"

"No. Not her. She has been with me since I was a girl."

"As it happens, the wine was poisoned prior to being opened. The cork was penetrated by a needle that injected the poison in the bottle," said Ispettore Del Favero. "Do you know what that means?"

"There was someone else who poisoned the bottle in my apartment?" Carlota questioned.

Ispettore Del Favero nodded. "Was there someone else in your apartment?"

"No, not that I know of. Besides, the sensors did not alert me."

"It seems that the entire video security of the building was sabotaged, as well as the sensors in your apartment."

Carlota widened her eyes in shock when she heard that information.

"Why didn't you call emergency when you saw that Prescott was unconscious?"

"Well, I am trained to give first-aid assistance. Besides, I didn't know we were poisoned at the time."

"What's the real reason you invited Prescott Alighieri over to your apartment?" asked Ispettore Del Favero raising his eyebrows.

"I like him. He's cute," said Carlota, blushing. "That's all. I wanted to impress him with a good bottle of old Chianti. To show him some Italian hospitality."

Travis and Claire observed the interrogation without saying a word. Their PAVs, however, were set on full analysis of her emotions, and, so far, she had told the truth.

"Where were you last night before you responded to the emergency call at Suore Mantellate Serve di Sofia?"

Carlota hesitated before answering, "It's a private matter." She seemed to be embarrassed about what she may have done during that time. "I have an alibi, if that's what you're after. But I'd rather not bring this person into the investigation. Also, if you think that I may be the killer, I'm not."

The corners of Ispettore Del Favero's mouth bent downward in disappointment when he heard about Carlota not divulging her whereabouts at the time Sister Terina was killed. With his head cocked to the side, he said, "Right now, it is all right not to give us that detail, but if the evidence will be stacked against you, I urge you to reconsider."

"I fully understand the implications." Carlota Romano crossed her arms.

Ispettore Del Favero glanced over at Claire and Travis. "Anything you would like to ask of Ispettore Romano?"

"Yes, I would," said Claire. "Carlota, about your maid, Edda: Where was she while Prescott was with you?"

"Most likely in her room. Unless I need her assistance, she usually watches her favorite shows."

"And the last time you saw her was when?" Claire asked.

"Shortly before Prescott arrived," answered Carlota. "I didn't kill my maid."

"We believe you," said Travis instead. "Who was the woman who called and distracted you from drinking the wine?"

"Hmm. I know she was talking about my recent interest in redecorating, but she was no one I recognized."

"Just audio, no video?"

"Yes, just audio."

"It's very coincidental that she called you just as you toasted and you were about to drink the wine, don't you think?" Travis paced around the room.

Carlota's eyebrows furrowed in alert. "Someone was watching us?"

Travis nodded. "Hold on a second, I have an idea." He input some coded commands into his PAV. "Prescott's PAV alert level was lowered, but its audio recording capabilities were on. I just downloaded from his PAV what he heard during your conversation." Travis gave another command to the PAV. "Prescott's PAV picked up the woman's voice, too, and my PAV will replay the conversation at audible volumes and equalize your voice and hers. Let's listen."

Travis's PAV initiated the broadcast of the conversation. It was in Italian, and Carlota and the other woman were speaking rapidly. Carlota was making efforts to conclude the conversation, but the other woman went on explaining decorating choices.

"Do you remember it?" Travis asked.

"Yes, that's her," said Carlota. "But who that woman is, I don't know."

"We weren't able to locate the caller. The call came via a disposable comm," said Ispettore Del Favero.

"Travis, please play it again, just the woman's voice," asked Claire. Travis complied and Claire listened intently. "That sounds like Lucia Pietro."

Chapter 38. Prescott Alighieri

"Are you sure?" exclaimed Carlota. "Lucia Pietro?"

Claire checked her PAV. "Ninety percent match."

"Incredible! Lucia Pietro strikes again," said Travis. "Judging by how she killed Sister Terina, she is a master of disguise and of bio-molecular stealth. And knowledgeable about disabling security systems. No wonder, Ispettore Del Favero, that your officers couldn't find traces of anyone else in Ispettore Romano's apartment."

"You're saying that Lucia Pietro was in my apartment all that time?" Carlota Romano asked.

"Yes," said Travis. "She probably came in through the dumbwaiter."

"Regrettably, we don't have any strong evidence connecting her to the crimes," said Claire. "Even the voice is only a ninety percent match."

Travis faced Carlota. "In any case, for our part, we are satisfied with the information you've given us, Ispettore Romano. Lucia Pietro is still the primary suspect, but without much hard evidence." He added silently in Claire's PAV, "Let's make sure that Lucia keeps away from the Pope. She seems good at avoiding detection." Travis sent a message to Oberst Glauser.

"Well, Ispettore Romano, I hope that you'll feel better soon and that you are discharged quickly," said Claire.

"*Mille grazie*, and call me Carlota."

"Sure, Carlota. But, if you'll excuse us, we need to attend to our colleague next door."

"Say hello to Prescott for me when he wakes up." Carlota looked pained when she mentioned Prescott's name.

"We will," said Claire.

Dottore Virgilio escorted Claire and Travis to Prescott's recovery room. A nurse was waiting for them near his bed. He had the respirator attached to his mouth and several IV tubes affixed to his arms. An apparatus performed blood filtration to remove the poison. Other sensors were attached under his gown, monitoring his vital signs. The life support systems blinked and beeped from time to time. His complexion was as white as the sheets of the bed, his lips purple.

"He's doing better, but it will take time," said Dottore Virgilio.

"That's what we don't have—time," said Travis. "We will help him recover faster."

Travis and Claire sat on the two lounges, which were positioned near the bed facing Prescott. They extended the backs of their hands to the nurse so she could attach the IV needles.

"What exactly are you going to do?" Dottore Virgilio asked.

"For an observer it won't look like anything unusual," said Claire, wincing as the needle penetrated the back of her hand. "We will be holding hands with Prescott, and we will infuse him with our life energy while we are in a trance. Our metabolisms will increase, therefore the need for IVs."

"Very unorthodox," said Dottore Virgilio.

"But effective," said Travis, taking Claire's hand across Prescott's body and also Prescott's hand. Claire took Prescott's other hand and relaxed in her chair, ready to start the life infusion. A few moments later, both of them had their eyes closed in a state of semi-consciousness.

"What are we supposed to do, Dottore Virgilio?" asked the nurse.

"*Niente, infermiera*. Nothing, nurse. We will leave them alone until they wake up. You may go back to your station and monitor Signore Alighieri's vital signs. I'll be on call. Don't hesitate to let me know if anything goes wrong."

It was eight o'clock in the morning when Travis and Claire opened their eyes. Their IV bags were empty. They removed the connections to the IV needles and visited the nearest bathrooms. When they returned, Prescott was awake. Based on his vital signs, he was doing well, and the nurse on duty had already removed his respirator. He had no difficulty breathing on his own. He looked around, disoriented, until he saw Claire and Travis, and then smiled on seeing them. They offered their hands to the nurse to remove the IV needles.

"How are you doing, Prescott?" Claire asked.

"How's your hangover?" Travis asked.

Prescott made as if to sit up, but the nurse pushed him gently back down. "Dottore Virgilio was notified, and he will be here soon to check you out. If he says you're doing well, we'll remove the catheter and all the other life-assisting apparatuses."

"Relax, Prescott," said Claire in a soothing voice.

Prescott nodded and closed his eyes. "How is Carlota?"

"She's doing well," said Claire.

Dottore Virgilio hurried into the room. "Prescott, you're looking well, and your vitals are almost back to normal." He inspected the screens on the life support machine. "Please excuse us, Claire and Travis, I need to attend to my patient."

Claire and Travis waved to Prescott and left the room. "Breakfast?" asked Travis on their way to the lobby.

"Even hospital food sounds good right now," replied Claire.

It was not until an hour later when they returned to see Prescott. He was sitting on his bed, feet dangling, enjoying his breakfast of solid food.

"Hungry?" asked Claire.

"Mm-hmm," he acknowledged, taking a long drink from his juice cup. "Thanks, guys."

"Don't mention it," said Travis. "How do you feel?"

"Good! A little drowsy from the medication they gave me, but, otherwise, I'm ready to roll out of here by noon."

"Prescott, we need to know what you remember," Claire asked.

"I remember arriving at Carlota's apartment with flowers." Prescott blushed, and Claire patted him on the hand. "We went to the terrace, and she received a call. I remember Carlota talking on her comm and I was drinking wine. That's all. The doctor told me that Carlota and I were poisoned. He said that Carlota was fine and she was released last night."

"Yes, she's doing OK," said Claire.

"Now it's your turn. What happened?" Prescott asked.

Claire and Travis alternated in telling him what had transpired since he was last conscious.

"So, the Monsignore had a gas mask with him," Prescott said, satisfied about his intuition regarding the gas mask under the Monsignore's hat.

"Right on the mark," said Travis.

"Lucia Pietro is a resourceful woman," said Prescott.

"Definitely," Claire said.

"How did she know about my lunch date with Carlota?" Prescott wondered. "And she poisoned the bottle before I arrived."

"Good point, and that's what worries me," said Claire. "So far she's been one step ahead of us. With the Dottore in custody, she may be handicapped now."

"If she's alone," speculated Travis. "I suspect she has help. Sister Terina's memory contains a secret that Lucia does not want us to discover."

Prescott sighed. "I'm not well enough right now to help with the séance. But I'll be alright by tomorrow."

"We have to stay together until this is over," said Claire.

"Indeed," agreed Travis. "We'll wait until you're released and can go back to the Vatican. We need to talk to Dottore Pietro."

There was a knock at the door and, a moment later, Carlota Romano came in holding a bouquet of flowers. Claire and Travis looked sideways at each other, smiling.

"*Ciao*, Prescott," she said shyly.

"Carlota, what a surprise!" Prescott opened his arms wide. Carlota did not hesitate; she embraced him, kissing him on the cheek. "I hope you are better than I am."

"I'm well, I'm well, and I'm so sorry for what happened," she said, smiling.

"I'm sorry, too, and especially for your maid," said Prescott.

Carlota saddened. "Yes, it's horrible. Edda raised me." She wiped away a tear.

"I see you brought me flowers," said Prescott to change the subject. "Last time I saw you, I did the same thing."

"*Sì*, I thought it might brighten your day," said Carlota.

"Yes, it will," said Prescott, smiling at her. "But I'll leave soon. No time to waste in a hospital."

"But are you well enough?"

"Well enough to report back for duty."

"You don't have to worry—the Rome police will arrest Lucia Pietro by the end of the day," said Carlota.

"Do you have new leads?" Travis asked.

"No, but she did not leave Rome," said Carlota. "We are narrowing the section where we believe she is hiding in Rome."

"Very good," said Prescott admiringly.

"It seems that you shouldn't be in any hurry to report back for duty," said Carlota, shaking her head. "Things are under control."

"Well, we still have a few ends to tie up," said Claire.

"With the Pope, no?" Carlota asked.

"Serious matters reserved for the Vatican," said Claire.

"Is Lucia Pietro a danger to the Holy Father?" Carlota pressed.

"Maybe. But whatever the danger is, it will all happen within the Vatican walls," said Travis.

"Not within my jurisdiction."

Travis nodded. "Of course, if you arrest Lucia, it will be of great help."

"Not necessarily for what she did, but for what she might do," said Carlota, as if understanding the magnitude of the crime about to happen. "This changes how eager we are in apprehending her. Dead or alive?"

"Preferably alive," said Travis.

Chapter 39. The Dottore's Interrogation

That afternoon, the Capuchin Trinity Team arrived back in the Vatican. The Swiss Guards and plainclothes Vatican police were on high alert and visible everywhere. The danger they were watching for was from within the Vatican, not from outside. However, the danger may or may not have had a face, which made every shadow a suspect.

"How is your prisoner, Albert?" asked Travis as they entered Oberst Glauser's office.

"Dottore Pietro is silent as a stone," Oberst Glauser answered. "He insists on seeing his lawyer, and he knows very well that we don't have any solid evidence against him."

"Can we spend some time with him?" Claire asked.

"Definitely. Maybe you can get something out of him," said Oberst Glauser.

"We will," said Claire.

A few minutes later, they were taken underground through many iron-barred gates to what were, once upon a time, the famous cells used by the Inquisition. This cold and humid jail has been closed for a long time, but Glauser thought it safest to hold Dottore Pietro there. There was only one-way in and out, unless one could dig through rock.

The Dottore sat on a wooden stool behind the iron bars. Only a dim light illuminated his dilapidated and foul-smelling, damp cell. He looked serene; in his Italian-tailored suit he resembled a televangelist missionary who had fallen out of favor with the locals.

"Please let us in and lock the door after us," Travis said to the guard who took them down there.

Dottore Pietro stood up and folded his arms defiantly. The CTT entered and the iron-barred gate closed with a slam behind them. The guard left, looking for cleaner and healthier quarters.

"What do you want?" the Dottore asked.

"Sit down, Dottore." Travis pushed him down onto the wooden stool.

Dottore Pietro regarded Travis with dark, murderous eyes. "You're the bad cop?"

"No, Dottore, all three of us are the bad cops," said Claire. "We're the closest things to hell, which you so much aspire to belong to."

"I don't know what you're talking about. I am an innocent man, held in here illegally."

Travis, Prescott, and Claire walked quietly around him.

"If you plan to torture me, I have nothing to say. Besides, I am our Holy Father's doctor. Wait until he finds out about this!"

"Really? Maybe he put you in here." Prescott bent down to face the doctor, nose to nose. "This is how the Pope rewards you after so many years of faithful service."

Dottore Pietro's appearance darkened instantly. Lightning roiled in his eyes.

"Yes, Dottore, this is how the Pope disposes of all the unfaithful," Claire whispered into his ear from behind. "We were hired as his Inquisition squad to exterminate you. Like a bug," she hissed.

"I have rights! You cannot do this to me!" the doctor screamed.

"No need to exhaust yourself yelling prematurely," said Travis, taking over Prescott's face-to-face position. "Besides, why do you think they brought you here, rather than to the cozy, glass-walled cells upstairs? Hmm? So no one will hear you when you spit out your lungs in anguish and pain."

There was a moment of silence, which was made worse by the sound of water dripping somewhere in the cell.

"Don't you dare touch me!" Dottore Pietro stood up.

"Sit!" Claire said, as if giving an order to a dog.

The Dottore collapsed back onto the stool. "What do you want from me?"

"To punish you," said Claire. "The Pope's orders."

Without warning, the CTT penetrated the Dottore's mind. He was unaware that the CTT had no power over his mind, but the penetration felt like a red-hot rod entering the front lobes of his brain, followed by the sensation of a cold ice cube running down his spine. He shivered uncontrollably and screamed at the top of his lungs. The CTT was quickly out of his mind, leaving him confused and fearful of what they might do next.

"How does it feel when the Pope wants to punish you?" Claire asked.

"The Pope is a just man. You are making a big mistake. Who put you up to this? God?" howled the doctor. Droplets of sweat formed on his brow.

"Why not Satan?" Prescott asked. "Your newfound god. Do you think he's testing you? But you've already failed him."

Dottore Pietro slid off the stool down onto his knees, hands together, head lowered, praying arduously in a strange tongue. But to whom was he praying? God or Satan?

Prescott and Travis didn't let the opportunity of his position slide away. Travis reached over and grabbed the Dottore's coattails and pulled his jacket over his head, immobilizing him. From behind, Prescott tore the doctor's shirt along the spine, exposing his bare back. There was no tattoo on his back, as they expected to see. Travis pulled him forward and flattened him on the stone floor, placing his foot on the back of his neck.

Claire leaned over him and activated her PAV's infrared sensor. There, in its entire dark splendor, was the tattoo of Satan that adorned the Dottore's back—a grinning, hideous, horned creature, baring his canine teeth. His eyes were ferocious and almost alive. Claire was not squeamish, but the sight of this hairy, scaly tattoo of Satan sickened her.

"And what do we have here?" wondered Prescott. "Your true master, Satan. Under your skin."

"Indeed," said Travis. "As ugly as he is in person." He lifted his foot off the doctor's neck.

The Dottore stood up slowly, pulling his jacket back down. He looked pitiful.

Claire had to remind herself that pitiful people make deadly servants of the devil. "Sit down," ordered Claire.

"Now we have proof that you are a Satanist," said Travis. "Drop all pretenses and tell us: Why did Satan recruit you and your wife to destroy the Pope?"

The doctor regained his coolness. "That pompous, pathetic, soul-manipulating man." He spat the words out. "Pretending to represent God here on Earth! He deserves what's coming to him and to his pretend-god under whose disguise he enslaves humanity. The true God, Satan, will rule the Earth. His time has come, the true Lord!" The Dottore's voice rose to a shout.

"But where is Satan? Why isn't he helping you now?" Prescott asked.

"He will, he will—he will accept me in his kingdom after we complete our task."

"After you're dead," said Travis. "Just like your sons."

"Don't you dare talk to me about my sons!" said the Dottore with his teeth clenched.

"Satan did not bring your sons back to life, did he?" Travis asked. "But you fool, together with your wife, you incinerated alive the other two boys."

"They deserved it."

"And Satan feasted on your crime," said Claire. "He did not intend to help you out, just to use you and Lucia to get to Sister Terina, to contaminate the Pope. We know about that."

"And he deserves it!" shouted the Dottore. "He did nothing for my boys. Just meaningless words muttered about a fake god's immense love." He snarled. "Satan kept his word. He helped us kill our sons' murderers, a down payment to us for what more is to come."

"You mean for you and Lucia?" asked Claire.

The Dottore clenched his teeth, wrapped his arms around himself, and bent down without saying another word.

"Your plan was undone by what you call a fake god," said Prescott. "He was more powerful than Satan. His chosen genes purged the evil genes from the fetus. The game is over."

Dottore Pietro started laughing in a sinister way. "No, it is not over yet. The best is yet to come. They will avenge me, and I will be set free in Satan's garden."

"They? Who else besides Lucia is out there?" Claire asked.

"Ahh! Worried, aren't you?" Dottore Pietro laughed maliciously. "Satan has many servants. What if there are more than Lucia out there plotting and carrying out the Pope's demise? You caught me, but I'm only one of many. You may catch Lucia, and so what? After we extract our revenge, we will be in Satan's hell, except it's not a hell for us, but a heaven."

"Will you meet your sons there?" Prescott asked. "Wait. They were good boys. Perhaps they are in God's heaven now."

Dottore Pietro stood up and screamed in shock, and then he started crying.

"It is not too late to ask forgiveness," said Claire, trying to persuade him to relent and confess.

Dottore Pietro stopped crying and wiped his eyes with the back of his sleeve. "You are fools, aren't you? Satan is not a choosy elitist like God. Everyone is welcome to come to hell. All we have to do, if our sons are in that fake heaven, is to tell them to leave and come join us."

"You're delusional," said Claire.

"I'm not delusional. My Lord Satan's work will be done. The head of the fake-god church will suffer from the wrath of the true god, Satan!"

"And?" Claire asked.

"The collapse of the Roman Catholic Church without a new Messiah." Dottore Pietro clasped his hand over his mouth. It seemed he had let a truth out.

"Excellent information." Claire smiled. "But the Church won't collapse and the new Messiah will be born."

"We brought our own medical team," said Travis. "The child will be born, and the Pope will be well, while you and Lucia will rot in jail."

"That will have to be seen." The Dottore laughed knowingly.

"Where is Lucia?" Claire asked.

"Under Satan's protection, intent on carrying out her mission."

"What's her mission?" Claire asked.

"Kill him. Her mission is underway, and you cannot do anything about it." The Dottore laughed hysterically.

Chapter 40. High Alert

"Albert, we're done here," said Travis into his comm.

"OK," answered Albert Glauser.

The guard came shortly after and opened the door to let them out. Dottore Pietro leaned against the back wall and stared into the distance. They didn't bid him farewell.

"I listened on the open comm," said Oberst Glauser, meeting them at the top of the stairs. "We need to talk."

"Yes, we do," replied Travis.

A few minutes later they were sitting in Glauser's office, with the door closed. Glauser looked intense.

"You realize you were not supposed to hear what he said," said Travis.

"But I did!" shouted Glauser. "I cannot do my job if I don't know the entire story. Satan worshippers are trying to kill the Holy Father? It is my solemn duty to protect him from harm. And who is that unborn child? An illegitimate child of the, of the . . ." It seemed that Albert Glauser was afraid to utter the words incriminating the Pope of fathering an about-to-be-born child.

"Albert, we have very little time," said Claire. "We need to let you in on the true nature of our investigation. However, you must be sworn to secrecy."

"Of course. I'm the Oberst. I've dedicated my life to the Holy See."

"Very well," said Claire. "It is worse than you can imagine."

"W-w-worse?" Oberst Albert Glauser, coolness gone, was trembling.

"The Pope did not father an illegitimate child. He is carrying a child."

"Carrying?" Glauser was stunned. "Is he a woman, like Pope Joan?"

"No, he is a man," said Claire. "And through no fault of his own, he's bearing a child."

The blood drained from Oberst Albert Glauser's face. "How could that be?"

"Satan planned to have a holy man carry his offspring. He selected the Pope. With the help of Angelo and Lucia Pietro, who are devil worshippers, Satan contaminated Sister Terina. She later transmitted the seed of the devil to the Pope. And the Pope, a man, had an immaculate conception of Satan's son. Monsignore Giuseppe, by choice or chance, transmitted counter genes to the Pope that destroyed Satan's genes. The healthy fetus continued to grow in the Pope's belly."

Albert Glauser swallowed hard, looking from one to the other, as if not comprehending what he was hearing.

Claire continued, "When the Dottore found out that Satan's child was destroyed, he wanted to abort the pregnancy. But the Pope, once assured that the child was not Satan's son anymore, refused. And that's when it seemed that the mystery was solved. All we had to do was find the culprits. Then Sister Terina and your officers were killed, we were ambushed, and Prescott almost died from poisoning. The perpetrators are adamant about eliminating us, which doesn't make sense at this stage. We don't see the purpose."

"Unless you already know who they are and their secret, but haven't yet put two and two together," said Glauser, somehow recovered from his shock.

"That could be a possibility, if we take into account that we have Sister Terina's memory," said Claire. "But we don't think that's the reason."

"Then what's the reason?" Glauser asked.

"The boy must not be born or live," said Claire. "Angelo Pietro lied about the Pope being their target."

"Besides Angelo and Lucia Pietro, there must be others who are afraid that we will foil their plan, and the boy will be born and survive," said Prescott.

"They're not after the Holy Father?" Glauser seemed to be hopeful.

"The Pope is still in danger," said Prescott. "They don't care if he lives or dies, as long as the newborn dies."

"Holy heaven," said Albert Glauser. "Do you know who else and how many are involved?"

"Besides Angelo Pietro and Lucia, we have no clue," said Prescott. "But we suspect that Lucia may not have done all the killings by herself.

And we don't know if there is another suspect or a fined-tuned organization behind them."

"The Vatican is safe," said Glauser.

"But if the Pope needs to go to another hospital in Rome, all bets are off," said Travis.

"That will be the last thing the Holy Father will do. He will not leave Vatican City. He is well-protected here," said Glauser.

"What if they are already here in the Vatican, waiting for the right time to strike?" speculated Travis.

"I doubt that, but if they are here, why haven't they killed the Holy Father yet, and the fetus as well?" wondered Glauser.

"Maybe they have only a certain window of opportunity to strike," said Travis.

"The most vulnerable time will be when Holy Father is in surgery," said Glauser, standing up and pacing around. "You requested your doctor to come here, a Dr. Stark, who doesn't seem to exist, according to my research. I need your corroboration."

"He's arriving tomorrow, and we vouch for him," said Claire. "How about the doctor Cardinal Bertrand recommended?"

"Yes, I checked Dottore Salmeri. She checks out. Very trustworthy," said Oberst Glauser. "I checked her assistant, Sister Fulvia, and she is trustworthy as well. She has worked with Dottore Salmeri for the past five years. Nevertheless, we are on high alert."

"We need to be," said Prescott. "I have a strange feeling about this."

Chapter 41. Lucia Pietro

Later that evening, a call came on the comm from Oberst Glauser, "We've just apprehended Lucia Pietro."

As they crossed through the courtyard returning to the Vatican jail, they observed the full moon rising. Was it an omen of another trial humanity would have to endure?

Oberst Glauser was waiting for them at the entrance. "We have her."

"How did you catch her?" Claire asked, as they walked toward the jail.

"She tried to enter the Vatican through the delivery gate, posing as a vendor," said Glauser. "She made it to the delivery dock, and then she went through the GeneID secure gates. The silent alarm activated, and she released a smoke bomb. She struggled when we tried to arrest her, but we were able detain her. Other than the smoke bomb she was unarmed. She must have been desperate to get in here."

"A smoke bomb," said Travis, perplexed. "Has she said anything yet?"

"No, she is silent and defiant," said Glauser. "She did not even ask about her husband."

Lucia Pietro sat like a stone statue in her glass-walled cell. Two Swiss Guard officers stood outside. Oberst Glauser gave them orders to open the cell door. The glass door slid open, while the guards stood at the ready, with their guns drawn, in case of trouble with the detainee. The four of them entered the small cell.

Lucia Pietro looked up at them. "Hello, Claire," she said as if greeting a friend.

"You have caused a lot of mayhem," Claire said coldly.

Lucia smiled. "I'm glad you weren't killed in that ambush. I wouldn't have been able to talk to you right now. And Prescott, you're alive. What a surprise."

"Let's talk," said Claire, ignoring her sarcasm.

"What would you like to talk about?"

"Besides your husband and you, who else is involved in this?"

"Just Angelo and I."

"Angelo said otherwise," said Claire.

"That would be your problem then. Go chase phantasms."

"You are a Satan worshipper."

"So what if I am? He provides better than God does."

"Why did you kill Sister Terina?"

Lucia smiled coldly.

"We have her memory," said Claire.

"If you do, why are you asking me questions? You should know most everything." Lucia looked intently at Claire. "But you don't—you haven't learned the secret. By the time you do, it will be too late."

Claire switched to mute conference with her partners through her PAV. "Do you think she is bluffing about the memory?"

"Yes, otherwise she would not have ambushed us," said Travis. "She hopes that we will unravel the memory too late."

"We are at the eleventh hour, and we still don't know the secret," said Claire.

"Are you conferencing?" asked Lucia, seeing them silent. "What else would you like to know?"

"What happens if the baby lives?" asked Travis.

"All hell will break loose."

Mit Sandru

Chapter 42. The Surgical Team

It was Friday, June 5. Earlier in the day, the technical team inspected the robo-med and gave the go-ahead for any surgeries. The Capuchin Trinity Team wasn't able to unravel any more secrets. Although they went over all the facts and suppositions, they could not determine with certainty what would happen.

Late in the afternoon, they were on their way to the papal medical quarters to meet Dottore Salmeri and Sister Fulvia, who were already in place in case of any premature emergency. Dr. Stark was due to arrive soon.

They found Dottore Salmeri and Sister Fulvia busy reviewing the Pope's medical records. The robo-med was deployed and ready to operate. Magdalena, the medical computer, was answering questions and displaying the information requested.

"Magdalena, please initiate the countdown for the fetus's full maturation," Dottore Salmeri asked, while turning to see who the new arrivals were. She seemed intrigued, seeing the three of them in their dark-gray uniforms and dark shades obscuring their eyes.

"Dottore Salmeri and Nurse Fulvia," said Claire. "Allow us to introduce ourselves. This is Prescott Alighieri, Travis St. John, and I am Claire German." Claire extended her hand, but the doctor raised her hands in objection.

"It's nice to meet you, but sorry—Nurse Fulvia and I can't shake hands. We've started our sterilization process," Dottore Salmeri said in English. She was a middle-aged woman, already dressed in hospital garb, including headgear that covered her hair. Her transparent face shield was raised, giving her the appearance of a space-age knight.

Nurse Fulvia nodded in salute. She was a petite woman, young by all appearances, and dressed for surgery. Besides her face shield, which was raised as well, she wore a surgical mask and an unusual horn-rimmed PAV. She didn't seem to be able to speak English, as she was listening to Dottore Salmeri's translation of what Claire said.

"We understand," said Claire. "And we will keep our distance. We just wanted to meet you and find out what you know about this emergency surgery."

"It is shocking, I'll say that much," said Dottore Salmeri. "Camerlengo Bertrand apprised us of the situation and, after reviewing the medical records, all I can say is that we will do the best we can, no questions asked."

"Thank you for your tactfulness, Dottore Salmeri," said Prescott. "Did Cardinal Bertrand tell you of our involvement in this?"

"Yes, you are a paranormal investigating unit," responded Dottore Salmeri. "From a professional point of view, I would be very interested to find out how this conception could have happened." She gave instructions in Italian to Nurse Fulvia, and she went to work.

"That's the billion-dollar question," said Prescott. "Our conclusion is a metaphysical intervention. When Dr. Stark arrives, he will tell you that whatever we find out is not worth anything scientifically."

Magdalena, the computer, reported her findings: "The fetus is maturing faster than previously predicted. The new maturity date and time of surgery should commence shortly after midnight."

"Yes, we continue investigating the paranormal aspects of this case." As Travis spoke, he walked closer to Nurse Fulvia, who was observing and reviewing the information provided by Magdalena. "Satan was responsible in causing the Pope to carry a fetus." He observed the nurse more closely, but she did not flinch. Maybe she did not speak English after all.

"Satan." Dottore Salmeri chuckled. "Always blame it on Satan. But I'm still interested in what agent he used to cause the spontaneous conception."

"As Prescott said, it is metaphysical," said Travis.

"And not worth any scientific attention," said Dr. Stark, who just arrived. "Hello everyone. *Ciao*, Dottore Salmeri. Ready for our important procedure?"

"*Ciao*, Dottore Stark." It seemed that Dottore Salmeri and Dr. Stark knew each other.

"I presume you've read Sister Terina's autopsy, so you know that no pathological agent was detected," Dr. Stark said to Dottore Salmeri.

"And yet the process started at exactly the time Sister Terina kissed the Pope's ring and finger," said Prescott, not giving up.

"Coincidence," argued Dr. Stark.

"Twice a coincidence?" said Prescott.

"A mystery, yes. But not beyond scientific explanation in due time." Dr. Stark was dismissive.

"In any case, I'm glad you're here, Dr. Stark. You've arrived not a moment too soon. Please, suit up and sterilize." Dottore Salmeri pointed to an adjacent room.

Dr. Stark looked as gaunt as ever. "I will be assisting you. The glory will be all yours." He left to get ready.

Dottore Salmeri instructed Nurse Fulvia to enter the operating room. Travis stood by the large window and observed the nurse doing her prep tasks inside.

"How long have you known your nurse?" Travis asked.

"Long enough to trust her," replied Dottore Salmeri.

Travis wasn't so sure. He was unnerved by the lack of progress in their investigation and suspected just about every woman under a certain height. This nurse was the right height, but he had nothing else to go on. He was sure that the mysterious woman was in the Vatican already. But where?

Chapter 43. Sister Terina's Memory

"One hour until midnight," said Travis. "We cannot wait. We must decipher Sister Terina's memory."

"Where shall we hold our séance?" wondered Claire.

"The best place on Earth: the Sistine Chapel," said Prescott.

"Indeed," said Travis, grinning. "Let's hope it is not too crowded at this time."

The Capuchin Trinity Team passed by the Swiss Guards and entered the historic chapel, which was deserted. In ordinary times, it would have been full of special, after-hours guests, but now, with the high alert, the Sistine Chapel was empty.

"Not bad—we have it all to ourselves," said Travis, walking around and studying the beautiful frescoes on the ceiling.

"Where shall we sit?" said Claire.

"How about under the temptation of Adam and Eve by the devil-serpent?" said Prescott.

"Good place," accepted Claire.

They sat on the floor in a circle with their legs crossed and joined their hands. This was the closest to a séance they would ever perform. They were not after spirits, but after a memory they jointly possessed and the meaning in it, which had evaded them so far . . .

Sister Terina's memory is a whitish puff, tumbling around raggedly as we remembered when we captured it, and as we approach, it becomes a convoluted mass of ether with a white, denser center. Her memory lies within the twisting mass, and we must enter it. It's a journey, not perilous, but confusing. Our task is to make sense of what the memory is.

We are within the memory. Flickers of places and faces. A dark alley. Feelings of fear and terror. Strong hands grabbing and groping. Soft cloth smelling aromatically. Sleep. A cold stone floor in a dark vaulted chamber. Candles flickering in niches on the walls. Lights and shadows dancing around. Flickering knives, blood flowing, salty taste. Cold and damp, and shackles on the wrists and ankles. Torture and anguish. Much pain and despair.

The jumbled memory suddenly reassembles into clear images, and we see what Sister Terina saw:

I am on a dark street in front of a tall stone wall. Someone is beckoning me. It is Lucia. Poor Lucia. Her boys are dead. The anguish she must feel about her loss. I'm so happy that I can comfort her. My heart is open to her. But why come here? Where are we? The dark clouds obscure the moonlight, and I can barely see.

Lucia beckons me again from the entrance in the wall. There must be a chapel inside. She wants to pray with me for her boys. I'm a nun and I can help her. She retreats in the shadow of the doorway. I step inside and strong hands grab me above the elbows. It's a man. He pushes me into the courtyard. I see Lucia and she smiles at me.

I hear an iron gate slamming behind me. What's the meaning of this? Who is this man behind me and what does he want? I open my mouth to call for Lucia to help. A soft cloth that smells medicinally sweet covers my mouth and nose. I . . .

I've been asleep. I had a nightmare. I'm cold. I need to pull my blanket over me. I feel nauseated. Someone bends over me, and I smell something awful. I'm shocked to full awareness. Where am I? I am cold. I'm lying down on a cold stone floor. My God, I am naked. Where are my clothes? What's going on?

My hands are stretched over my head and I cannot bring them to my breasts. My wrists are held in handcuffs tied to iron spikes on the floor. Why am I naked? My legs are spread and my ankles are in shackles. I try to wrestle free. I can't. I'm immobilized on my back on the cold floor.

I am in a stone vaulted-ceiling chamber. I can see a little from the candles flickering in niches on the wall. My God, what is the meaning of this? I'm afraid. I cry with terror. What happened to Lucia? Was she taken, too?

I see her. She stands at my feet and she smiles. She is naked, too. What have they done to her? Wait, she is not shackled like me. She stands there of her own free will and smiles bitterly. I shout, "Lucia, help me!" She raises her hands and chants some obscure words, which I do not understand. She screams, and her screams resonate within the room.

Two hands grab her breasts from behind. She bends down and kneels between my legs, looking at me and smiling evilly now. A naked man is behind her and he mounts her. Is that Dottore Angelo Pietro, Lucia's husband? What is he doing to her? Oh my God, they're having intercourse. They both stare at me with burning eyes.

"What is the meaning of this?" I scream.

"You must pray for redemption," they both tell me.

"God, please help me!" I close my eyes and I begin praying as I've never prayed before.

"Lucrezia, set her eyes open," shouts Dottore Pietro.

Someone else pulls my eyelids up and tapes them open. I cannot close my eyes and avert them from the grossness of the rocking bodies between my legs.

"Pray, Sister Terina," they both demand. "Pray for our savior."

"What? What do you mean? Jesus Christ?"

"Satan is our savior," they all say.

"No, no!" I scream from the top of my lungs. My screams bounce around the chamber and no one answers. "Is there anyone there who can help me? Please help me!" No one answers, just the echo of my pleading words.

My eyes fill with tears. I cannot see well, which is good, but someone wipes my eyes. She wants me to see. The other woman, Lucrezia, naked, crawls over me, and she exposes her anus as she squats over my face. Please God! Help me! I am so afraid I cannot even breathe. I don't understand the meaning of this torture.

Dottore Pietro, Lucia, and Lucrezia, whose face I cannot see, are standing up, embracing, kissing, and rubbing each other's genitals. I can see only their lower bodies above me. I cannot shut my eyes. They stand over me and perform gross sexual acts. They moan and howl like beasts. Suddenly, they stop. I see their arms raised as they chant and chant and chant in tongues I don't understand.

Silence.

Lucia bends down and kisses me on the mouth. I've never been kissed by another woman on the mouth. Why is she doing this? I keep my lips tight. I feel the cold blade of a knife between my teeth. Lucia is prying my teeth apart, opening my mouth. She puts something rubbery in my mouth to prevent me from closing it. My mouth is held open, just like my eyes.

Dottore Pietro crawls on all fours to me. He is on his knees between my legs. He licks my inner thighs, and then up between my legs; I feel his tongue inside me. No! I feel disgusted by what he's doing. He goes up, licking my belly, my breasts, and my nipples. He sucks hard on each nipple, after which he bites me. I scream. It hurts. Lucia is holding my head to look at Angelo Pietro. His mad, bloodshot eyes stare at me; his tongue waggles.

"Are you ready, Sister, to take Satan inside you?" He slobbers.

I'm afraid that I will be raped. I maintained my virginity to serve God. But now it will be all over. I'm afraid these people are devil worshippers and I am their sacrifice to Satan. Although gagged, I pray, "Our Father, who art in heaven, hallowed be . . ."

"Sister Terina, are you ready to take Satan inside you?"

I shake my head, no, no, no—

The women are chanting in shrill voices.

"Satan will be inside you." He lifts me under my buttocks, and, in one brutal stroke, he penetrates me. I feel a burning pain between my legs that brings a long scream from me. They laugh and shout, "Hail to Satan! Hail to Satan!"

Lucia kisses Dottore Pietro, as he forcefully goes in and out of me. It burns. I feel the hot blood escaping from me. Oh God, what have I done to deserve this?

Lucia squats over my face. She holds my head steady and lowers herself over my mouth, holding my head between her thighs. My mouth is open under her vagina and she rocks on my face and mouth. The awful taste, the wetness, the excretions flow into my mouth, and I have no choice but to swallow them. I'm choking. Please God, please God, help me!

I'm in hell. I can barely breathe. Lucia is on top of my mouth. Dottore Pietro is raping me. I'm hurt. I'm in agony. I feel pain on the bottom of my feet. Someone is burning the soles of my feet. I scream from underneath Lucia. Dottore Pietro thrusts even harder and faster in me. It huuuurts.

At the last stroke, I feel him inside me, quivering. He screams. Lucia screams. The other woman screams. I feel something cool flowing inside me. Darkness . . .

I feel warm, salty liquid spilling over my face. Dottore Pietro and Lucia hold a goat above me with its throat slashed, convulsing in the grip of death. Its blood covers me. My mouth is held open and I have no choice but to swallow the goat's blood. They laugh and rejoice. I lose consciousness.

Candles surround me now. Lucia and Dottore Pietro sit at my feet and eat the goat's heart and liver and eyeballs and tongue and brains. I hear the other woman over my head eating her fill as well and burping with satisfaction. She reaches down and removes the rubber mouthpiece. I can close my mouth now, painfully. I am thirsty for water. A metal canteen is shoved in my mouth and I drink, but it tastes awful. It is alcohol. I turn my head and close my mouth. I'm gagging. They let me be, but I'm getting dizzy.

Dottore Pietro brings up a long silver knife. He twists it in the air and growls like a beast. His eyes are the eyes of a madman. Lucia kneels in front of him and he inserts the blade in her mouth, down into her throat. He takes it out, but she is not hurt. She only swallowed the blade. The other woman, naked, kneels in front of him. She is with her back to me. Dottore Pietro lowers the knife down her throat as well.

Lucia places a satchel over my head. I cannot see. I feel two sharp pains in each of the crooks of my elbows. They've opened my veins. They are bleeding me to death. They are drinking my blood.

Chapter 44. Midnight, June Sixth, Sixty-Six

A bell was tolling somewhere in the Vatican. Claire, Travis, and Prescott woke up, startled from their nightmare trance.

Claire buried her face in her hands, horrified at what she had witnessed.

"Damn monsters," whispered Travis. "Satanic rituals."

"Poor Sister Terina," lamented Prescott. "She opened her heart to Lucia, and Satan took her."

"There is another accomplice out there. Another woman." Travis stood up, followed by Prescott.

"We need to go to the medical quarters!" Claire ran out, followed by the men.

"I bet the other woman is already here in the Vatican," said Prescott as he ran alongside them.

"That was my feeling all day long," said Travis. "Lucia was not captured—she gave herself up to lull us into a sense of false security and to create a distraction for the other woman to slip in." Travis opened his comm. "Albert, what's the situation with the Pope?"

"They're ready for surgery. Where are you?" came the reply.

"We're on our way to the medical quarters," said Travis. "Albert, there is a high possibility that another suspect is in the Vatican, planning to do harm to the Pope and the baby. She is a woman and her name is Lucrezia."

"What? Why didn't you tell me earlier? I scaled down the security."

"We just found out," said Travis. "She has about the same physical build as Lucia."

"Stigmata!" Oberst Glauser gave the order "Stigmata" to start the highest alert in the Holy City and commence the shutdown of all exits. Red lights located at strategic places began pulsing to indicate the alert mode.

"Anything we need to do now during Stigmata?" Prescott asked.

"No, it is an automatic process," said Glauser. "In essence the Vatican is on lockdown. First the Italian police, then the *carabinieri*, will soon encircle the walls of the Vatican, sequestering it from the world."

"What are Angelo and Lucia Pietro doing?" asked Prescott.

"Both of them have been praying in tongues for the past hour. To Satan, I presume," said Glauser. "The computer is monitoring what they're saying, and, just as you contacted me, it identified a name. What do you know? Lucrezia. Just what you said."

"Yes. Lucrezia. We couldn't see her face," said Prescott. "Can your computer put a face with that name?"

"No, no such woman has access to the Vatican," said Glauser. "Wait! This is something new. The computer shows that Dottore Pietro put in a request for a Vatican pass for a certain

L. Infermiera, or L. Nurse, but then he cancelled it."

"How long ago?" Prescott asked.

"Three months ago. Do you think it is the same woman?"

"It could be. Probably a nurse to assist him with the delivery of the baby. For some reason, he changed his mind. In any case, Lucrezia is a dangerous suspect," said Prescott.

While Prescott was talking to Oberst Glauser, Claire asked in her comm, "Dr. Stark, what is the situation?"

"All normal," replied Dr. Stark. "The Pope is under general anesthesia, and Dottore Salmeri will begin the removal of the baby in a few minutes. Is something wrong?"

"Yes, there is another suspect, a woman. Her name is Lucrezia," said Claire. "And we are certain she is in the Vatican."

"Another woman? You realize that the surgeon and the nurse in here are women, and they are about to laser-cut the Pope open?"

"You need to be vigil," said Claire.

"That's your job. Where are you?"

"We're on our way. Running."

"Make it snappy, boys and girl. Even the small nun here could take me out."

"We'll be there in less than a minute," replied Claire.

On their way toward the papal apartments, they crossed the inner square, which was storming with armed guards, taking positions at their pre-assigned posts. Oberst Glauser had cleared their passage through all checkpoints, and no one stopped or delayed them.

The CTT burst into the medical quarters and found Cardinals Navarro, Cellini, and Bertrand in front of the glass wall, viewing the operating room. The cardinals turned, startled at their brusque entrance.

"Your Eminences," said Prescott as a greeting, breathing hard from the run. Dr. Stark from across the window seemed relieved to see them.

"What's going on?" asked Cardinal Cellini. "You look as if you were being chased by the unholy one."

"Just about right, Cardinal Cellini," said Prescott. "We have reason to believe that there is another suspect here in the Vatican, intent on doing harm."

"How could this be? Is Oberst Glauser aware of this?" Cardinal Cellini was indignant.

"Yes, Your Eminence. Oberst Glauser is fully aware of the situation and is taking the right measures as we speak," assured Prescott. "But this woman, she is a crafty criminal."

"Why don't you search for her?" Cardinal Cellini sounded even more indignant, pointing outside.

"That's why we're here, Your Eminences," said Prescott.

Cardinal Bertrand turned quickly and looked into the operating room. Cellini and Navarro turned slowly and looked through the glass wall as well.

"Do you suspect one of these two women?" asked Cardinal Navarro, turning back to face them and raising his eyebrows in shock.

Dr. Stark said over the private comm, "Don't tell me one of these women is the criminal you're looking for?"

"No, neither Dottore Salmeri nor Nurse Fulvia are the suspects," said Claire to the cardinals and Dr. Stark. "We know her physique, and it does not match those of the medical team. Also, we just found out her name is Lucrezia." Two of the cardinals showed no sign that they knew a woman by that name, but Cardinal Cellini's eyes opened wide.

"Sounds familiar, Cardinal Cellini?" Claire asked.

"Yes, I've heard that name associated with Satan worshipping," said the cardinal.

"Any other information you can give us about her?" Claire asked.

"No, just the name." Cardinal Cellini shook his head in disbelief.

By now Dottore Salmeri and Nurse Fulvia had stopped what they were doing and were watching with dismay the commotion behind the glass wall. "Is there a problem?" Dottore Salmeri inquired over the intercom.

The cardinals and the CTT looked back into the operating room at the confused medical team. "No, nothing's the matter, Dottore," said Cardinal Bertrand. "I'm just curious, Dottore, how much longer can you delay the operation?"

"Delay? Not much longer, Your Eminence. Why?"

Cardinal Bertrand cleared his throat, more to gain time to think of a response than to clear his voice. "Well, we're discussing some security issues."

"May we know what those security issues are?" Dottore Salmeri asked.

"Your Eminence, we must let them know the concern we have," said Claire.

Dottore Salmeri approached the glass wall.

Cardinal Bertrand glanced at Cellini, who nodded in agreement.

Prescott opened a private comm with Dr. Stark. "Keep your eyes on those two."

"Why, are they dangerous now?" Dr. Stark asked, getting closer to the operating table as if to protect the Pope.

"Depends on how they react after we tell them our concern," replied Prescott.

"Dottore Salmeri," said Claire. "There may be nothing to worry about in the operating room, but we have reason to believe that there is a suspect, a woman, on the loose in the Vatican who may want to harm the Holy Father and the child. Her name is Lucrezia."

Dottore Salmeri looked at Nurse Fulvia with an apprehensive look. "What are we supposed to do?" Dottore Salmeri asked. She turned to face Dr. Stark. "Dr. Stark, did you know about this?"

Before Dr. Stark could open his mouth, Claire said, "Yes, Dr. Stark was informed of the situation. That's why he's in there with you."

"Are we in danger?" Dottore Salmeri asked Dr. Stark.

"No. Not as long as the Capuchin Trinity Team is here." He motioned toward the CTT.

"Capuchin Trinity? They'll protect us through prayers?" Dottore Salmeri looked aghast.

"No, no, no. They are a special investigation team," said Dr. Stark in a serious voice. "They are here to protect the Pope."

"I see. Very well. Capuchin Trinity Team, I need to operate and remove the fetus—" She turned and looked at the medical dashboard hologram hovering above the Pope's body to inspect the vitals for both the Pope and the fetus. "We cannot delay this procedure any longer."

"Please go ahead, Dottore Salmeri," said Travis with assurance.

Dottore Salmeri returned at once to the operating table. Nurse Fulvia took her position by the surgical instruments table. "Ready, Dr. Stark?" Dottore Salmeri asked.

"As ready as I'll ever be." Dr. Stark took his position opposite Dottore Salmeri.

"How do you know it is safe to start the surgery?" Cardinal Bertrand asked Travis. "There could be a sabotage in the operating room."

"It is safe until the baby is born," said Travis.

The cardinals looked inquisitively at Travis. He opened a private comm with Dr. Stark for him to hear as well what he was about to say. "This woman, Lucrezia, does not want just to kill the baby, but she must follow a certain ritual when she does that. She worships Satan, and the ritual is very important. I believe that she will have until sunrise to perform this act."

Chapter 45. Past Midnight

They looked at the digital clock in the operating room. It was 00:00:00. Midnight. The operation began. Using the robo-med, Dottore Salmeri made a precise laser incision in the Pope's belly, right below the bulge containing the amniotic sac, but not through the sac membrane. There was very little bleeding, as the laser cut and cauterized the flesh almost instantly. She—or the robot—did not have to do any guesswork as the laser cut through the layers of skin and flesh. The holographic display above the Pope's body indicated exactly how deep the cut was. Magdalena the computer was monitoring the incisions as well, responding to the doctor's commands to assess or to simply turn the image to the right angle for a better view. All the vital statistics were displayed above the patient, and Dottore Salmeri never had to turn her head to see the status and progress. With the help of Dr. Stark, she began inserting micro-tubes and robotic surgical instruments into the amniotic sac. The delicate procedure began.

The glass wall had holographic display capabilities, so the cardinals and the CTT were able to watch the operation. With her fingers, Claire expertly changed the angle and zoomed in for a more detailed view. This was independent of what Dottore Salmeri was doing, seeing, or commanding Magdalena to do.

The cardinals watched with their hands on their crucifixes, praying silently.

Prescott and Travis stepped away from the glass wall display for a private conference. Claire was better qualified to supervise the operation, and she would intervene and instruct Dr. Stark in case of any issues.

"If your supposition is correct—" began Prescott.

"Which it is," said Travis.

"—then the suspect will not act until the baby is born," said Prescott.

"She needs the baby alive," agreed Travis.

"What would we do if we wanted to snatch the baby and take it to an altar for the killing ritual?" wondered Prescott.

"I like your evil way of thinking," said Travis, not as a joke but to acknowledge they had to adjust their mind-set to the dark side. "The first element of surprise for all of us is when the baby comes out of the womb, or shortly after."

"Uh-huh, let's follow that plan," said Prescott, as if pretending to be the villain.

"In that case, when everyone has their guard down, I would create an even bigger surprise."

"How?" Prescott speculated. "Cut off the power? Inject a sleeping gas? Incapacitate or kill the medical team? Come from an adjacent room? Blast your way through the walls from above, sideways, or below?"

"That's movie stuff," said Travis. "This is a very cunning woman, helped by Satan."

"Or by an insider?" proposed Prescott. They both turned and looked at the surgery team. Could it be that another accomplice was already in there?

"And even if I snatch the baby, where would I go?" Travis said. "The Vatican is sealed. No one can get out by road or air or—"

"Via underground," Prescott completed Travis's thought. "There must be unknown tunnels leading out from the Vatican."

"Yes, the way out could be underground. But how would I get there? We're two stories high." Travis pondered. "The medical quarters were Dottore Pietro's domain, and he planned accordingly. He knew of a passage or built one from here to there." Travis pointed down with his finger.

"Very possible," said Prescott. "No blasting, no noise, just a clean abduction. And the baby disappears down a magic hole."

"Indeed." Travis activated the comm to Glauser. "Albert?"

"*Pronto*, Oberst Glauser here."

"I presume everything is quiet on all fronts?"

"Eerily quiet, except for the media, which are swarming toward the Vatican. Armageddon is expected. What's the situation in the surgery room?" Glauser asked.

"As we said, the suspect is already in the Vatican. This plan was in place before any of us were aware of it. We suspect Dottore Pietro built a secret access route to the surgery room already and his accomplice is in place, ready to act," said Travis.

"No wonder we couldn't detect her." Oberst Glauser sighed. "I'll send a search team to determine if there is a secret passage from the operating room."

"Good idea, and hurry—the operation is under way," said Prescott.

"What areas of the Vatican don't you monitor?" Travis asked Glauser.

"A few places that are hard to reach from the outside and some of the underground," replied Albert Glauser.

"Can you find out which area of the underground has chapels or altars?"

"Hmm. I'll have to check. I'll get on it right away," said Glauser.

"Lucrezia may not have to exit the Vatican, if an altar is available below," said Prescott.

"Your Eminences," Travis addressed the cardinals. "Do you know if there are small chapels or altars underground?"

The three cardinals looked at Travis, confused. Cardinal Bertrand was the first to speak. "Well, yes, some entombments have alcoves for praying, but not chapels with altars."

"How far underground?" Cardinal Navarro asked. "There are long-forgotten crypts and passages down there."

"Do you know if there is a chapel dedicated to Satan?" Travis asked.

"How dare you ask such a question!" Cardinal Cellini was incensed and turned as scarlet as his zucchetto.

"I meant no disrespect, Your Eminence," said Travis. "Even enemies have lines of communication with each other for special circumstances—why not the Vatican?"

"Nonsense!" erupted Cardinal Bertrand. "We don't worship or communicate with Satan."

Cardinal Navarro cleared his throat. "Actually, there is such a place."

The other two cardinals turned quickly and stared at him. They looked flabbergasted—it was news to them as well.

"Very few in the Holy See know about this, but there is a chapel for Satan down there," Cardinal Navarro said in an even voice, motioning down with his head. "There are many reasons why there is such a place within the Vatican, but to enumerate them would not be prudent. Travis, are you suggesting that the baby will be taken to that place and ritually killed?"

Travis nodded. "Everything about the devil worshippers is ritual. That's why they haven't killed His Holiness yet."

"The baby is out," announced Claire. They all crowded toward the display. "Oh my God! It's a girl!"

Mit Sandru

Chapter 46. Satan's Chapel

"What?" Cardinal Cellini shouted. "A girl? Wasn't it supposed to be a boy?"

"Dottore Salmeri, how is the baby, and is she a girl?" Claire asked.

Nurse Fulvia was holding the baby and Dottore Salmeri was checking her. "Yes, she is a girl. Born at 00:06:66 on June sixth, 2066. Surprise, surprise! She is healthy, and I have no idea how she changed from a boy to a girl."

"I'm happy to hear that, Dottore Salmeri," said Claire.

"What's the meaning of this?" Cardinal Cellini asked Claire.

Before Claire could answer, someone screamed in the operating room. They looked at the glass wall display and saw nothing abnormal. Nurse Fulvia was holding the baby, but then the image flickered, and Nurse Fulvia returned from the surgery table holding the baby . . .

"The display is looping!" shouted Travis. He ran to the surgery's door, which was locked. He kicked it open and entered, followed by Prescott and Claire.

The air in the room was hazy, as if some gas had escaped from a pressurized bottle. Nurse Fulvia was crying, empty-handed. Dr. Stark was flat on his back on the floor. Dottore Salmeri was bent over the Pope on the operating table. A sword penetrated the doctor's back and went through the Pope. The blood from the two stabbed victims was pooling under the table.

"Emergency help!" shouted Claire into her comm. "Emergency medical help!"

"Medical help on its way!" No sooner had Glauser said it than the clinic doors opened and two teams of medics burst in. Travis and Prescott came out of the operating room to make room for the medics.

Claire shouted, "Magdalena, give me vitals on the surgery team!" The medics came in swiftly and immediately unfolded their gear to help the victims. Orders were snapped, gear was deployed, and the medics, helped by nurse Fulvia, began to untangle the gruesome mess.

Two officers entered the room. *"Signori* Travis, Prescott?"

"Yes," replied Prescott.

"We are here to look for secret passages."

"Right in here." Prescott took them into the surgery room. The two men paled when they saw all the blood around the operating table. "The passage must be somewhere in this room." Prescott flung his arms open wide. The officers deployed their handheld detectors and started scanning the walls.

Travis turned to Cardinal Navarro. "Your Eminence, you must take us to Satan's chapel. Right now."

"Please follow me." Cardinal Navarro walked out of the medical quarters, followed by Travis and Prescott. Prescott called for Claire, who ran to catch up with them.

"Dr. Stark is fine," Claire said. "The Pope and Dottore Salmeri are both in critical condition."

On their way, they came across Oberst Glauser and two other officers.

"What's going on?" he asked.

"Come with us!" Travis shouted without slowing down.

Glauser took one of the officers with him and dispatched the other one to the medical quarters.

"Where are we going?" asked Glauser from behind.

"To the underworld!" replied Travis.

Cardinal Navarro took them down by elevator. The lowest level, which was displayed only for certain cardinals with secret access codes, like Navarro, showed "–VI," which was presumably six levels underground. They exited the elevator into a vaulted stone room, and the automatic lights turned on, one by one, as they descended by stairs to even lower levels in the crypts. Marble burial boxes lined the corridor.

At an inconspicuous niche, Cardinal Navarro stopped and placed his palm on an engraved Vatican seal on the wall. Clicking sounds could be heard as if a vault lock were unlatching. The wall swung open into a dark passageway.

Cardinal Navarro entered and took an unlit torch off the wall. "This may look strange, but we cannot continue unless we have fire-light from the torches. Please take one, and I'll light them for you." Cardinal Navarro sparked a lighter and ignited his torch.

They all took a torch and lit each one from Navarro's torch. The cardinal took the lead, walking deeper underground. The vaulted, narrow stone passage allowed only one person at a time. Cardinal Navarro led, followed by Travis, Glauser, his officer, Prescott, and Claire. Niches on the wall contained skulls, and the deeper they advanced, the more such niches appeared, until the walls were made entirely of skulls.

"The skulls are protecting us. They belonged to the Christian martyrs during the Roman Empire," said Cardinal Navarro. Most of the skulls were blackened by age and decay.

A heavy, double-paneled bronze gate, embossed with an image of none other than Satan himself, blocked their way. Navarro raised his hands and began an incantation. The heavy doors opened slowly. Travis did not detect any mechanical or electronic apparatus that controlled the doors. They passed through and arrived in a stranger-than-strange hall.

By the dim light of the torches, they could see a stone hall with a round, vaulted ceiling. It seemed to be taller than it was wide. They were standing at the top of a circular, black-veined marble stairway. On the floor at the bottom stood a chapel, its roof resembling a Thai pagoda. It was an open chapel, and five jagged columns supported its dome. The entire chapel seemed to be made from basalt—black as night and sparkling with cold, silver specks.

"There is no one here," said Cardinal Navarro, looking around the hall. His voice echoed in the cavernous hall.

Travis placed his torch on a ring on the wall. "Not yet, or maybe she is already here." He walked down the stairs toward the chapel. Claire and Prescott placed their torches on the wall as well and followed Travis. They descended thirteen steps to the circular pathway encircling the chapel. The mosaic on the pathway depicted a giant snake. They crossed the scaly path and climbed five steps to the chapel with no walls.

Cardinal Navarro, Glauser, and his officer stood at the top of the circular stairs, their torches in their hands, lighting this eerie and ghastly place. The smoke from the torches settled in eerie layers in the giant hall. Travis, Prescott, and Claire activated their PAVs to adjust for the dim light in the chapel. They moved quietly on the smooth stone floor of the chapel. In the center stood a pentagon-shaped altar table. Judging by the amount of dust on it, it didn't seem that anyone had been there in a while. Except...

Faint chanting could be heard under the cupola. Satan was being summoned, and it was Lucrezia who was chanting. But where was she? Not anywhere in the chapel. Prescott pointed to the floor. She was somewhere down under it. A baby started crying.

Claire bent down to inspect under the altar. On the floor, in the middle of the five legs holding up the altar, a round opening led down to a spiral staircase. Followed by Prescott and Travis, she slid under the altar table and took the stairs down. The spiral staircase was enclosed in a stone block shaft, dotted with occasional triangular-shaped openings. Through them they could see into another chamber, similar to the one above them.

They walked carefully down the stone stairs. The satanic chanting and the baby crying continued emanating from down below. Occasionally, they peered through the openings, but there was no sign of Lucrezia or the baby. The spiral stairway ended, and two openings led outside the stairway shaft. Rail-less stairways on top of arched, stone gangways, resembling flying buttresses, reached the opposite wall of this round sub-chamber. At the wall, the stairway bent and followed the contour of the wall in a counterclockwise direction, descending to the floor below. This chamber seemed to have been carved out of solid rock, just like the one above.

Travis crawled a few steps down on the left stairway and Prescott on the right, and they peered down over the edge. They were at least ten meters above the floor. Down below, in the center of the room, they saw Lucrezia dressed in a red robe, walking around yet another black, pentagon-shaped altar. She was chanting while holding with both hands a silver knife over her head. Five candles on each corner of the pentagon altar lit the sinister event. The baby girl, wrapped in a bloody blanket, lay on her back in the center of the stone table. She was whimpering, too tired to cry anymore.

And then they saw Lucrezia's face. It was Lucia. It couldn't be. But Lucrezia resembled Lucia. Prescott pointed down, signaling to Claire. She slid next to him, looked down, and stiffened. She looked at Prescott and raised her eyebrows in dismay. They returned back up in the spiral-stairs shaft.

"Lucia?" Travis whispered.

"Or maybe her twin sister," speculated Claire.

"I think you're right. Lucrezia is Lucia's twin sister," agreed Prescott.

"Time to take her out." Travis gave the signal. He and Claire would each take a stairway, while Prescott would stay at the top as a backup in case of trouble, which was sure to come.

Prescott kept his eyes on Lucrezia down below, bending over the edge of the stairway while pointing his wrist gun at her.

Claire moved quickly and silently down the stairs along the flying buttress gangway. At the wall she stopped and watched Lucrezia continuing her Satan worship. The knife Lucrezia held worried her. The baby was on the altar among the candles, within easy reach of Lucrezia and that knife. Claire lay down on her stomach and slid down the final flight of stairs to the floor. She extended her left-hand gun from under her sleeve, and extracted a knife from the side of her right leg. Crouched, she aimed her gun at Lucrezia.

On the opposite stairs, Travis reached the wall in a flash. He peered down and saw the baby safe on the altar and Lucrezia walking around it, chanting and brandishing the silver knife. He waited until Lucrezia had her back to him, and then he jumped to the floor. He landed as quietly as a panther. He crawled quickly on his elbows and knees toward the altar while Lucrezia still had her back to him. He reached the shadow of the altar just as she turned around a corner of the altar. From that point, he moved quickly and got underneath the altar table.

"I'm under the table," Travis informed Claire and Prescott.

"I'm aiming at her head," said Claire. "Shall I shoot?"

"Why hasn't she killed the baby yet?" Prescott wondered. "What is she waiting for?"

"A sign from Satan?" Travis speculated.

"Maybe she just wants the baby to die from exposure," said Claire. "It's cold down here."

"Prescott, we need you down here," said Travis. "Come down the same stairs I did, and take position at the bottom of the stairs."

"OK," replied Prescott.

"Is it me, or is it getting colder in here?" said Claire.

"It is colder," said Travis. "I don't like this. Prescott, what do you sense?"

"I'm at the bottom of the stairs," said Prescott. "She's definitely summoning the devil. I suggest we take her out."

"When she faces me, at my command, we'll both shoot her," said Claire.

"Agreed," replied Prescott. "Travis, get ready to grab the baby."

"Yes. Don't miss," said Travis. "What the hell? Now it's getting hot in here."

"Never mind the heat," said Claire. "Get ready, Prescott. I have her in my crosshairs. At three. One, two—"

Claire didn't get to say "three." The chamber shook as if an earthquake were taking place. Her hand swayed. She lost her balance and leaned on her left elbow, her gun hand. The shaking continued, and she was forced to lie down on her side.

Prescott was on his belly, leaning on his elbows. He had the back of Lucrezia's head in his PAV's crosshairs. Suddenly, he felt a tremor. The floor was moving, and a rumble thundered in the chamber. Satan was interfering. Calmly

Prescott issued the command, "Fire." But
Lucrezia's head did not explode. She was still
standing. He was sure his aim had been perfect.
"I missed," he hissed.

Travis felt the temperature getting hotter
than on a summer day in Death Valley at high
noon. He touched the bottom of the table and
almost burned his fingers. The tremor began.
That was not a good place to be at that
moment, under a stone table weighing a ton
and supported only by five slender stone legs.
He slid out from under the table not a moment
too soon. The altar's legs crumbled as if they
were made of sand, and, as the table collapsed,
it made a sound like "boof." The baby started
crying in earnest. Travis eyed Lucrezia, who
was crazed with joy. He pointed the gun at her
and commanded it to fire, but the gun didn't
shoot. His sensors told him that Prescott had
missed when he fired. Their firearms were
useless.

Claire felt red-hot light descending into the
chamber from above. She looked up and saw a
snake of fire coiling downward on the outside
of the spiral-stairs shaft. When it hit the two
gangways, it split in two and followed the
curved gangways like rivers of red lava. The
two flows hit the walls and splashed into
rivulets of fire. Claire jumped to her feet and
shouted, "Satan is here!"

Lucrezia raised her arms up straight and burst into mad laughter. She held with both hands the silver knife, which gleamed red from the fires surrounding the chamber. She shouted, "Lord Satan, I'm awaiting your command to kill this child!"

Prescott saw Travis escape just in time from under the altar. The fire descended from above. Satan had decided to intervene and claim his victim. If they didn't act fast, they and the baby would be dead. "Form a triad!" Prescott shouted.

Before the fire could engulf the entire chamber, Prescott, Travis, and Claire positioned themselves around the altar, Lucrezia, and the baby. Travis was closest to Lucrezia. She lowered her knife and, aiming for his heart, stabbed him in the chest. But the knife did not penetrate his jacket. She looked at the knife and then Travis, bewildered. She stabbed him again, but to no avail. Travis, without remorse, kicked her in the solar plexus. He wished to kill her, but Satan was surrounding them and would not give him time to finish her off.

Prescott, Travis, and Claire opened their arms, forming a protective shield between Satan, and Lucrezia and the baby. Satan's fire could not penetrate the life shield that they established. The fire encircled them and moved like a vortex. Their special suits protected them from the searing heat, and their life shield protected Lucrezia and the baby from the fire. By chance and for the sake of the baby, the Capuchin Trinity Team saved Lucrezia from Satan's flames, which would have consumed her as a reward for her devotion.

Lucrezia got up and regained her breath. Staggering, with the knife in one hand and uncertain what to do, she approached Claire, raised her knife, and struck at her. Her arm stopped halfway down, blocked by the life shield. "Lord Satan, help me!" she shouted, looking desperate. The fire vortex raged all around them.

"We cannot hold this much longer!" Prescott told his partners.

"And Lucrezia is free to do as she wishes inside our shield," assessed Travis, worrying about the baby.

"We have only one choice," said Claire. "Let Satan kill her."

Lucrezia moved around with her back to the altar, where the newborn lay whimpering. She looked confused and helpless. Satan, her lord, was just on the other side of these three despicable humans and could not reach her. And she could not get through the Trinity barrier. She stopped, lowered her head for a moment, and then raised it. She shouted, "Kill the baby!" She grabbed the knife with both hands, towering over the baby and ready to strike her in her tiny heart.

"Now!" shouted Claire.

Lucrezia was facing Travis and Prescott across the altar. They saw her grinning with the expected pleasure of killing the newborn and carrying out Satan's command. The knife began descending toward the baby.

Travis and Prescott concentrated and opened the shield between them for a fraction of a second. A jet of plasma broke through and hit Lucrezia in the chest. She caught on fire, lost her balance from the blast, and fell backward. She screamed in pain and agony as the flames consumed first her hair and clothes, and then her flesh. She collapsed on the floor, dead and sizzling. Satan's fire dissolved her to ashes a few seconds later.

The baby lay unharmed on the altar.

"Give it up, Satan. You've lost!" shouted Claire.

"I have until sunrise to destroy you!" boomed a malicious voice in the chamber.

A thought came to Claire: What difference did the sunrise make here underground? Like a vampire, Satan couldn't face the white light of the sun, but here the sun would never rise. She communicated to Travis and Prescott, "Let the sun rise here."

Claire, Travis, and Prescott concentrated and imagined the sunrise. Within their triad, a globe of red, then yellow, and soon white light appeared. It was the sun of their imagination.

A thunderous scream that shook the chamber signaled Satan's defeat. The fire vortex died instantly.

Chapter 47. The Aftermath

It was quiet in Satan's chamber, but it was hot as an oven. The Trinity Team was safe, but the baby was not. Claire opened her jacket and placed the baby inside it. Travis and Prescott opened their jackets and shielded Claire and the baby. They moved slowly toward the stairs and climbed them cautiously. They reached inside the spiral-staircase shaft, where fortunately the temperature was not as hot.

The narrow, spiral rail-less stairs made it impossible for the three of them to climb as a trio. Prescott took the lead and communicated with Glauser. Claire followed, holding the baby inside her jacket against her breast. Travis was last, walking sideways and keeping an eye out for Satan's possible return from down below. They finally reached the top and crawled out from under the onyx altar in Satan's chapel.

Cardinal Navarro, Oberst Albert Glauser, and his officer stood at the top of the circular stairs, pale and visibly shaken. Neither Glauser nor his officer had their weapons drawn. They probably figured that whoever was coming out from under the altar could not be harmed by bullets.

When Cardinal Navarro saw them, he kneeled, raised his arms, and exclaimed, "Thank you, Lord, our Heavenly Father, for protecting the innocent and the just."

Oberst Glauser and his officer kneeled and made the sign of the cross.

"It is a miracle that you came out of there." Oberst Glauser wiped a tear from the corner of his eye. "We were frightened out of our boots up here. I can't imagine the hell you encountered down below."

"Indeed," said Travis, and then he noticed Claire.

"We need emergency help for the baby!" she shouted.

"Right away," said the officer, opening his comm.

"Hold it," said Cardinal Navarro. "Help can only come from within the Holy City. We will not take this baby outside its walls."

"There is an infant incubator in the medical quarters. Tell them to bring it down. Stat," said Claire, using medical jargon. "Find an obstetrician," she added.

Claire began running down the corridor for the exit. The others followed with Navarro trailing far behind, and they eventually lost him.

Travis addressed Albert Glauser. "Lucrezia is dead. Satan burned her alive. And she is—was—the spitting image of Lucia. We suspect she was Lucia's twin sister."

"Unbelievable!" exclaimed Oberst Glauser. He turned his comm on and issued orders about Lucrezia's identity.

At the elevator, they pushed the up button. Luckily, a secret code was not necessary to call the elevator down, which arrived shortly.

"Where is the emergency team for the baby?" Claire inquired in her comm, and after hearing the answer she said, "Good, stay where you are—we are coming up." She checked on the baby, who seemed to be OK. At the top, the emergency medical team received them with the incubator. They took over from there. Glauser's officer accompanied the medical team and the baby back to the clinic.

"Dr. Stark, how are you feeling?" Prescott inquired in his comm.

"I'm doing as well as can be expected after a concussion. I heard that you rescued the baby."

"Affirmative," said Prescott. "How are the Pope and Dottore Salmeri?"

"Dottore Salmeri is in critical condition. They took her to another hospital here in the Vatican for emergency surgery."

"And the Pope?" asked Travis.

"He didn't make it." Dr. Stark sighed.

"Oh, no," lamented Claire.

Oberst Glauser was following them while talking into his comm and getting the status of the surgery room massacre.

"Where are you, Dr. Stark?" asked Prescott.

"In the medical quarters."

"Are the cardinals there, too?" asked Travis.

"Yes. They're praying."

They arrived shortly at the medical quarters where the Swiss Guards stood sentry outside. Inside, they found Dr. Stark sitting near the glass wall, holding an ice bag behind his head. He looked even paler than usual. Another officer, who was with him, stood up when they entered. In the surgery room, a white plastic sheet covered the Pope's body, which remained on the operating table. Cardinals Cellini and Bertrand were kneeling beside it, praying.

"Oberst Glauser," saluted the officer. "We have confirmation that Lucrezia is Lucia's twin sister and Dottore Pietro's second wife."

That was a big surprise to all. Angelo Pietro was a polygamist, married to both sisters, who were devil worshipers.

"That was unexpected. Please give us a report of what you discovered, Officer." Glauser looked gray.

"Certainly, Oberst. The perpetrator, Lucrezia, entered the surgery through a recently constructed secret passage. It was well concealed, and we had trouble finding it with our sensors. The passage was connected to the wet wall, the interior passage that houses the plumbing. We lost the trail behind the wet wall, but we have sniffers searching for the escape route."

"No need to do any more searching. Cancel it," said Oberst Glauser.

The officer gave a few short commands in a small device he retrieved from his pocket.

"Before entering the surgery, the perpetrator activated a looping hologram for the glass wall display. Anyone looking at the display may not have realized immediately that they were watching previously recorded images. While this was happening, she entered the operating room through the hidden access hatch, managed to knock out Dr. Stark, and impaled Dottore Salmeri with a *spatha*. Unfortunately for Dottore Salmeri, she was hunched over the Holy Father at the time, and the blade penetrated through her and into the heart of the Holy Father. Lucrezia Pietro snatched the baby from Nurse Fulvia and retreated through the secret access, which had an automatic closing mechanism, leaving no visible opening afterward."

"Was there any hope of saving the Holy Father?" Oberst Glauser asked.

"No, Oberst. After they extracted the sword to help Dottore Salmeri, the medics declared him dead with no chance of revival. Cardinals Cellini and Bertrand asked us to leave him in place until Cardinal Navarro returned."

Oberst Glauser picked up the clear plastic bag holding the bloody sword used in the murder of the Pope. He looked at the straight edge blade with its stubby guard. "This seems to be something from our armory. Bastards! They used our own weapon to kill the Holy Father."

Cardinal Navarro came in, flushed from the fast pace he must have taken. Without a word, he entered the operating room, kneeled alongside the other two cardinals, and began praying with them.

"Where is Nurse Fulvia?" asked Claire.

"She went along with the medics to help Dottore Salmeri," answered the officer. "She gave us her account of what happened inside the surgery. Lucrezia pulled Dr. Stark backward by the scruff of his neck. He fell and hit his head. Then she impaled Dottore Salmeri as she was hunched over the Holy Father, and she pushed the sword down to the hilt. It penetrated both bodies. Nurse Fulvia said that it all happened so fast she froze with fear. Lucrezia came to her, pulled a silver knife from her waistband, and grabbed the baby from her arms. According to her, Lucrezia disappeared with the baby. She recovered from the shock long enough to scream, after which you came in."

Travis looked around and sighed. "I don't think there is anything we can do here tonight."

"Dr. Stark, are you OK to walk? Were you given accommodations?" Prescott asked.

"I am OK to get the hell out of here," he said grimly.

The Pregnant Pope

Chapter 48. Christ or Antichrist

Travis, Prescott, and Claire were having a late morning breakfast after they had reviewed the latest information about Lucrezia, Lucia, and Angelo Pietro. The mystery made sense now—who did it and how. And, of course, why.

They each checked the news about the Pope in their PAVs. At ten o'clock, on the steps of Saint Peter Basilica, Cardinal Bertrand addressed the thousands of people in St. Peter's Square: "Dear brothers and sisters in Christ, it is with great sorrow I announce that, at 00:07 of June 6, our beloved Holy Father, Pope Julius Urban Pius, has entered heaven and the house of our loving God. Our silent prayers will guide our saintly Holy Father to join our Lord Jesus Christ in eternal life."

The people in the square were in a state of shock, crying and praying. Pope Julius Urban Pius was a beloved pope who had worked hard for forty years to restore much of the Roman Catholic Church to its former glory after the near end-of-the-world in the 2020s. Most young Catholics had not known any other pope but Julius Urban Pius. He had been an iconic figure, and his death, shrouded by the lockdown of the Vatican the night before, raised questions and suspicions from the outside world.

"We are summoned for a 10:30 meeting with the cardinals," said Claire, listening in her PAV.

391

They concluded their breakfast and headed to the conference room. It was going to be fascinating observing, for the near future, a Vatican headed by Camerlengo Cardinal Bertrand and the powerful Cardinal Cellini.

In the center of the room stood an ornate table with three red velvet high-back chairs. In front of the table were three humbler armchairs, presumably for them. In a corner of the room, four priests stared uncomfortably, as if caught in a very secret conversation. A few moments after the CTT arrived, Cardinals Cellini, Bertrand, and Navarro, dressed in their black cassocks and scarlet zucchetti, entered the room and took their seats at the table. Cardinal Cellini sat in the center chair, with Bertrand on his right and Navarro on his left. Prescott, Claire, and Travis sat down as well.

Cardinal Cellini addressed the four priests: "You're excused for now." The priests bowed and exited the room. Cellini waited until the door closed behind them. "As you may have heard, Cardinal Bertrand made the official announcement in Saint Peter's Square about the passing of our Holy Father." He looked at them with tension showing on his face. "Needless to say, this was not the outcome we expected."

The Capuchin Trinity Team listened quietly.

"You were unable to find the culprits in time and prevent our Holy Father's murder," said Cardinal Bertrand. "Because of your panicked warnings, which were futile, the Vatican was locked down, and now the whole world wonders what really happened inside here and how the Pope died. We have a situation to contain, besides getting ready to elect a new pope." Cardinal Bertrand fingered his rosary. "Why did you pursue this Lucrezia and save the newborn, and, in turn, summon Satan? My God, if the word gets out that under God's cathedral lies a chapel for Satan, our cause is finished." Cardinal Bertrand raised his eyebrows, demanding answers.

"Your Eminences," Prescott began. "We are deeply sorry for the Pope's death. We offer our condolences. We understand your dissatisfaction with the outcome. Although it ended tragically, we accomplished what we were hired to do."

"Please explain, because we're not sure about that," said Cardinal Cellini.

"Our directives were to find out the circumstances under which a man, the Pope, became pregnant and carried a human fetus. And, if there were wrongdoers, to find out who did it and bring them to justice. We did all that," said Prescott. "You are witnesses to what I say."

The cardinals shifted in their seats but did not say anything, as if expecting to hear more.

"Very well," said Prescott. "The following is our report. Satan sensed that humanity's world is weakening and that it is ripe for ending—"

"That's preposterous!" exploded Cardinal Cellini.

"It could be, but look around you," said Prescott. "Half the world's population does not believe in God. The other half is fragmented among many religions, some even worshipping Satan as a new and better god."

The three cardinals seemed to be uncomfortable. Cardinal Bertrand ran a finger inside his collar, as if to relieve himself of some unknown heat.

"Pope Julius Urban Pius accomplished tremendous deeds in restructuring and reforming the Catholic Church," continued Prescott. "We were at the abyss in the '20s. Our faith in God kept us from annihilating each other. Pope Julius Urban Pius became a threat to Satan, and the year 2066 was to be, and it might still be, Satan's year. The time had come to give birth to the Antichrist.

"Who should carry this child, I ask you? A woman? Why not a man? A holy man, for that matter. The Pope. But to accomplish such a feat, Satan needed help from a few humans. In spite of what you may think, Satan can influence most of us, but he has difficulties with the religious, especially the clergy. To be able to seed the Pope with his essence, he needed a religious person. A nun was ideal for that task.

"Who else to help him with his mission but the Satanists? And if the Satanists were also close to the clergy, Satan's treachery would be stronger yet. Dottore Pietro, the Pope's personal doctor, was a Satanist. His wife, Lucia, was converted to Satanism by her twin sister, Lucrezia. When his sons died in the auto race, which Satan probably caused, Dottore Pietro was ready to be converted as well.

"He renounced Christianity and took a second wife, Lucrezia, his wife's sister. No law enforcement agency keeps track of Satanists, and therefore the Vatican didn't know about the Dottore's newfound religion. Catholics don't allow polygamy or group marriages, but other religions and Satanists do. We don't know at this time if Angelo Pietro was in a group marriage and if other members of his cult were involved in this crime.

"Angelo, Lucia, and Lucrezia Pietro, as instructed by Satan, targeted Sister Terina to be the carrier of the evil seed. We learned from her memory, which she preserved for us, how she was infected through a satanic rape ritual. The next step was for her to touch the Pope's flesh, and that event was already scheduled. Sister Terina was not alone. The devil Zepar was inside her, guiding her on what to do. At the ceremony on March 6, she transmitted the evil seed to the Pope.

"The Pope became pregnant with a parasite, Satan's son, the Antichrist. God intervened and instructed Monsignore Giuseppe in his dreams to visit a saint's site, that of Santa Francesca Romana in Rome. He disobeyed God's instruction, and, being infatuated with Pope Joan, he visited her alleged burial site instead.

"Monsignore Giuseppe defied God and acquired the essence of what was supposedly Pope Joan. We don't know if the woman was Pope Joan or someone else, or what different effect it might had have on Satan's fetus. But it worked, killing Satan's genes and reverting it to a human fetus. The fetus evolved much faster than a normal human fetus and was, all along, a male.

"In the last hour before surgery, the fetus transformed itself into a female. Maybe that was the effect of not bringing the essence of Santa Francesca Romana to the Pope, but another woman's essence instead. That we may never know." Prescott took a break and, with a gesture, invited Claire to continue.

"I hope it makes sense so far," Claire said to the three cardinals, who nodded, acknowledging their understanding of what had happened. "As for the culprits, as Prescott said, it was the Pietros' satanic trio. They were the operatives who carried out Satan's mission. Dottore Pietro was in an ideal position to help bring Satan's son into the world. Later, Lucia Pietro joined the convent to keep an eye on Sister Terina, in case she remembered the satanic ritual the Pietros had performed on her.

"If the Dottore hadn't been absent when the Pope didn't feel well, and if Monsignore Giuseppe hadn't performed the tests on him, the Dottore would have kept everything a secret until the day of the surgery. However, unbeknownst to Dottore Pietro, the Pope was not carrying Satan's son, but a human son. Again, because Monsignore Giuseppe did not visit Santa Francesca Romana as he was instructed, we cannot call the child God's child.

"When Dottore Pietro found out from our research that the fetus had devolved, he wanted it aborted. He was afraid that a new Messiah might be born instead of the Antichrist. Satan and the devil Zepar had no more use for Sister Terina, and Zepar began annihilating her soul. That's when Prescott accompanied Cardinal Navarro to see the exorcism, and, soon after, the Capuchin Trinity Team drove the devil out of Sister Terina.

"No longer possessed by the devil, she became a problem for the Pietros. Sister Terina might have remembered what happened, and so she needed to be killed, fast. But Oberst Glauser's men got in the way. Lucrezia on the outside arranged with assassins to kill Sister Terina with frozen mercury bullets. Lucia managed to get into Sister Terina's room, hide under the bed, and later, when it was quiet, she stabbed her to death. When she came out, the assassins shot Glauser's officers and eliminated all witnesses."

"I'm confused. If Lucia Pietro was able to kill Sister Terina, why the need for the assassins?" Cardinal Bertrand asked.

"The Pietros needed absolute assurance that Sister Terina was dead. I think the assassins were backup, as they would have been able to kill her in the room with the mercury bullets. Since Lucia was successful, they just killed the guards, eliminating all witnesses," said Claire. "Lucia was afraid of us, and she was sure that we had begun to suspect her. We were in possession of Sister Terina's memory, and we had to be eliminated. She instructed Lucrezia and the assassins to ambush us under the railroad underpass. They failed.

"We still needed to be eliminated urgently, to stop us from interfering. I'm sure Cardinal Cellini and some of the other twelve cardinals know something on this matter." Claire smiled coldly at Cardinal Cellini, who turned red with embarrassment. Cardinal Bertrand and Navarro looked at him with confusion.

"In any case," continued Claire, getting enough satisfaction for the moment, "not all of us had to die or be incapacitated, just one of us. The Pietros decided to act against Prescott when he visited Ispettore Carlota Romano. Lucrezia and Lucia accessed the Ispettore's apartment via the dumbwaiter, disabled the building's surveillance, poisoned the Chianti, and killed Edda Passarelli, Carlota Romano's domestic help.

"It would have ended there, if Travis and I hadn't detected through our PAVs Prescott's distress. We helped Prescott recuperate, and after interrogating Angelo Pietro, we realized that someone else was involved in this plot besides him and Lucia. We unlocked Sister Terina's memory and confirmed that Lucia and Angelo were involved along with another woman, Lucrezia, who we didn't know at the time, was his second wife. I'll let Travis take it from here."

"The time for preforming the surgery and removing the baby from the Pope was approaching fast," said Travis. "Since we had arrested Dottore Pietro, we requested Dr. Stark to help with the surgery, and you, Cardinal Bertrand, suggested Dottore Salmeri to perform the operation."

Cardinal Bertrand bowed slightly.

"In the meanwhile, the Swiss Guards arrested Lucia, giving us a false sense of security. And by creating confusion with the help of a smoke bomb, Lucrezia entered the Vatican at the time Lucia was arrested. It was not until the last minute that we figured out what would be their desired way to kill the baby. But we were too late—Lucrezia was waiting in the secret passage built by Dottore Pietro for this occasion. She had rigged the glass wall display to mask her entrance into the room. While we thought we were watching live images, she struck.

"She knocked down Dr. Stark. Then she saw Dottore Salmeri bent over while attending to the Holy Father, and she stabbed them with a spatha. After that, she grabbed the baby from Nurse Fulvia, retreated to her access hatch, released a small fog bomb, and ran underground to offer the baby to Satan. Thanks to you, Cardinal Navarro, we were able to find her there. Satan did appear. Fortunately, we tricked him into killing Lucrezia, and we saved the baby. Also, the Holy Father may not have been the intended victim. Lucrezia stabbed Dottore Salmeri to prevent her from interfering, and, in the process, she stabbed the Holy Father in the heart, killing him. And that's about it," concluded Travis.

"And you want us to believe that Satan was involved in all this? That he appeared down below and you stood up to him?" Recovered from his previous embarrassment, Cardinal Cellini gave a small, sarcastic chuckle.

"Yes, Satan appeared down below in his chapel, and we defeated him. For now," said Prescott. "As for Satan instigating these tragic events, it was him. Unless you don't believe in Satan at all, and, if that's the case, you will not have a Church of God, Cardinal Cellini."

Cardinal Cellini made a gesture as if he were about to excommunicate Prescott, when Cardinal Navarro intervened. "Yes, Satan was there, Cardinal Cellini. I witnessed it along with Oberst Glauser and his officer. Our prayers kept us safe from his fire. I cannot even begin to imagine what the Capuchin Trinity Team did down below to avoid Satan's wrath."

Cardinal Cellini shrank in his chair, deflated.

"I understand now that Lucrezia summoned Satan," said Cardinal Navarro. "And yes, Satan's chapel has a purpose under Saint Peter's Basilica. We must be reminded at all times about the evil that faces us, and we must fight it every day."

"I, too, have a better understanding of the events now," said Cardinal Bertrand. "It is tragic that our Holy Father was killed." Cardinal Bertrand and Navarro exchanged glances as if to approve the explanation given by the CTT.

"Your Eminences, what explanation will you give to the world about the emergency response and the Holy Father's death?" Travis asked.

Cardinal Bertrand glanced at Cardinal Cellini, who made a gesture with his hand as if to say, "It's all yours. I don't care anymore."

Cardinal Bertrand sighed. "As far as the Church is concerned, a man conceiving a baby is unnatural. For all practical purposes, the fetus might as well have been a tumor. Our Holy Father died in surgery while being operated on to remove that tumor. Security precautions were taken for that reason, which, due to a glitch in communications, were misinterpreted as force majeure."

"What about the newborn girl?" Claire asked. "What will happen to her? She is flesh of the Holy Father."

"She will be taken to a convent to be raised by nuns," said Cardinal Navarro. "We will not divulge to her how she came to be born. As far as she will know, she is an orphan who the

Church cares for. Do you have an opinion on whether this child, this girl, is—how shall I say it—is she special?"

"We don't know what she might become when she grows up," said Claire. "She may grow to be a perfectly ordinary woman. Only time will tell if she will be a common person or the new Christ."

Chapter 49. Cardinal Le Pere

The CTT mission was complete, except that they didn't divulge all they knew about Satan's secret.

Prescott, Clair, and Travis stopped in the corridor as they walked away from the conference room when a call came into their PAVs. "Good morning, CTT. This is Cardinal Le Pere." The deep voice of a reassured man introduced himself. "I'd like to congratulate you and thank you for an excellent job done." The mysterious Cardinal Le Pere, who they never saw or talked to, decided to contact them.

They exchanged surprised looks. They switched their PAVs to silent.

"Your Eminence, what a surprise!" said Claire. "Good morning to you, and I'm glad we have a chance to, at least and at last, talk."

"I apologize for not meeting face to face, but as you see here in the Holy City, we are going through turbulent times."

"We understand, Your Eminence," said Prescott. "And on behalf of our team, I would like to express our sincere sorrow for His Holiness's premature passing."

"I know you did your best, and sometimes tragedy strikes, even when the best Trinity Team is working to solve Satan's evil doings. Our Holy Father was a great man, and I will miss him, just like all faithful Catholics will."

"Thank you, Your Eminence, and, again, we are sorry about His Holiness," Claire said.

The cardinal took a moment to say a quick prayer, after which he continued, "The reason I called is because, somehow, I feel that we haven't heard a valuable piece of information. Yes, we prevented the murder of the child and foiled Satan's plan. We discovered who the culprits were, and at least one faced an early demise. However, the three Satanists went to great pains to kill you and, in the process, killed Sister Terina. May God protect her in eternity."

"That is very perceptive of you, Your Eminence," said Travis. "Satan had a secret. As it happened, we were aware of it all along, but we did not realize until this morning what that secret was. It was unacceptable for Satan to allow a human to possess a certain capability."

"Travis, you sound as if Satan allowed the fruit of knowledge to escape from, in this case, hell," said Cardinal Le Pere.

"Just about," said Travis. "He wanted very much the death of the child. The child has inherited a unique ability. The girl's mind has a link to the White Energy Mind Realm and to the Dark Energy Mind Realm. That is a unique ability that very few humans have ever had. Jesus Christ was one of them."

"It's a miracle," said Cardinal Le Pere, and he prayed. "Aside from bringing into this world a new Messiah, why would Satan be so concerned?"

"Your Eminence, in the case of Jesus Christ, God granted Jesus access to the two realms," said Travis. "In the case of the girl, Satan did."

"Excuse me, but I don't understand what the problem is."

"The problem is monumental, Your Eminence," said Prescott. "Satan really wanted to bring the Antichrist into this world. The world is ready for him. God foiled his plans. Satan gave the gift, but God and the people of Earth will reap the benefits through the works of this newborn child, a girl."

"I don't know what to say," said the cardinal. "Is the girl a new Messiah?"

"We do not know that," said Prescott. "In the past there were a few other select people with that unique ability. Unfortunately, they were misunderstood."

"I understand," said the cardinal. "However, why does Satan fear the child so much? He can kill her anytime he wants to."

"Yes, he could," said Prescott. "But in order to undo the damage he set in motion, the child needed to be killed before the first sunrise after birth. He failed."

"Thanks to you, for which the Holy See will have eternal gratitude. God bless you," said Cardinal Le Pere.

"Your Eminence," said Claire. "What will be the girl's name?"

"Giovanna Magdalena."

Chapter 50. The Villains

Oberst Glauser moved Lucia Pietro to the underground jail into a cell adjacent to Angelo Pietro's. They talked little, probably because they knew the cells were bugged. A guard kept watch on both of them, just in case they tried to commit suicide.

Claire, Travis, and Prescott, accompanied by Oberst Glauser, went down for the final interrogation of the Pietros. Oberst Glauser asked the guard to move both detainees into a larger cell, which, unlike the others, had a heavy wooden door, not bars. Several wooden folding chairs were brought in, and Glauser closed the door after the detainees were inside, along with himself and the CTT.

"This is your last chance to come clean," said Glauser with steely eyes. He sat down in front of them, flanked by Travis, Prescott, and Claire.

The Pietros, seated, exchanged quick glances. "Come clean about what, Oberst?" the Dottore asked.

"About your attempt to kill the Holy Father and the child."

"I hope the Pope is doing well," said the Dottore. "However, we are innocent. I did nothing, although I said whatever needed to be said to stop those three from hurting me." He motioned with his head toward the CTT. "Torture is not allowed, even at the Vatican. As far as Lucia, she came to the Vatican to contact me." He and Lucia smiled confidently.

"It seems that way. Now, aren't you curious about what happened last night while you were here alone?" Glauser asked.

"What could possibly have happened?" said Lucia innocently. "Angelo told me that the Pope had a condition that may require surgery. He did not tell me what kind of condition on the basis that it was confidential. I hope everything went well." She smiled.

"Everything went well," said Oberst Glauser. "The baby was born and it is a girl and she is alive." Glauser stopped and watched them. Angelo and Lucia were blinking fast and started perspiring. "Yes, the baby was born in spite of how much you wanted her dead."

"You're lying!" shouted Lucia.

"Lucrezia—" Oberst Glauser paused. Claire observed that the Pietros' blood pressures were rising fast. "Lucrezia is dead."

Lucia buried her face in her hands and wailed. Angelo looked stunned. Their arrogance disappeared.

Travis spoke, "We know everything there is to know about what you did. Satan killed your sons with Lucrezia's help, Dottore Pietro, to make you and Lucia his subjects. You fell for it, and Lucrezia, already a Satanist, married you and converted you to Satanism. You were the brains of this crime. Lucia killed Sister Terina. Lucrezia killed Oberst's officers and Edda Passarelli. She attempted to kill us, and almost killed Prescott and Claire. It was all for nothing."

"And the Pope?" Angelo asked darkly.

"Lucrezia killed the Pope," said Travis.

Angelo and Lucia Pietro started howling with pleasure. "Praise Satan!" they cried together.

"At least the Holy Father is in heaven. You two, on the other hand, will join Lucrezia in hell," said Oberst Glauser.

"We will be given eternal rewards in hell!" screeched Lucia with a sinister laugh.

"When our time to die comes," said Angelo Pietro calmly. "You have nothing against us. *Niente*. Nothing."

"Aren't you in a hurry to die and join Satan?" Prescott asked.

"Life is to be enjoyed," said Angelo Pietro with a confident smirk. "And Lucia and I will do exactly that, for a long time to come."

"Maybe I should tell you how Lucrezia died," said Prescott. He got their attention. "Satan killed her. She failed in her mission, and Satan burned her alive. Satan does not tolerate failure. You failed as well. Do you think Satan will reward you? Think again."

Lucia and Angelo looked horrified at hearing that outcome.

"The only hope for you is to ask God for forgiveness, and, for as long as you live, you should live near God's church," said Claire.

Angelo was hesitant. "Will our confession help us?" he asked timidly.

"No, Angelo!" shouted Lucia.

"Everything you said we did, it's true," confessed Angelo Pietro.

Lucia exploded with rage and started hitting him. "Stupid, they have no proof!" she shouted.

"I actually don't need proof," said Oberst Glauser. "You are in deep shit with Satan. If I were you, I'd pray to live for as long as possible to avoid Satan's wrath in hell."

The Pietros looked distraught. Failing Satan was not acceptable, and no rewards awaited them in hell. For all their hard and faithful work, after they died, only eternal pain and suffering would be their reward.

"I would like to say 'God help you,' but I can't," said Oberst Glauser darkly. "We have concluded our discussion. After you die, may you burn in hell for eternity."

The Pietros looked as if they had just received the death penalty.

Oberst Glauser, Claire, Prescott, and Travis gathered outside the cell, leaving the Pietros to contemplate their future, burning in hell for eternity.

"We don't have much hard evidence against them," said Claire.

"The Vatican will not allow anything to be divulged in court about what really happened," said Oberst Glauser grimly. "Those two evil people will walk, and then they will talk." He sighed.

"That's always the case when the devil is involved," said Travis.

"His Holiness's legacy cannot be tarnished by these Satanists." Oberst Glauser looked tense and thoughtful for a moment, and then his appearance relaxed. "If you'll excuse me, I have something to take care of." He opened the door and entered the cell. A second later, Lucia screamed, and two distinct gunshots boomed in the cell.

Oberst Glauser came out, his smoking gun pointing up. "Now, Lucia and Angelo Pietro can join their beloved Satan." He rotated the gun in his hand and offered it to the guard, handle first. "Guard, I surrender my firearm to you. Please take me into custody. I executed the two suspects."

Mit Sandru

Chapter 51. Habemus Papam

The CTT mission was finished. The outcome was a tragic one for the victims and the villains.

Travis, Claire, and Prescott sat at an outdoor café in Piazza Venezia. They were dressed as civilians: Prescott and Travis in slacks and sport shirts, Claire in a white blouse and miniskirt. She had tinted her brown hair blond.

Claire was nursing a gelato. Prescott was enjoying an espresso and a creamy dessert, while Travis was savoring a cappuccino. He loved his cappuccinos. That's why he had suggested the name for their Trinity Team, the Capuchin Trinity Team.

"Satan never sleeps. If he did, we would all be in heaven," said Prescott philosophically.

"Amen to that," said Claire.

Their case solved and closed, it was a good opportunity to take time out to appreciate the Eternal City. They were in Rome, it was June, and they were unharmed. Satan could go to hell.

"The College of Cardinals got together in a hurry to elect the new pope," said Prescott.

"I wouldn't be surprised if Cellini set this express conclave in motion," said Travis. "He doesn't want Bertrand to get used to being the acting Pope."

"I give Cellini the lowest chances of becoming the next pope," said Claire.

Travis nodded in agreement.

"Who do you think will be the next pope?" Prescott wondered.

"The enigmatic candidate," said Travis.

Claire and Prescott smiled mysteriously.

"What do you think will happen to Giovanna Magdalena?" Claire had some more gelato and remarked, "What a fitting name."

"Indeed," Travis said.

"It depends on how paranoid the priests in charge are or will be," speculated Prescott.

"I hope Navarro makes it safe for her," said Claire.

"I hope so, too," agreed Prescott. "At least until she grows up."

"After what Navarro witnessed in Satan's chapel, he'll tread as carefully as walking on egg shells when it comes to that girl." Travis took a sip of his cappuccino.

A convertible red Ferrari pulled up by the sidewalk, and the driver honked. "*Ciao, bella!*" saluted the white haired, distinguished gentleman driving the car.

Claire waved to him. "Gianni!" She smiled, pleased to see him. "Well, boys, Claire has an engagement to attend to."

Prescott and Travis looked dumbly at each other. "Who's the ancient guy?" Travis managed to ask.

"That is my sugar daddy." Claire winked at them and turned toward her sugar daddy. "Gianni, these are Prescott and Travis."

"Hello, *ragazzi!*" Gianni waved to them. Travis and Prescott waved back, like two schoolboys in the presence of the principal.

Prescott whispered to Travis, "Sugar daddy?"

Travis seemed to be at a loss for words.

"OK, guys, I've got to go. Gianni and I have a busy agenda ahead of us," said Claire, grabbing her handbag.

"Sugar daddy, Claire?" Prescott had to ask.

"A sophisticated woman requires more than just brawn for companionship," said Claire. "Gianni is a professor of Roman history and an archaeologist. He's taking me on a trip to see ruins that are not shown to regular tourists. *Ciao, ragazzi!*" She blew them a kiss, pirouetted on her white sandals, and got into Gianni's red convertible. The Italian men around them did not miss admiring the blonde Claire in her white miniskirt and see-through blouse, with her gorgeous legs and slim figure. A few gave appreciative whistles.

Travis and Prescott watched Claire and her sugar daddy disappear in traffic, their mouths hanging open long afterward.

Travis cleared his throat. "Did you know any of this about Claire?"

"Nah-huh," said Prescott, still staring in the direction of Claire's departure. "Do you think she was referring to us as being the brawn?"

"I'm sure she was," said Travis. "We should get ourselves some women, some cougars."

"Cougars?" Prescott gazed mischievously at Travis. "Well, I've got mine, and I've got to go. Carlota is waiting for me."

"Ispettore Carlota Romano?" Travis didn't know how to feel anymore. He usually had at least two women at his beck and call, and now he was outdone. "You son of a gun! Watch the *vino.*"

"I'll bring my own bottle and an opener." Prescott winked at him. "Sorry to leave you all alone."

"Oh, I'll manage somehow," said Travis, faking loneliness. He watched Prescott get into a robo-taxi to meet Carlota. Lucky guy.

Travis took another sip of his cappuccino and admired the sites around him, considering what to do on his own.

"*Scusi,* could you take a picture of my friend and me?"

Travis turned to see the woman who addressed him. A voluptuous blonde sat at the next table with a cute brunette. God works in mysterious ways. And rewards always await.

"I'd be glad to," said Travis. He moved around the table to frame them with Il Vittoriano's white marble building in the background. "Smile." He took their picture with his PAV and transmitted it to their commercial PAVs. They looked attractive, both of them. "Do you have any plans here in Rome?"

"No, just sightseeing," said the brunette. "I just joined Tessie yesterday." Tessie was the blonde, Travis gathered.

"Hi, I'm Travis." He extended his hand.

"Nice to meet you, Travis. My name is Kathy, and this is my friend, Tessie."

Travis felt Kathy's soft hand. It felt like a promising beginning. "Can I join you in sightseeing? I'm by myself, and I've studied history, among other things."

"Wow! Sure," said Tessie. "An educated man." She smiled pleasantly at him.

It was time to use his magic. "I hope you get good vibes about me."

"Yeah, definitely. I feel good about my impression of you," said Tessie, and she asked her friend. "What do you think? A threesome?"

"Why not?" agreed Kathy, smiling sweetly at him.

A threesome was a good beginning, thought Travis.

Car horns started blaring in the piazza, and people were shouting jubilantly. A waiter announced, "*Habemus Papam*! *Habemus Papam*! We have a new Pope!"

"Who did they elect?" Travis asked.

"Cardinal Le Pere."

The End

Other Books by Sandru

Sferogyls (Timurud Bk. 1) by Mit Sandru

The gods resurrect Tim Andrus from the dead. To his surprise he finds out that he is a god himself, and his name is Timurud.

But, the life of a god is not all heavenly. Timurud must protect weak and powerless civilizations against ferocious galactic empires. His first mission is to defend the peaceful and unarmed Sferogyl race against the Maggotroll Empire, warlike hominids who come to enslave the Sferogyls and capture their planet.

Fighting is the only solution to stay free, but the Sferogyls have no space warships. How will Timurud help them out?

Gold Rush Mystery (Terraspantion Chronicles, Bk. 1) by Mit Sandru.

America is back on the Moon, and we intend to stay and establish a self-sustaining permanent base for tourism and mining. The work is challenging, the environment is deadly, but the astronauts Mia, Geo and Roby succeed in building the moon base, even if they landed in a mysterious crater.

Time Hole, (Terraspantion Chronicles, Bk. 2) by Mit Sandru.

Mining on the moon is a hazardous affair. Deedee and Arno, two lunar generalists, find perils beyond what they signed up for when they travel on the lunar surface at night . . . on the dark side of the Moon. Time will not be the same after they fall into the *Time Hole.*

Folding Reality, by Mit Sandru, a Paranormal, Time Travel Adventure.

Experiencing a new reality is just a paper-fold away for Mike the insurance salesman. But those realities are not by his choice and he ends up being crucified, or gassed at Auschwitz, or marooned in space in a Russian capsule.

Arboregal, the Lorn Tree, by D.G. Sandru.

Four youngsters, Melissa, Perry, Nathan and Michelle materialize in a desolate world where giant, mile-high trees, support all life. They find shelter in the Lorn Tree among the Lorns. Soon after they discover that an evil spirit, Hellferata, wants them dead. Fearful Lorns want to expel the youngsters from their tree, which would be a dead sentence since monsters roam the land at night.

Will their ingenuity, cunning, and courage help them escape, or will Hellferata mete out her wrath before they can escape?

Vampire Thriller & Romance

Vampire (Vlad V Series), by Mit Sandru, a Vampire Romance.
Meeting a vampire isn't something that happens every night, even on the New York City subways. Even in her wildest dreams Cat never expected to meet a vampire or survive an encounter with one. Instead, she becomes his confidant. Why is she so lucky?

R.I.P., The Death of a Vampire (Vlad V, Bk 2) by Mit Sandru.

Vlad V Draculesti is dying because of an incident that happened decades ago. Unfortunately for Vlad V, the US intelligence agencies investigate him to find out his true identity, and centuries old life. Will Cat Sanders and vampire friends be able to help him die in peace, or will Vlad be discovered for being a vampire and die in a US Federal research laboratory?

Vampire Slayers (Vlad V, Bk 3) by Mit Sandru.

Cat Sanders is a billionaire, but not all is well. Her nemesis, Veronica Seyler, allied with a vampire-slayer drug cult, demands extortion money or she will be killed.

Cat's vampire friend, Angelique, comes to her aid. But the cult is more cunning and dangerous than even her vampire friend could handle. Would Cat and Angelique be able to come out of this alive even if Cat pays the ransom?

Vampires of Transylvania (Vlad V, Bk 4) by Mit Sandru

Cat Sanders has a simple task: spread Vlad V's ashes in Transylvania at midnight, during full moon. But in Transylvania Vlad V has centuries old enemies who take her and her friend Tudor hostage, placing them in iron cages among zombies and proto-vampires. Will they be able to escape from the blood sucking proto-vampires and flesh-eating zombies, or become zombies themselves?

The Queen of Vampires: A New Queen Arises (Vlad V, Bk 5) by Mit Sandru

The Vampire Queen, Eleonore von Schwarzenberg, is bloodthirsty and vengeful on Cat Sanders and her friends. She plans the most painful death for them. Cat and her friends find themselves entrapped and helpless to avoid her wrath.

Will Cat and her friends be able to escape and survive the Queen of Vampires' fury?

Other Books:

Escape from Communism, by Dumitru Sandru, a True Story and Commentary.
Life under communism is cruel and inhumane. Communist countries have a "Berlin Wall" around them, and the whole country is a giant concentration camp. I risked my life to escape from hell and reach freedom.

Abstract Dreams: Coloring Book 1 (Sandru's Art)

Reward your soul with the smooth and pleasing lines of Abstract Dreams

T-Shirts and other stuff:
Sandru's Shop or Sandru's Products

Visit my e-Gallery at:
http://dumitru-sandru.artistwebsites.com/
http://www.artistrising.com/galleries/Sandru

About Dumitru "Mit" Sandru

Dumitru "D.G." "Mit" Sandru was born in the greater area of Transylvania in the last century. He is an artist, composer, and author. He paints in the classical, surreal, and modern styles, and most of the music Dumitru composes is of the New Age flavor. As an author, he prefers to write Science-Fiction, Paranormal, and Teen/Children Fantasy & Sci-Fi novels.

Dumitru resides in California with his wife. They have one daughter and two grandsons.

Visit him at sandru.com